Endangered Fae

NO FAE IS AN ISLAND

ANGEL MARTINEZ

No Fae is an Island
ISBN # 978-1-78686-387-4
©Copyright Angel Martinez 2019
Cover Art by Emmy @studioenp ©Copyright January 2019
Interior text design by Claire Siemaszkiewicz
Pride Publishing

Published in 2019 by Pride Publishing, United Kingdom.

Pride Publishing is an imprint of Totally Entwined Group Limited.

NO FAE IS AN
ISLAND

Dedication

For my readers, the ones who've stuck by me
through all the twists and turns, and the ones
who joined us more recently — thank you.
Without you, I'm just a crazy cat lady talking to
my imaginary friends. And for Melyna, who gave
me the perfect name for Nusair.

Chapter One

Sidhe
Classification: Dual-nature fae *shifter*
Appoquinimink social scale: 7
The sidhe are arguably the most ancient fae race, suggested by their creation of the Veil between the worlds. Each sidhe possesses a dual animal-fae nature, exhibiting behaviors associated with that animal even in fae form. While they are social fae with a complex, closed-group structure, over the centuries they have adopted other beings into their court system, even certain humans.
The Compendium of the Magically Sensitive, 4th Edition, Dr. Nathan Cooper

Late-morning sun glinted off the rainbow sand. Diego let the grains run through his fingers, smiling at the tropical-bright shades. Once, he would have wondered at the colors. By now, he knew that the rocks under the restless sea weren't gray, as they were at home, but painted in riotous brilliance. He had swum in these waters and seen it for himself. Why this was, no one could tell him. There seemed to be no geological explanation because the Otherworld often refused to conform to such trivial things as science.

Though the dragon lord would have an explanation.

Squinting, Diego searched the waves for the sleek, black shapes leaping and arrowing through the surf. It wasn't fair to say the Otherworld had no natural laws. They simply followed different paths. In three years, a man could learn enough to know he would need several hundred more to claim he understood them.

He stood and brushed the sand from his skin. *It'll be strange to wear clothes again.* Some of the black heads turned toward him and he raised an arm to wave the pod to shore. In a gleeful surge, the seals became their own wave, barking and cavorting up the beach, an impending onslaught of noise and joy.

The first of the pack reached the sand, flippering their way out of the foam, all so alike and yet he knew them. Whelk with the gray spot on his nose. Lyonsia with her slender flippers. Murex with his overlarge eyes. Limpet with the white scar on the side of his head.

In the middle of the pod, a larger seal, coal black and shining, galumphed along, barking and nudging at the rest. Oh, yes, he knew that one, too.

The seals stopped on the sand, bumping into one another, complaining and barking seal laughs. As if shot, they suddenly flopped over on their sides, while the larger one in the center reared up on his tail, a blue glow surrounding him. His flippers elongated. His tail began to separate.

Disturbing enough, if one had never seen such things, but the seals on the sand did something far more distressing. The fur on their abdomens split in a neat line from chin to tail. The slits grew as the seals wriggled and squirmed, their skins wrinkling as if they were suddenly loose. Feet and hands emerged from the openings and the pod transformed into a group of selkies standing or kneeling to wriggle the rest of the way out of their sealskins.

The one in the center had no sealskin to shed, a lone pooka standing hipshot in their midst, watching their more arduous transformations with poorly concealed amusement. The ocean back home would have made him ill, but the oceans of the Otherworld, abiding by their own laws, affected him only after several hours of swimming. Here, he could live among marine people and play to his heart's content.

"I could have devoured the lot of you by now." Finn made a snapping motion at the nearest selkie, who reached over and smacked him on the back of the head.

"You could never, Fionnachd," she said on a laugh. "You would talk us to death first."

"And we'd be back in our skins and out to sea before you could even finish chewing on Limpet," the tallest male added as he kicked sand at Finn.

Limpet, the youngest, made a strangled sound. "Me? Fionnachd would never...would you?"

He clutched his sealskin to his chest, black eyes huge in shocked recrimination. Lean and sleek like his pod mates, wild unruly hair the shifting color of waves falling to his waist, Limpet did his best to appear wounded. He ruined it by snickering as he compressed his sealskin into as small a parcel as possible and tucked it into the little marsupial-like pouch on the side of his right thigh.

"Never." Finn ruffled his hair. "I would much rather eat Cerith, who has a bit of meat on his bones."

Cerith pounced and knocked Finn to the ground, which only encouraged a selkie pile. All the wrestling kicked up more sand and Diego waited until they had expended enough energy to collapse into a giggling heap.

"*Mi vida*?" he finally ventured. "We should probably start on our way."

Finn's dark head popped up from the selkie pile. "So soon?"

"Don't you want to go home?"

"Of course! But right this moment?" Finn struggled to free himself from the tangle of naked limbs.

"People might worry."

"Oh, bother." Finn stepped through sprawled selkies with astounding grace. "I suppose there will be anxious handwringing if we're not there on time. We can fly, though? None of this paddling upstream in a boat nonsense?"

Diego turned his gaze inland, his heart aching at the thought of home. His time among the wild fae had taught him so much, but three years without the company of another human was a long time. There were people he longed to see, dear friends and family. The terrible memories still haunted him, though, the guilt still sharp inside him.

He wasn't certain he was ready to face the world again. He was even less certain if the world would want him back. *I could always return here, I suppose.*

The selkies picked themselves up to hug Finn one last time. Then they scampered up the beach to smother Diego in warm embraces as well. He turned to find Limpet at his elbow, with the selkie holding Diego's pack out to him.

"Are the waves there like ours, Light Wielder? Do the humans swim? Is it true that there are boats larger than kraken?"

Selkies, like most fae, had few children. Limpet was the only child born to the pod after the Veil had closed. Even though he was over a hundred and fifty years old, he had yet to visit the human world.

"They are." Diego took his pack and zipped it closed. "Many do. And all Finn has told you is true, oddly enough."

Finn gave an offended sniff. "The human world needs no embellishment. It's quite unbelievable all on its own."

"Yes. Sometimes." Diego managed a smile, tamping down on the melancholy threatening like a summer squall. "How shall we go? Dragon?"

Instead of answering, Finn gave him a wink and walked off a few steps. He dropped his head back and spread his arms, a sign that he was shifting into one of his less usual forms. His body increased in size as he pulled magic and mass from the world around him, his limbs changing, his neck stretching. For a moment, Diego was certain the gleaming black hide and four limbs would resolve into Finn's version of a dragon after all, but then the ends of Finn's new feet resolved into hooves.

Diego stared, slack-jawed, as the familiar pooka horse took shape but with one astounding difference. Enormous black wings fanned out on either side of powerful flanks. Finn flapped those huge appendages a few times, raising tiny sand devils. Despite his horsey face, he managed to look smug as he settled his wings against his back.

"I didn't know you could do…that."

Finn stamped a hoof. "I've learned things, too, bucko. Did you think I was sleeping all this time you were receiving instruction?"

"No, but..." Diego waved a hand at him, trying to find an appropriate word. "You're magnificent."

"My heartfelt thanks." Finn bent a foreleg in an elegant equine bow. "Your steed awaits. Though you may wish to wrap your beautiful bits in something. Cold aloft."

Diego laughed as he pulled the blue kilt and a blanket from his pack. This was their gift to him, his lesson from the selkies, his ability to laugh again. He still caught himself sometimes. That he had no right to make such a happy sound nagged at him, but it was a normal, human thing to do, despite and sometimes because of tragedy.

After everything he had done, everywhere he had been, he was still human.

He closed up the pack again, slung it on his back and climbed up onto Finn. They had a moment's clumsy maneuvering as Diego puzzled out where to put his feet. By sliding up toward Finn's neck and tucking his feet up, though, he managed to keep them out of the way of those shining black wings.

Lyonsia, the selkie matriarch, put her hand on his calf. Her seal black eyes shone up at him, so familiar and alien at once. "Listen, Light Wielder, and I will tell you a truth."

"I'm listening."

"The oceans of both worlds understand regret. They are mother and destroyer, bringers of joy and despair. Their deep, dark places and restless natures contain all of time's regrets and they have room for more. Always room. Ever shifting. Ever sifting. Give yours to the waves as we have done. It is a stone you drag behind you. If you cannot cut it loose, you will drown."

"Someday, maybe. Thank you. For letting me stay with you a while. For all you've done for me."

Cerith let out a deep, barking laugh. "Oh, yes, we let you fish for us and let you bring us a new playmate. We are so very generous."

"I'll miss you. Come to the *sidhe* lands and through the door to visit me. I'd be happy to see all of you," Diego offered.

The selkies shifted uncomfortably, looking away or at the sand. "Perhaps someday. When the oceans of the human world are quieter again."

He gave a final wave then clung tight to Finn's mane as the pooka-Pegasus leaped skyward. The knot of selkies grew gradually smaller below, some of them turning to embrace their neighbors. Diego wondered if they wept.

* * * *

"What is it? The Light Wielder left it." Limpet held out the strange hide case to his father.

Cerith took it and turned it over. "It's called a 'knife'. An extra sharp tooth for humans to use since their teeth are flat like deer."

"We should take it to him, shouldn't we? Won't he need it? How far of a swim is it? If he needs it to eat, why haven't I seen it before?"

"I didn't say he needed it to eat," Cerith said with an exasperated chuckle. "I'm sure he has others. You keep that one as a remembrance."

Limpet turned the long, razor-clam-shaped case in his hands as he wandered down the beach. *It wasn't a gift.*

Isn't keeping it the same as theft? Why couldn't we go find him and give it back? What are they all so frightened of?

The pod's hesitance over returning to the human world both puzzled and irked him. They had been there. *They* had seen it, but they wouldn't give him the chance. This was certainly not the first time he had asked.

He fiddled with his scarred right ear as he let the waves lap over his toes, his resolve growing. He wasn't a child any longer. Perhaps he would never reach his father's height or Whelk's breadth of shoulder, but he was grown, by all the water goddesses. If he wished to see the world, he would simply do it. The door lay in the *sidhe* court lands. Everyone said so. If he swam up the Alainn, he would reach those lands and the door to the human world, or so he'd been told.

He glanced back at the pod, getting ready to settle in for the night. *Perhaps, though, it will be best if I wait until it's dark so no one sees me go.*

* * * *

"Odd. I wonder what I did with it."

"With what, beloved?" Finn flopped down on the grass by their rest-stop stream. At the halfway point to home, they'd both agreed Finn needed a break.

"My penknife."

"Ah, well. You dropped it somewhere, I expect. We'll be home soon enough where you've no more need of it. Plenty of pens at the embassy."

Reams of notes took up most of the space in Diego's pack, records of conversations and lessons from the wild fae over the last three years. At first, he had used a ballpoint and notebooks he had brought. But when

14

the ink and paper ran out, he had used the penknife to sharpen reeds into pens, using whatever berries were at hand for ink and large Otherworld leaves and rolls of fae flower silk as paper.

Diego dumped out the rest of his pack. "I know, but I've had that one a long time. It's just…distressing."

"My heart, my own, will you be angry with me if I suggest your distress is not caused by lost small objects?"

"Are you hungry?" Diego stood and brushed off his knees. "I saw a stand of golden berries over there."

"Diego…"

"Or maybe there are some of those red pods around here. The ones that taste like *chorizo*?"

Finn surged up and seized Diego's head between his hands. "Beloved, stop. Please. Tell me."

He gazed up into Finn's coal-dark eyes that looked human until one knew the wild magic fires that simmered within. Pooka's eyes that burned red in anger and glowed blue at the height of passion. His husband's eyes had seen every moment with him, good and bad.

"I'm… All right, yes. I'm nervous. Anxious."

"We go back to friends. To the home we built. Are you afraid you won't be welcome?"

"I don't know." Diego gripped Finn's wrists. "Things change. I don't know what's happened. How the world's changed. How people will react. How I'll…fit."

"We'll find our way." Finn's thumb brushed his jaw, his hand sliding into the curls Diego had let grow to shoulder length. "I'm right beside you."

"I know. It's… Thank you." Diego leaned in to lay his head on Finn's shoulder. "You're what keeps me moving forward. Without you—"

"Without me, you would go on," Finn whispered, his voice tight and fierce. "Don't say otherwise. You would find a way to go on."

Diego nodded, swallowing against the stone in his throat. Without Finn, he would have ended things three years before, but he couldn't tell his pooka that. It would break his heart. He was done breaking Finn's heart.

* * * *

It's today. Zack chewed on his bottom lip but it didn't help him concentrate on the long-winded email on his screen. He really was supposed to be working but what if Diego came home early? It was the last day of his exile. Would he come back before noon when he'd left? Would that be allowed? Would anyone care?

Most of the fae, except for the few with jobs at the embassy, didn't have to watch the clock in the human world. They could sit by the Alainn and wait for Diego's canoe for a week in anticipation if they wanted to. Hell, for all he knew, waiting *sidhe* and Fomorians packed the banks already.

He could just...but, no, he was the Consul for at least another few hours and, damn it, duty came first. Not to mention there was no guarantee Diego would want his job back. Zack's cracking knuckles echoed like rifle fire in the deadly quiet office and he tried once more to absorb the information from the Canadian ambassador. Something about detained magic users...isolation camps that sounded more like concentration camps... *Oh, here we go.* None of the details of the camps were news to him, but apparently some Canadian college students had managed to get themselves snapped up by the authorities while visiting the kingdom of Shera'alej. Sounded like the kids had pulled some illegal magical prank and got themselves thrown in the magic user zoo there.

"And you want me to do what, Mr. Ambassador?" Zack muttered to his screen. "Get my super ninja fae commando squad together and save these boneheads?"

The purpose of the email wasn't entirely clear, something Zack was used to by now in diplomatic missives. So often, the real meaning lay in what was *not* said. Implication. Obfuscation. Allusion. The ambassador couldn't ask directly for the Fae Collective to intervene but that was what he was asking, all the same.

For this, he needed to consult. Before he even composed an 'I received your message' response, Zack needed to talk to the fae authorities, namely the *sidhe* and Fomorian rulers and their ambassador to the human world, Prince Lugh.

His phone chirped the first notes to the *Battle Hymn of the Republic*, his signal that one of the security staff was on the line.

"Morrison."

"His Highness is on his way back to you, Consul," Theo Aguilar's soft voice came through.

"Why aren't you with him?" Zack tried to modulate his tone but the sharp edge made him cringe. It wasn't Theo's fault that he was Lugh's bodyguard now and not Zack. Also it wasn't their newest bodyguard's fault that Zack still resented not being able to watch over his royal lover personally.

"He's on the ferry. I still have line of sight. Marcus is with him."

"Not an answer, Theo."

"Kevin's taking me to the range for my qualification."

"Oh. Damn it. I knew that. Sorry, kiddo." Zack pinched the bridge of his nose. "You all right out there today?"

"Yes, sir."

Zack waited but that was all he was getting. Theo would never complain about sun headaches, nausea or any of the other symptoms vampires suffered in full daylight. Truth was, even feeling poorly, Theo was more deadly unarmed than any other security officer with an arsenal.

"Sir?"

"Yeah?"

"Is he home yet?"

"Not yet." *Carol would've told me, right?* "Theo, you all right with him coming home?"

There was a long silence on the line. Finally, Theo said in that quiet, expressionless voice, "I am. I know…he won't be the same."

"Not the way you first knew him, no." Zack spoke carefully but firmly. "That's really a good thing."

"Yes, sir." Theo hesitated. "Still, it will be strange."

"I think it will be for him, too. Good luck on the range. You got this."

Zack knew Theo well enough by now to hear the hint of a smile. "Yes, sir. Thank you."

He'd had serious reservations about taking a rogue vampire on as security. Inexperience aside, Theo had made some bad choices as a lone vigilante and some not much better ones working for Diego in his soul-shredded state. Still, Theo wasn't a monster, and a kind heart lurked under his chilly, laconic exterior. These days, Zack worried more about Theo as Theo. Was he happy? Was he getting what he needed, this young man who had been thrust out into the dark without a safety net?

Legally, Theo was an adult but Zack couldn't help feeling like a surrogate parent sometimes, especially since Theo didn't make friends and didn't seem interested in having them. The cliché phrase one heard on the news when someone snapped kept nagging at Zack. *He was a nice kid, kept to himself.*

When the phone rang again, it was the internal line with Carol's extension. "We have word?"

"Hello to you, too, Consul," Carol said at her driest. "Angus spotted them. They're about fifteen miles from the ford, airborne."

"You think I have time? Can I—" *Blow off the rest of my day, be a friend instead of a diplomat?*

"I've cleared your schedule, Zack. I think a fit man, jogging, could probably make it in time."

"Thanks, Carol. I owe you."

"Again." Her voice quieted as she said, "Tell them welcome home from all of us."

"Yes'm."

Zack left his dress shoes under the desk and stripped down to his T-shirt and boxer briefs as he hurried down the hall, through the kitchen to the basement stairs. The fae wouldn't bat an eye if he arrived in the Otherworld naked, but Zack hadn't managed to let go of his modesty that far yet. He hesitated at the silver door that led through the Veil. Should he wait for Lugh? But no, the big guy was on his way and would zap himself right to the riverbank when he heard. Zack didn't have the whole teleport option thing going for him.

The heart-stopping blue of the sky, the riot of lush grass and wildflowers stretched out before him, nearly blinded him as he stepped through to the *sidhe* fields.

He didn't stop to let his eyes adjust, though. He put his head down and ran flat out, heading for the river and Cian's Ford. That was where Diego and Finn would come. That was where everything seemed to end and begin.

Fae had gathered on the banks, just as he'd predicted, restless tides of *sidhe* in both humanlike and animal shapes, eager knots of Fomorians in all their multiformed splendor. King Balor towered over them all, his sharp tusks catching the sunlight as he tossed his head.

"Zack!" A blur of red hair and pale skin slammed into him, stealing his breath in a bone-creaking hug. "They're coming!"

"Hey, there." Zack set Sionnach back, chuckling at the way the little fox fae's tail waved madly behind him. "I heard. Spotted them yet?"

Sionnach pushed the wild red hair from his eyes. "Not yet. Oh, you will know, Consul, the moment someone has."

He linked his arm through Zack's, weaving through the growing crowd where hands reached and petted in greeting. It had taken some getting used to, the touchy-feely, we-don't-know-what-personal-space-means social interactions. Even for physically demonstrative humans, it was overwhelming at first, but Zack had grown accustomed and simply petted back, touching arms and shoulders and gripping hands as he passed.

At the river, a flat protrusion of granite jutted out over the rushing water. Zack tugged Sionnach up with him, shielding his eyes against the sun, searching downriver for any sign of movement. He twitched when a large hand clasped his shoulder but the wonderful, earthy-male scent of Lugh settled him.

"Warn a guy, maybe?" Zack tipped his head back, trying to scowl at his *sidhe* lover but the damn prince had the nerve to laugh and pull him into a fierce hug.

"Are you happy? That they'll be home soon?" Lugh murmured in his ear.

"Yeah. Happy. Nervous, though. I don't know…"

He couldn't finish the thought but Lugh nodded, a shadow of sorrow under his bright smile. "It will never be the same. But all things change, my braveheart."

Several of the excited *sidhe* shifted to their animal forms, the avian ones taking wing to keep an eye out aloft. Angus, the *sidhe* court's herald, already circled overhead in golden eagle form, possibly with the sharpest pair of eyes in the Otherworld.

Zack tipped his head up to watch his friend's flight path since Angus would spot anything approaching long before he could. He leaned back into Lugh's arms, soaking in his heat, letting the strong heartbeat against his back calm him.

High above, Angus stopped his circling and arrowed forward in a flash of golden feathers. He let out an aquiline scream, all the other winged *sidhe* hurrying in his wake.

"There." Lugh pointed, his deep voice caressing Zack's ear.

Zack squinted and spotted a black dot in the sky, maybe half a mile downstream, growing steadily larger as it headed toward them. At first, he thought maybe Finn had flown ahead in crow or falcon form with Diego following more slowly in their canoe. But the shape grew larger and larger.

"That's no bird. What the hell…?"

Lugh chuckled. "It most certainly is not. Our Finn has learned a thing or so in his travels."

How Finn had learned this, Zack couldn't imagine. What swooped down toward them was something out of myth, and not the sort Zack had met in his years of dealing with the fae. Finn's horse form, sure, he'd seen that plenty of times, but not with these shining black wings, a full twenty feet across if they were an inch. A pooka Pegasus. A Pookasus?

"Wow."

On the near bank, the fae cleared a space, shielding their eyes from the wind kicked up by Finn's back winging as he landed. If there had been any doubts about this beautiful, impossible creature being Finn, Diego sat astride the beast. Who else would it be?

The fae let Diego dismount, then mobbed him, nearly burying him under a tide of overeager bodies crowding in to welcome him home. Zack took Lugh's hand and stepped off the rock, making his way slowly through the crowd. It was hard to make out in the mob of voices, but Diego's was definitely becoming more stressed by the second.

"I think we need to mount a rescue," Zack muttered.

Lugh shot him a grin and bellowed over the tumult, "Gently! Quietly! Let the man breathe!"

A path opened up for them and, though the fae still thrummed with excitement, the mob around Diego retreated far enough so Zack could see he was still standing. A little shaky, a little pale, but on his feet. A mixed pile of *sidhe* and Fomorians, on the other hand, had tackled Finn, though he took it all in good humor, laughing and wrestling in the grass.

"Zack?"

Oh, that voice broke his heart, so uncertain and anxious. "Diego." Zack approached with his hands held out, overjoyed when Diego took them without hesitation. He yanked Diego closer into a hard embrace, whispering, "Damn, but it's good to see you. You don't even know."

Diego clung to him, shivering. Maybe the flight had been too cold. Maybe he fought tears. Zack wasn't going to embarrass him and ask.

"It's good to see you, too. I...didn't expect all this."

"Sorry. I would've tried to keep it quieter, but they've just all been so excited."

"I just don't understand it. Why would they...? After everything..."

Lugh wrapped his arms around them both. "You have served your exile. It is done. We have all missed our Taliesin. Welcome home."

"Thank you." Diego lifted his head from Zack's shoulder. "Should I say something?"

"Only if you want to. Then maybe they'll simmer down and we can get you settled." Zack kept a hand on Diego's shoulder as he turned to take in the assemblage.

Shoulders squared, Diego took a breath and pitched his voice to reach into the crowd. "Thank you for coming to greet us. Thank you for..." Diego hesitated, apparently stumbling over what word he should use, "all your kindness. It's good to be home."

Cheers, roars, shrieks and squeaks erupted after his words, but the fae allowed him to pass now and let go of Finn so he could catch up.

Zack flanked him on the left, Finn on the right, with Lugh taking the rearguard so Diego could walk up the bank toward the door in relative peace.

"It is. Good to be home."

"It better be." Zack growled. "And don't you ever leave me alone with these damn loonies again."

Diego laughed and things felt right once more. Just like that, the world turned the right way up again.

* * * *

If Zack hadn't been so preoccupied with being happy, he might have noticed the dark shape sliding along in the reeds near the shore.

Chapter Two

Selkie
Classification: Dual-natured fae *shifter*
Appoquinimink social scale: 8
Selkies are of that unique class of fae shifter that requires a
pelt or second skin to shift to animal form, in the selkie's case,
to seal. Found in large family groups, selkie pods readily
interact with each other and visiting fae, but are wary of
humans and magically altered humans, with whom they have
a long and rather unpleasant history.
The Compendium of the Magically Sensitive, 4th Edition,
Dr. Nathan Cooper

"You want to try the Sig?" Kevin gestured to the handguns lined up on the counter, all carefully pointed downrange.

Theo picked it up gingerly. He wasn't certain he'd ever be comfortable with it.

"You're not gonna break it, kid," the range instructor, a bald bulldog of a man, growled.

"I'll try not to." The problem was that Theo *had* broken three smaller handguns before Kevin had finally taught him to shoot using a larger .44 Magnum. He would tense so badly when firing that he gripped too tightly. Sig Sauers weren't designed for vampires.

He kept his two-handed grip gentle and tried to relax, but he hated the noise of gunfire. Even with protection on, it hurt his sensitive ears. The target popped up. He let out a breath and fired six shots in quick succession.

The range instructor grunted and pressed the button to retrieve the target, shaking his head as he glanced at the shot grouping. "Maybe slow it down. You only hit once."

Kevin let out a strangled cough. "Better look closer, Murphy."

"At what?"

"That's all six shots in that one hole."

"What the...fuck?" The man turned to him, tight-jawed and angry. "Pick up the damn Magnum. Let's see you do it again."

Why is he angry if I'm doing well? Theo swallowed a sigh and picked up the heavier weapon, the one that felt less like a toy in his hands. He took up his stance, both hands on the grip, though he could easily fire with one, and found the calm space inside him. When the target popped up, the Magnum roared six times, barely kicking back in his hands.

He could see the result from where he stood, but his eyes were much better than the instructor's. The man retrieved the target, stared at the single, larger hole through the center, and muttered, "Freak."

The fae security staff used several different weapons. Theo qualified easily with each. The man was still muttering about him having cheated somehow as they left.

"Asshole," Kevin snarled as they climbed back into the van. "You did good, kid. I won't make you carry a Sig, but I do want you carrying when you guard His Highness."

Theo nodded. They both knew his weapon of choice, if he had to carry at all. He had tried to argue early on that he didn't need a gun, but Kevin had remained firm on that point.

"I know you're pretty damn close to indestructible, but I'm willing to bet if some jackass puts a bullet in your heart, you're as dead as the rest of us. How about we not give him that chance?"

That was that and Theo had soon learned when and how one could argue with Kevin. At least Kevin accepted him as he was, for whatever strange reason. Many of the fae did, too. They were better adjusted to the weird parts of the universe. The human security officers, except for Kevin and his husband Marcus, were more wary, some because he was a vamp, some because they saw him as an Angelino punk, and some because he had, for a short while, been the enemy.

The last one he understood. He might have to keep proving himself to them for a long time before they fully trusted him.

"I hear those gears grinding in your head, Aguilar," Kevin said as they parked his truck in the ferry's lot. "Don't let that asshole at the range get to you."

"No, sir." Theo chewed his bottom lip, careful of his fangs. "I'm not. I won't."

"But? I hear a thing you're not saying."

A half-smile tugged at Theo's mouth. Kevin was getting too good at this, hearing between the lines. "People will always stare. Say things. Be afraid."

"You make it sound like bigotry is normal." Kevin shook his head at Theo's shrug. "Look, Theo, I'm a gay retired Marine. I grew up in red-as-patriot's-blood Nebraska. You think I don't know? Don't think I ever had to fight my way out of a bar 'cause someone didn't like faggots?"

Theo winced at the word, the one he hated more than *freak*. "No, sir."

"Sure. The world has assholes. But it's not *normal* and you don't have to accept it."

I have to pick my battles, or people die. Theo shivered, the memories of a hot Los Angeles night ambushing him, the screams, the bones splintering, the horror on his sister's face when she'd realized the monster slaughtering her attackers was her brother.

"No, sir."

Kevin gave him an odd sideways glance. "You give me one more 'yes, sir' or 'no, sir' and I'm partnering you with Vivian."

I would die from auditory overload. Vivian didn't treat him badly, but she never stopped talking. "*Sí, jefe.*"

"Smartass."

When they had docked on the island and cleared the security checks — yes, Kevin insisted on protocol, even for familiar faces — Kevin stopped in the doorway of the pier-side command center. "You need a rotation change? Meal break after being out in the sun all day?"

Theo took off his hat now that the sun was setting. The top of his head felt tight and achy still, but bearable. If he begged off to go feed, he would inconvenience the person who would have to take his place.

"I'm fine. Feeding's scheduled tomorrow."

Kevin narrowed his eyes. "Go see medical first. They clear you, fine. If not, we're pulling you."

"But—"

"Your 'I'm fine' is on a level with most people's 'I feel like crud'. No arguments."

Theo nodded, keeping his face carefully neutral, and set off down the pier toward the path that led up the hill. There really was no medical department on the island, so he would need to find one of the fae healers or the consul himself for clearance, since Consul Morrison had been a medic and a nurse during his military career.

His steps slowed as he neared the consulate. The cozy, two-story building didn't seem impressive or official. It looked like someone's grandmother lived on the island in isolated splendor. Occasional visitors would see only that, the cozy house with offices at the front and common living spaces at the back. If they were important guests, they might be treated to tea by the lovely garden fountain out back. But few humans, even magically changed humans, knew the extent of the consulate, the network of caverns running underneath, the secret door that led to an entire separate world.

If there was anywhere a vigilante vampire belonged, it was here. At least, it had been. Now, Mr. Sandoval was home…

"Theo?"

He had stopped on the pink cobbles outside the front door. Carol, the consulate's administrative supervisor, had her purse over her shoulder, obviously leaving for the day.

"Mrs. Arseneau." He nodded, twisting his hat in his hands.

"Are you all right?"

"I—" *I'm afraid to go inside. I'm not sure I can do this.*

Somehow, she knew. She placed a hand on his sleeve, on an arm strong enough to snap her spine with a careless blow. "He's probably just as worried about seeing you."

Theo nodded, his eyes glued to his hat. "Mrs. Arseneau? Could I ask you something?"

"Of course."

"Why aren't you afraid of me?"

She smiled, though there was something sad and fierce in her gaze. "I know better than to be scared of the good guys, Theo. Take care on patrol tonight. There's a storm moving in."

"Yes, ma'am." He stepped aside to let her by, watching her for a few moments as she made her way to the dock. The backs of his eyes stung. Maybe he was more tired than he realized.

Murmuring carried through the walls as he padded silently through the consular offices. Within a few moments, he knew who had left for the night and who was still in the building. Wolf scent crept down the hallway from the kitchen. Consul Morrison was there. Had he been alone, Theo would have stopped in for some water. But Mr. Sandoval was with him and Finn the pooka, their voices rising and falling in quiet conversation.

I just can't yet.

Taking the cowardly route, he turned right and headed downstairs toward the fae caverns where he had his own room. It wasn't that he blamed Mr. Sandoval for what he had been. A spell gone awry had temporarily stolen part of his soul and left him without compassion. His quick intelligence, his ability to sway people, though, those things had remained intact, and Theo had swallowed his version of the universe, this dark Mr. Sandoval's. He would have followed the dark mage into hell because he'd been able to make his mad plans all sound so reasonable, so *sane*.

That was the problem. It wasn't Mr. Sandoval's fault, but Theo had been ready to obey him of his own volition. He had been ready to become a true monster for the promise of a better world.

He couldn't quite name the lead ball in his stomach. Shame? Anger? Fear? Dark and tangled, he didn't want to face it, not yet. The caverns were cool. The lights dim and soothing. He closed the door to his cave-room and drew an easier breath. *Sanctuary*.

"You're not Quasimodo," he muttered as he shrugged out of his leather jacket and yanked off his boots.

Black. Unrelieved black, every piece of clothing he owned except for the white dress shirts he had for diplomatic security details off the island. He supposed he could start adding color again, but the black felt comfortable now, as if a perpetual state of mourning was natural for him.

He thought about stretching out on his bed for a rest. The sun did take a lot out of him and the shelf of books beside the bed tempted him. No. He wanted to do something with his hands. His fingers itched. After a moment's thought, he opened the trunk at the end of his bed, pulled out the hoop with its attached piece of linen and his bag of thread. Sitting cross-legged on the bed, bent close to the fabric, he let the stitch and tug rhythm of his embroidery calm his aching heart.

* * * *

Diego lowered his mug to the table. "Someone just went downstairs."

"Fae are up and down that staircase all the time." Zack was watching him carefully, almost warily.

"This person wasn't fae."

Zack quirked an eyebrow at him. "You can tell that from here? Even with your new shields up?"

"I…" Diego glanced over at Finn, who rolled his hand in a *go on* motion. "Yes. I can… Feel isn't really the right word. I sense living currents better now. The *bane sidhe* taught me to listen. That person wasn't fae and he wasn't human, precisely. But you're not alarmed, so I'm trying not to be."

"I'm not 'cause I could smell him." Zack smiled behind his coffee mug as he took a sip. "That was Theo."

"Theo? *My* Theo?"

"Yeah. Why?"

"I don't recall him feeling…" Diego trailed off again. It was hard, trying to communicate with humans again, all the things he wasn't sure they would understand. "He's very…solid." *And so damn sad.*

Zack shook his head. "He really hasn't changed much since you left."

"I should probably talk to him." Fingers tracing the rim of his mug, Diego fought against squirming. He was responsible for leading Theo in the wrong direction, for all the pain he had experienced after. It wouldn't be a comfortable conversation.

"Maybe let him come to you?"

"Ah. Of course." Diego's face heated. He hadn't thought of that. Theo probably didn't want anything to do with him or his apologies. Three years, *Dios*. "How has he been?"

"He's a good kid, you know. Went through his training. Settled in. He's reliable. Good at what he does—" Zack broke off with a chuckle, wagging his finger at Diego. "I remember that look. The 'that's not what I asked you' look. He's doing okay, Mr. S. I think he's kinda lonely, but it's hard for him. His family—"

"Was everything to him." Diego knew that much, at least. He wished he had taken the time to learn more, but the partial person he had been hadn't been interested in his minions as people, just as chess pieces.

Finn's hand closed over his and squeezed. "He is different in so many ways. He is the youngest here. Of a different human type from the others. And vampire. Humans don't do well with different."

"Says our resident human expert." Diego managed a chuckle and leaned over to plant a kiss on Finn's jaw. "You're all too right. Speaking of which, what's happening in the world, Zack? With magical laws and such?"

"Yeah. About that." Zack blew out a long breath. "I have a briefing ready for you and everything. If you can wait until morning when the staff's here. You know, do the whole hand-off thing right."

"Hand-off?"

"The consul job? Your job? You're…" Zack trailed off, his fair skin becoming a few shades paler. "Aw, hell, Mr. S. You're gonna tell me you don't want it back, aren't you?"

Here it was, then, the first of many difficult conversations Diego knew he would have. "Zack, I'm sorry."

"Damn it." Zack's hands were flat on the table. He stared down at them as he spat out, "Three years. I waited for you for three years. And somehow I knew."

Anger laced those words, frustration, yes. Resignation. That hurt more than Diego had anticipated. He had rehearsed speeches, explanations and arguments, but for Zack, who had risked life and sanity for him, plain, undiplomatic truth was best. "I can't. I think you know that. Zack, I'll help. I'll advise as best I can. I'll give you my opinions. But I can't step back into those shoes and be the human voice of the fae again. Not out in front of the cameras. Not after all the horrible things the world watched me propose."

"But wouldn't that be a good thing? Let people see you changed your mind?"

All his life Diego had tried to make things better for others, make things easier. He wanted so badly to wrap his arms around Zack and tell him he would take the burden from him, that he was here to make everything like it was. Nothing was harder than trying to resist a lifetime's worth of instincts. "From what you've said, it doesn't sound as if the issue of magic legislation has gone away. Or that the world has accepted magical beings as part of life."

"That's what the briefing was supposed to be about." A muscle jumped in Zack's jaw, his expression trapped between amusement and irritation. "No, damn it. No, it hasn't. They haven't. I mean, yeah, some countries are great. Denmark. Germany. Hell, most of Europe. But here's still a mess. Asia's kinda half-and-half. And on like that."

"We knew." Finn reached across the table to grip Zack's arm. "Human governments are strange and needlessly complicated. We knew the storm would not have calmed. And that certain humans would welcome it and stir the storm."

"Zack, listen. You put me in front of a camera, remind the world about me, and they'll pull out all the footage from three years ago. I'll just become a flashpoint for anti-magic factions. They'll point to my long absence. Say I've been brainwashed or that I'm under a spell or worse."

"But that's...backwards!"

"I know that. You know that. The fae and everyone who was at Heersford knows that. The rest of the world?" Diego shook his head, the hard ball of regret in his stomach heavier by the second. "I hate that I had to abandon my post. That I left all this on your shoulders. But you can't put me back out there in front of the world as Consul. Nothing good will follow."

"Oh." Zack's broad shoulders folded in, as if he were deflating with his arguments.

"I'm sorry," Diego whispered on a hard swallow.

Zack held up a hand and flopped back in his chair, staring up at the ceiling. "Not like I didn't know this was coming. Well, maybe not *know*. I wondered if you'd be able to take your job back. But when you came back healthy and strong, head up and talking like yourself again...guess I hoped, was all."

Diego shot a quick glance across the table at Finn, reaching mind to mind to speak directly to his husband. *"Selkie hug?"*

"The perfect thing." Finn tipped his head toward Zack, who still studied the light fixture above his head. *"One... Two..."*

"Three!"

Finn lunged from his chair and Diego scrambled after. They slammed into Zack, one then the other, the dual impacts knocking a shocked *oof* from Zack and tipping his chair. They hung suspended for a moment, a tangle of limbs, until Zack's chair lost the battle with gravity and fell to the kitchen floor with thuds and clatters, pooka, human mage and werewolf consul in a flailing heap.

"The hell?" Zack growled from his spot at the bottom of the pile.

"Selkie pile," Diego mumbled against Zack's shirt. "It means we love you."

The growl turned into a choked laugh as Diego had hoped and Zack's arms wrapped around them both in a fierce hug. "Love you, too. Missed you so goddamn much."

Finn nuzzled his nose against Zack's throat. "This is nice. You still smell the same."

Diego untangled them far enough to help Zack sit up and get off the chair. "I would still like that briefing, though. Could we still do that? If I'm going to try to be useful again?"

"Well, yeah. I wasn't gonna let it go to waste."

"Good. Thank you. Come on." He stood and offered a hand up to first Finn then Zack. "Let's grab some beers and go out by the fountain. I'll tell you about your favorite subject."

"Dragons?"

"What else?"

* * * *

Theo blinked at the embroidery in his lap, then snapped his head to the left to check the clock. He hadn't meant to nod off. It had only been a few minutes, though. Plenty of time to see one of the healers and make it to his shift.

A short search revealed his fallen needle on his blanket, gleaming against the black cotton. He retrieved it and carefully folded his work before he placed it back in the trunk. The good thing about working security was that one never had to decide what to wear to work. The uniform of close-fitting pants and BDU shirt, both black, was comfortable and practical. Com unit, ID badge, zip ties and Swiss Army knife all went in the pockets of the short jacket. His newly issued weapon he would pick up at the command post that evening, since guns weren't permitted in the fae caverns.

As he caught his hair up in a band at the base of his neck, Theo froze. He had lived among the fae long enough to learn their scents — *sidhe*, Fomorian, *féileacán* — he knew them all. The being who had just passed his door was none of them. Salt and the strange, unsettled scent of the seashore, those could have been from a fae just back from a swim. But this was something else, something so new and alien.

Theo opened his door slowly, peering out into the empty corridor. The scent grew stronger as he followed the trail soundlessly, flitting from shadow to shadow. Whatever it was, it either had the arrogance to move so openly or lacked the intelligence to hide. Either one could be equally dangerous.

It's headed for the stairs, for the consulate.

Fear drove him, panic spiking through his chest. If the thing meant harm, if he arrived too late… No, he would be in time. He hurled himself through the invisible barrier and up the stairs faster than a human could blink. It would *not* have a chance to do harm. He would see to it.

Damn. The beast, thing, whatever it was had moved through the kitchen. The back door into the garden stood open and soft laughter drifted through. The scents of human, wolf and pooka reached him.

"No." Theo hurled himself through the doorway, out into the garden where crickets and frogs sang in happy ignorance. Consul Morrison was out there, with Mr. Sandoval and Finn. Even off duty, he had to protect them.

There. Along the wall, under the kitchen window, a darker shadow slunk in the gloom, headed toward the trio perched on the edge of the fountain.

The consul turned suddenly. "What the — Theo?"

"Stay there, sir!" Theo shouted as he closed in.

He dropped to a crouch, gauged the distance and leaped the ten remaining feet, bringing the intruder down beneath him. Whatever it was squeaked and snarled, writhing madly like an eel. With a knee on its back, he managed to tangle his fingers in the thick mane of hair and hauled it to its feet.

"Theo, what's going on here?" Consul Morrison was on his feet, teeth bared. Good, he was a superb fighter, backup if Theo needed it.

"This...whatever it is was stalking you." Theo growled low in the being's face and shook it roughly. "What are you? Assassin? Thief? What are you doing here?"

It squeaked again and found its voice, breathy and rushed. "I was returning Diego's tooth! He left it! What sort of guest greeting is this? Diego, why is there a Nightwalker in your home cave? And a Devourer? Will they eat us?"

The rush of strange questions confused Theo but not enough for him to loosen his grip. He would hold tight until they could call reinforcements and contain the threat. Why wasn't anyone calling it in? His confusion turned to irritation when the pooka doubled over, laughing hysterically.

"Sir." He glanced toward the consul, who watched Diego with raised brows. "We should —"

"Um, hold that thought, kiddo. Diego, you know this little guy?"

Little? Yes, it wasn't terribly tall or broad. But small things could be dangerous. Lila had been small.

To his horror, Mr. Sandoval came forward and took the creature's hands. "Limpet? *Dios,* how did you get here? Theo, *cuidado, por favor.* He's a friend."

"Poor little selkie." Finn came forward, still wiping his eyes. "At least we know where your penknife went, love."

Selkie...selkie...the seal people? That explained the black eyes and the sea smell. "If you're a friend, selkie" — Theo infused his voice with enough ice to freeze Long Beach Harbor — "why skulk through the embassy? Sneak through the garden?"

"It reeks of Devourer! Please, please, don't let it eat me!"

"*Hola,* Theo. It's good to see you." Mr. Sandoval caught his gaze, his stare no less compelling than it had been before his cure. "It's safe. Please let him go. Please. He was just frightened."

He had no verification that the situation was secure, and yet he released his grip before he could stop himself. That voice had once commanded him. He had sworn obedience. It was still the same, and yet...not. "Sir?"

"Stand down, Theo," Zack ordered. "I think we're all right here."

Theo twisted his head to the left. "And if not?"

"Really think you and me couldn't handle this little guy?" Consul Morrison's smile and wink said he wasn't worried, so Theo backed off and tried to stop bouncing on the balls of his feet.

Mr. Sandoval wrapped his arms around the selkie, making little shushing noises and rocking him. When the frightened gasping slowed, he pointed to the consul. "Limpet, this is Zack Morrison, the fae's human consul. Remember what that is?"

"The human who speaks for the fae in the human world. But he's—"

"I know. He is a werewolf but he's a good man and my friend. He makes certain he's somewhere secure when the change comes. He would never hurt you."

"And the...the Nightwalker?" Limpet eyed Theo suspiciously.

"Is also our friend. This is Theo Aguilar. He helps keep the island safe."

"Is it usually *not* safe?"

Finn kissed the top of the selkie's head. "The human world is a dangerous place. Your parents were right about that. This island is safe for us because of the vigilant and valiant warriors who keep us safe."

"Who keeps you safe from *him*?"

Theo wrestled his anger down, though he had to take it to the mat three times. *Don't react. Don't react. It gives them power if you react.* The taunts, the jeering calls of — damn it, he wasn't a kid walking to school anymore.

"We know more than they did in the old days," Consul Morrison said. "When a human changes because of magical...illness, we try to teach them how to live with it. It's only when people are hunted and desperate that they get crazy and hurt others."

No, some people are simply bad. Theo didn't think this would help the current conversation, though, so he kept silent.

"Speaking of. Isn't this a feeding night?"

Theo twitched and blinked at being addressed directly. Had he lost the thread of conversation? "Tomorrow, sir."

"You're looking a little strained and tired." Consul Morrison stepped up to him, put a hand on the side of his head and shone a penlight in his eyes.

"Ah!" Theo cried out and batted the light away, turning so no one would see him breathing through the pain.

"Sun headache?"

"Yes, sir. It's not bad."

"We really should move your feeding up."

"Sir, please. I'm on duty in fifteen minutes. I can't do that on a fae feeding."

Mr. Sandoval's eyes widened in alarm. "A fae feeding?"

"Vampire anesthetic," the consul answered after a slow breath. "The fae volunteer and once Theo feeds, he's out for the night. Happy and full, but not useful on duty."

Theo glanced at his watch. "Please, sir. I need medical clearance."

"I should declare you unfit, kiddo. You work yourself too hard." Consul Morrison puffed out his cheeks on another hard exhale and waved a hand at him. "Go on. Go. I know why you do it. I'll call your clearance in. Go patrol and we'll make sure you get fed as soon as you come off shift."

"Thank you, sir." Theo turned to try a dignified retreat.

"And Theo?"

"Sir?"

"Thanks for watching over us."

That stopped him short. It was his job and he did the best he could. The thank you settled as a warm glow in his chest, but what was the proper response?

"Sir." He nodded and walked away.

Chapter Three

Werewolf
Classification: Magically altered human
Appoquinimink social scale: traditionally rating from 2-4,
modern advances in support systems have caused increased
variations
Another alteration often classified as a kelan structure
disease, werewolves are among the most maligned of altered
humans. While potentially destructive, a Were who
understands his or her cycles is able to manage the violent
stage of the change effectively and safely.
The Compendium of the Magically Sensitive, 4th Edition,
Dr. Nathan Cooper

Diego had arrived in the dining-room-turned-conference-room early, wanting the advantage of terrain. Travel mug of coffee on his right, Finn dozing on his left, he was able to greet every newcomer individually, shake hands and reestablish contact. If he had waited until the room had filled, he would have had to rush through greetings, forced around the room from person to person without a chance to reconnect on a personal level.

Both Kevin and Marcus gave him bone-creaking hugs. Carol had greeted him the day before but embraced him again anyway, lingering for a kiss on the cheek. Stacy and Dan, newer office staff at the time of the incident, settled for handshakes, as did the rest of the security staff. Theo, he was sad to see, kept his distance and offered only a nod in greeting.

"I thought you said he needed to feed?" Diego whispered in Zack's ear.

"We put it off a few hours. He wanted to be here."

Lugh arrived last, his presence making the room feel half its size, his smile a miniature sun. He showed no discomfort greeting a room full of staff but then, he had no reason for lingering guilt and shame, no reason to doubt his welcome. He wrapped his huge arms around Diego and pulled him close, holding him for longer than human social expectations would have allowed. The *sidhe* prince, whom Diego had imprisoned in iron chains and had caused such terrible pain and anguish, forgave him and would forgive him as many times as he needed to hear it. He only wished the rest of the world had such immense, loving hearts.

"Morning, Highness, so nice of you to join us." Zack received a kiss instead of a hug or a clap on the shoulder, so his gentle sarcasm obviously wasn't taken seriously. "I think we're all here. Settle, people, please. I know we're all excited. Someone want to wake Finn up, maybe?"

Finn snorted and jerked awake at the sound of his name. "I put it back! Blood and bone, I swear I did!" When Diego patted his arm, he blinked, looked around the room and offered a disarming grin. "Hello, everyone."

"Are you all right?" Diego twined their hands together as he spoke to Finn mind to mind. The trembling in those long fingers worried him.

"I dreamt of something...I don't recall now." Outwardly, Finn still smiled, but Diego felt his unease as a cold trickle down his spine. *"I'm a mite tired."*

"All the flying. Of course, mi vida.*"*

He squeezed Finn's hand in reassurance as an odd shiver in the flows of magic passed from his pooka lover to him. Premonition, precognition, whatever the human world was calling it these days, Finn joked that they could feel disturbances in the Force when they were together. Trouble was, the feelings were rarely specific enough to glean any useful warnings.

Zack paced by and patted Finn on the shoulder. "I know you're probably wiped. Promise to keep this short as we can."

"My undying gratitude," Finn said.

"You want coffee, sir?" Dan asked, pushing his chair back from the table.

Several voices cried out, *"No!"* before Diego waved at the young man to sit back down. "Thank you. That's very thoughtful. But pookas and caffeine don't play well together."

Zack took his place at the head of the table in front of the presentation screen, new since Diego had last been in the room. "Good morning, everyone. Now, we're here to catch Mr. Sandoval up on where things stand, but I know some of you only get the immediate, need to know briefings, so if you have questions along the way, now's the time. Carol?"

At the far end of the table, Carol tapped on her laptop and the screen behind Zack blinked into glowing life to show a political map of the world, the countries color-coded in green, blue, orange, yellow and red.

"Stacy's been working on keeping this updated, but this is how magical legislation stands right now out there." Zack pointed to Sweden. "The green countries are where magical creatures are allowed the same protections as humans and where human citizens with magical abilities and syndromes are supported and offered equal rights."

Diego frowned. The proportion of green was distressingly small—much, but not all, of Europe, Canada and a few scattered bits in Asia. He squinted to be sure, afraid he might be mistaking one shade for another, but the US was blue rather than green.

"I know. I wish we could've been farther along with some of this." Zack's ears had turned pink, his expression mirroring Diego's distress.

"These things take time," Diego offered softly then gestured to the map. "What's the blue? There's a good deal more of that."

"Ah. That's not a bad thing. Progress, at least. Blue is where nonhumans are granted certain diplomatic immunities and where efforts are being made to address the needs of magic users."

"Not fast enough for senmajes to be safe," Dan muttered.

Diego half-turned toward him. "Pardon? The what? Sen Madges?"

"Um, Dan?" Zack's ears had deepened from pink to scarlet. "How about we stow the slang in the conference room. At least until Mr. S has a chance to catch up."

"Which does not answer the question," Finn said in his driest tone.

Zack cleared his throat again. "It's what magic-sensitive humans have started to call themselves. Ourselves. One of those Internet things that stuck.

People had long arguments over what to use. Witch. Mage. Magic user. No one agreed. They still don't, but senmaj is what most prefer now."

"Ah." Diego nodded his thanks. "Sorry. Didn't mean to derail you."

"Happens a lot around here." Zack grinned when he said it, though.

Diego understood that perfectly. Around fae, staying on topic could often be a challenge.

"So the yellow are those countries where there might be some education and support, but with certain restrictive laws in place, such as where fae are permitted and where magic-sensitive humans might live, what jobs they can have, that sort of thing."

A few countries in South America stood out as bright yellow against the blue, with other patches scattered worldwide.

"The orange, you've probably figured out, are more restrictive countries and the red are those countries where magic has been outlawed. Which, to me, is sort of like outlawing air, but it scares some governments. Things they can't control."

"We do our best not to frighten them further." Lugh's deep voice carried hints of sorrow and long-suppressed anger. "Though sometimes we have intervened."

That sounds alarming. "Intervened?"

"Diplomatic rescue missions," Zack supplied, a muscle jumping in his jaw. "If we hear about a detained fae in one of these places, though that's rare. The fae know better. Or if someone else's citizen is wrongfully detained, or we hear about someone seeking asylum, we try to work the channels to get them out."

"Does that work?" Diego tried to imagine going into a country hostile to magic and being able to talk the government out of a prisoner.

"We don't often have success directly," Lugh explained. "We appeal to friendly nations' consul authorities, ones with better relations in that country, to influence the outcome. The process is tedious, but we are often successful."

"That's really good to hear. I know you're trying to do everything you can." Diego stopped. He didn't really want to ask, but if he was going to work with the consulate again, he had to know. "But when it's not successful?"

Lugh's sorrow rippled out across the room in heavy, lead-apron waves. The fae present, and Dan, Carol, Zack and Theo, all cringed. Zack strode to him and put a hand on the prince's shoulder as Lugh leaned back against him.

"Sometimes we're too late," Zack said softly. "Some countries hold their executions within hours of arrest. A couple of times, we've had to use…non-diplomatic resolutions."

Diego shivered at the possibility of implied violence in that statement, his fingers tightening involuntarily on Finn's. He had no right, no room to find fault, since he hadn't been there for them and had contributed to a large portion of the political mess.

"Has anyone…? Has there ever…?" He shook his head, finding he had neither the will nor the breath suddenly to ask.

"Rescue missions," Zack said gently. "Quick extraction. The Silver Adepts made the doors we need, those couple of times. We've only done it when we had to and one of the fae was in trouble."

Rather than reassure him, those statements taken together only made Diego dizzy with anxiety. The Silver Adepts were the young coven who had been the catalyst to the incident three years before. He didn't like to think of them at risk. Besides that —

"I don't understand." Diego tried to control his wavering voice, steadying a little when Finn slid an arm around him. "The fae go into dangerous places? They leave Tearmann Island to go abroad to these countries where we know they're at risk?"

Zack blinked at him in obvious confusion. "Well, some of our staff certainly go abroad. His Highness, of course. Lots of invitations. And they love Sionnach in Japan where he's been helping set up magic schools. They call him *kitsune*, though they know he's not." He bent down so Lugh could murmur in his ear. "Oh! Sorry, Mr. S. Wasn't tracking. We've found isolated individuals and small pockets of nonhumans around the globe. Kind of like Finn was when he woke. Those who were stuck when the Veil closed. Not fae like the ones closest to our door, the ones we know, but different sorts."

It was something Diego had suspected but hadn't investigated, since he'd had other things on his mind. "The Otherworld is larger than we thought."

"Just a little," Zack said with a rueful smile. "And none of the fae ever told us how big. They thought we knew. But, yeah, we rescued a tengu from Mauritania and a simurgh from Iran. No losses, no casualties."

While Diego couldn't say he approved of putting the youngsters at risk or any of the consulate staff and allies, he breathed a sigh of relief. No bloodshed. He nodded, studying the map, trying to absorb this new world. "The US, Australia, Brazil — why are so many countries still blue?"

"Well, it was tough, you know." Zack spoke gently but a bit of reproof still seeped in. "Three years ago. So many people screaming to have everything magical rounded up and contained. There were militias cropping up that wanted to hunt us down. It was hard to get things calmed down."

Diego waited patiently. He could see there was more.

Lugh went on when Zack only stared at the floor. "Registration acts did go into effect, Diego. In many of these countries shaded in blue. There are still, in most cases, efforts to develop education and support programs. But magical beings, human or otherwise, must be registered."

"And how, pray tell, is that accomplished any better than catching water in a spider's web?" Finn asked. "I can see spotting one of us, perhaps, if not under glamour. But one can hardly tell magic-touched humans from non-magic on sight."

"Ah. Fionnachd, humans are ever resourceful. They test the children in their first year of school. They have dogs, trained by the magically sensitive, who can tell the difference. I'm sure they miss some. But the fact of registration by law remains."

"We did what we could," Zack added softly. "I'm sorry."

He looked so ashamed, so completely mortified by failing to do the impossible, Diego wanted to sink into the floor, preferably thirty feet down. No one else should have been accepting blame for any of this. "You've been here, trying to do what's right. I'm the one who started it. The one who spread detailed plans for these laws at their feet."

Lugh waved a dismissive hand. "The grass was tinder dry. All that lacked was a spark. There are plenty of others, we know now, who were contemplating such things before you spoke a word of it."

"Still—"

"You cannot call back breath, Diego. The places in the world where differences are not tolerated are the same, before and now. This is nothing new." Lugh gestured at the map. "The shape of the world would be much the same today had you never been soul-shattered."

Diego nodded, though he didn't agree, since arguing with Lugh would only waste time. Better to catch up, to bury himself in research, so he could begin to help straighten out the mess. Behind the scenes. Quietly. *They obviously don't need me, but maybe there's something I can do.*

A few more maps showed where countries had established schools for the magically sensitive and magic support systems, including werewolf transformation safe houses and vampire feeding rooms, both government-funded and self-supporting.

"I've reactivated your consulate email and accesses, Mr. S.," Carol said as Zack finished his prepared statements. "All the maps and stats are in the shared files if you need them. Anything you need, you just ask. We're glad to have you back."

"Thank you, Carol." They were ready for him. Wanted him to dive in. Maybe they needed him after all.

When everyone had left the room, returning to work, or in Theo's case going to feed, Diego stood staring at the color-coded map.

Finn slid up behind him, wrapped long arms around him in a tight hug and rested his sharp chin on Diego's shoulder. "What it is you see, my hero? What will it show you if you stare long enough?"

"Nothing useful, probably." Diego shivered and leaned back against Finn's solid warmth. "I just wish it didn't look like the world was screaming at us."

* * * *

The moon scattered pearls across the waves that evening. Sometimes Theo allowed himself a moment or two to enjoy the beautiful solitude of the island. A few years ago, this had been a bird sanctuary, the dock used only by marine biologists and ornithologists coming to do counts and studies. Even now, with the consulate built at the far western tip and the fae tunnels carved out of the rock beneath, Tearmann Island was mostly wild. Fae left the consulate sometimes to gaze at the stars of the human world, but they respected the quiet desolation of the island.

Whenever Prince Lugh went out into the human world, Theo went with him as part of his personal bodyguard. But the prince didn't need him while in residence and Theo took more patrol shifts than required while he was on the island. He needed this peace, this cocoon of isolation away from humans and their scents, away from things that sparked unwanted memories and pain. Other security staff paced the island perimeter in the opposite direction, usually a pair of them while Theo was allowed to work alone, but he saw them only once every two hours.

He needed the quiet more than ever that evening, his brain churning and crashing louder than the waves on the rocks. At least he had seen Mr. Sandoval, had even spoken to him briefly. That wasn't hanging over his head anymore. But he was so strange, quiet to the point of nearly being shy. He seemed uncertain and muted. Theo let out a long breath and turned away from the shore to continue his patrol. The Diego Sandoval he had first met...that man had *blazed* with magic, fierce and bright. Yes, he had been sharp and often impatient, impulsive sometimes to the point of being reckless, but he had been so confident, so sure he was right.

This man, the one everyone said was the real Mr. Sandoval, seemed broken. It was difficult to see the great man everyone else talked about. Incessantly. Theo wasn't sure if he resented the fact that his version, his *jefe*, was gone, or if he was just uncomfortable with the jarring reminder of the things he had done. They excused him here, said he had been misled, but little worms of doubt crawled into his brain still. He'd been given a position of command, of trust, had felt himself part of something important.

Yes, it'd scared him. Part of him had enjoyed the power, the inside knowledge. *Superior. I liked feeling superior. In control. I'm a monster waiting to happen.*

Theo blinked at the waves, realizing he'd stopped again. People counted on him to do a job, not a very complicated one, and here he was drifting off again. What if some crazy militia group decided to row up and attack the island from a boat offshore? What if something dangerous lurked out there under the surf, just waiting? He'd heard about the wendigo. It could happen.

A pebble rattled on his right. Theo tensed and shoved his hand inside his jacket, fingers closing around the grip of his Magnum. A shadow detached from a rock twenty yards away, partially hidden in the striated bright and dark patches of full moon and racing clouds.

"Stop where you are and identify yourself!" Theo yelled as he pulled his gun in the recommended two-handed grip. Humans didn't come out on the island at night and the fae knew better than to sneak around. Sometimes Consul Morrison walked the beach at night, but he always announced himself and this time the scent of werewolf was conspicuously absent.

The figure froze, half crouched as if preparing to flee. Then it stood, hipshot, arms crossed, and asked, "Are you always so unpleasant?"

Theo lowered the gun with a snort. "You." He holstered the weapon as the selkie, Limpet, walked cautiously toward him. "You can't sneak around out here at night."

"I wasn't sneaking. I was watching the waves, these strange, dim-gray waves that mutter ancient secrets. This is a strange ocean."

"There's security patrolling. Someone might shoot you."

"It's hardly secure if someone shoots at you. You're not making sense."

Theo ran a hand over the side of his face. "I'm security. I help guard the island."

"Why would you shoot me? Do you dislike me that much? You don't even have a bow."

"No. I don't." Theo walked around the selkie, an ache starting at his right temple. "I'll tell the other patrol you're out here."

"Oh, that's kind of you. Patrol? Other guards?"

To Theo's dismay, Limpet turned and scrambled after him, skipping along the rock-strewn beach. "I have work to do."

"But you're all alone. That can't be much fun. I'll go with you. Is this what you do? Walk about the island? Is it very large? I haven't swum all the way 'round yet, so I've no sense of it. The water's quite cold. Bracing, isn't it? Do you swim around it sometimes? You do swim, don't you?"

"You don't need to come with me." Theo fought clenched teeth. The selkie was a friend of Mr. Sandoval's and Finn's, too—Finn who had been so kind to him after accidentally squashing him in dragon form. No need to be rude.

"Quite all right. I've nothing better to do."

"You can't come with me," Theo said in the chilliest, sternest tone he could muster.

"Oh, of course I can. I see quite well at night."

Theo squeezed his eyes shut against the headache. It shouldn't have been there. He'd fed that morning and napped the rest of the day in lethargic, sated bliss. *Fine. He'll get bored and leave soon.* "All right. But you have to be quiet."

"Yes, yes, of course. In case something bad is here. A pack of nixes maybe. Oh, they're bad. Or a kraken tries to swim close and ambush you, yes? You're a real warrior, then? Have you seen many battles? Do you have scars? I have scars, but only because I was very young—"

"Limpet." Theo stopped and took the selkie's chin in his hand, holding his head still. "Whispering is not being quiet."

"Right you are. Sorry. You have beautiful eyes."

Theo dropped his hand and walked away, shaking his head. It was going to be a long night.

Chapter Four

Pooka
Classification: Omni-form fae *shifter*
Appoquinimink social scale: 2-9
Pookas are a rare fae *with only four known individuals identified. They are additionally rare in that they are one of the few* fae *able to shift into any form with which they are familiar. Many* fae *can cast glamours to change their appearances, but the pooka actually changes shape, gathering mass from the surrounding world or storing mass in what we will refer to here as the "pooka pocket" – a parallel holding dimension researchers believe related to the Dreaming (see Introduction to the* Fae, *Section 6).*
The Compendium of the Magically Sensitive, 4th Edition, Dr. Nathan Cooper

"So let me go instead," Diego said, his throat as dry as library dust.

Zack stared at him from the other side of the oak desk, the consul's seat he'd campaigned all morning to give back to Diego. "But I thought you said —"

Diego waved a hand to prevent having his words thrown back at him. "Putting me in front of the camera as the voice of the fae is one thing. Sending me on a quiet recovery mission? That's where I might actually be helpful."

"But we can't put you at risk like that."

"First of all, the full moon's only a week away. Cutting it a little close if you can't get in and out in a couple of days." Diego spoke gently, evenly, though he shook inside. He wanted to go through paperwork, to read legislation and business proposals, not go out into the hostile world. "And from everything you've told me, this country's practically on an information lockdown. If you go in officially, who knows what they'll do? I go in, make contact with the Swiss embassy, and if I run into trouble, I can get out."

"Sure, as long as you're conscious, you could make a door and get back here. But you wouldn't have backup. What happens if someone recognizes you? If they try to arrest you? You need to take some of the kids with you, at least."

The kids were the Silver Adepts, who were young adults now, most of them finished graduate school. While they had their own school and research center to run, Diego understood that they had worked closely with the consulate over the past three years when Zack needed them.

"I don't like putting them at risk." Diego dropped his gaze to his hands. "I think I've done enough of that."

"Mr. S…. Diego." Zack came around the desk to lean against the front edge, his hand on Diego's shoulder. "You didn't. You have to get past that. It's like saying it's your fault for breaking a lamp when you're sleepwalking."

"It's not. But thank you for saying so." Diego patted the hand on his shoulder. "It's not important. What's important is that it's not their job. Let me take some security with me. Should be all I need."

"Don't remember that I agreed to this yet."

Diego squeezed his hand. "Who else do you have to send? Really? Zack, it can't be you. Just by existing, you're against the law there."

"So are you."

"Only if I actively practice magic. I've read their magical laws. It's legal to be magically sensitive. Just not to actively engage in *witchcraft and abominations resulting in witchcraft*, I think was the actual language."

Zack let out a long, slow breath. "We just got you back."

"I won't be gone long. If it's an impossible situation, I'll come back home and the Canadian government can try a different route."

"You know this feels weird, don't you?" Zack offered him a crooked smile. "I've been waiting all this time for you to come back and take charge. This is all backwards."

Diego shook his head. "Never again."

"But you want to come back and top from the bottom, is that it? Let me lead until you need to tell me I'm not doing it right?"

"Zack… I'm… Is that what I'm doing?"

Zack leaned back again, arms folded over his chest. "Maybe not that bad. I'm teasing. Mostly. You're my friend. I need you to tell me when you don't agree with me. And I'm freaking overjoyed that you're enough *you* again to fight me when you think I'm wrong." The half-smile vanished. "But let me ask you this. What about Finn?"

"I suppose he'll have to stay —"

"Hell, no. You made him a promise never to leave him behind again. Gonna break it that quick?"

That stopped Diego, heat crawling up his face. Not two days home and he was on the verge of doing just that, as if he had learned nothing in the last three years, forging ahead with his need to save the world despite what Finn thought or how it hurt him. "No. I can't do that."

"Good." Zack walked back behind his desk to type as he talked. "I'll ask him. That way, he won't be saying yes just 'cause it's you. If he says he'll go, then I guess I'm out of reasons to tell you not to."

"Fair enough." Diego stood, feeling as if he'd forgotten something. Halfway to the door, he remembered. "Oh! About Limpet. Could we send someone to his pod? Let them know he's okay?"

"Yep. Angus sent someone off this morning. Peregrine *sidhe*. Don't remember his name."

That was a definite dismissal, Zack's blond brows already drawing down in concentration as he read something on his screen. It hurt. Of course it did, to feel shunted aside like that, but it was good to see Zack so comfortable in his role. Diego had known he was a born leader years ago, selfless and devoted, able to spot the best qualities in any human or fae and to delegate accordingly. By now, Diego could admit that his own leadership style had been *get out of the way, I'll do it*. No matter that he'd always tried to be kind and considerate, that was how he had done things. He wasn't a leader. He was a doer.

This he had also learned among the wild fae. Along with so many complicated things — how to shield himself, how to hear the songs on the world's magic flows, how to see without sight, to feel what vibrated beneath the surface, to call on only what he needed. But in all these complex teachings, two simple things wove through them all. The first was that Taliesin had never led. He advised, traveled, discovered, created, but he did not lead. In this life, this incarnation, he had forgotten that. The second was that nothing, *nothing*, was worth breaking a promise to Finn. Never again.

In his excitement to be home, to be useful, he had nearly forgotten. *It won't happen again.*

* * * *

"Until he was four years old, James Henry Trotter had a happy life…"

Finn curled up in his seat, letting the reader's soothing voice vibrate through his bones. This machine, this little flat square with all of its hundreds of uses, was one of the best humans had ever devised. He needed help finding what he wanted, but he could have music or listen to people argue or he could have a stranger with a beautiful voice read him a *book* when Diego was busy. It certainly made flying in a blasted airplane more pleasant.

This particular book, which Diego said had a giant peach in the title, started out in quite a dreadful place, though he doubted a rhinoceros would actually *eat* people. But he had enough experience of human stories to know that many were more fantastic weavings of familiar truth and fabrication than he could ever concoct.

It was most likely an *interesting* story, but he found it hard to concentrate. The whole situation made his skin itch, this flying to a country where magic itself was against the law. All the nice, sane humans he knew had assured him those days were long gone, but here they were again, the same laws that had, in his last life, cost him Diego and left Finn mutilated and quartered. It was enough to make any self-respecting pooka want to shift to otter and hide in the reeds.

For anyone other than Diego, he would have hidden. Oh, yes, if someone had come to him and said, "You are the only one who can get these young humans out of danger," of course he would have gotten on the plane. Perhaps. Unlike other fae, at least he appeared human when he wished to and Zack said his accent would lend the delegation a more 'international' feel, for whatever good that would do. His passport listed him as a 'consular officer' and, since it was a Tearmann Island passport, made no mention of species.

Diego sat beside him, reading something official and most likely terribly boring on his lap machine. Finn always expected the thing to act like a pet and was always disappointed when it didn't. A lap anything should have been something cute, furry and wriggly…and just like that, he had completely lost the thread of the story. With a little sigh, he turned off the book and got up to stretch his legs. The lovely thing about a charter flight was that one had more space to move and the only other passengers were their own security.

The three regular humans sat together toward the front, talking and laughing quietly. The fourth, Theo, sat a few seats back, alone. Finn leaned against a chair back, head cocked to one side. Difficult to say whether the others avoided Theo or whether he just liked being alone. The boy's head was down, his frown of concentration certainly not inviting conversation.

Finn slid into the seat next to him, ignoring the cold sidelong glance he received. Theo had a piece of cloth secured in what looked to be a wooden hoop. On it were beautiful colors, glorious skeins of fine thread, orange, red, yellow, green. Finn leaned in closer. He was certain it was a picture, but he couldn't quite make it out. On the tray in front of Theo sat a container of these threads and shining—

"Don't touch those." Theo's voice barely broke a whisper but the words had knife-sharp edges.

"Your pardon. I didn't mean any offense," Finn offered with a little seated bow as he prepared to get up to leave.

"They're steel needles, Mr. Shannon. You'd burn yourself," Theo murmured in a milder tone, not once glancing up from his work.

"Ah. My thanks, then." Finn tilted his head to see the picture again. "You make art with thread. Is it like a tapestry? A hunting scene? Or is it abstract?"

Theo lowered the work with a little sigh, straightening it out so Finn could see. It was far from finished, but Finn could see by the sketched outline on the cloth that it would be a dragon in flight over a mountain range. One wing, head and shoulders were complete, picked out in astounding detail so that the thread appeared to be shining scales.

"Your color palette is quite beautiful," Finn said as he ran a finger reverently along the dragon's jaw.

Theo's pale complexion gained a hint of pink, his normal stoic, unreadable gaze suddenly shy. "Are you an artist? I didn't know the fae…"

"Some are. Different sorts." Finn smiled for him, hoping to ease his discomfort. "I wasn't until I started to live with Diego. I paint. Oils, most times."

With a nod, Theo bent his head back to his work, though he seemed more relaxed. After a moment, Finn asked, "Is that what you wanted to be? Before the change? To make beautiful things with your hands?"

The flash up and down of Theo's needle slowed then stopped again. "It doesn't matter."

"Why?"

"They don't accept vampires at California Polytechnic."

"I don't unders—" Finn broke off on a sudden urge to sneeze. "Do you smell something odd?"

Theo lifted his head, nostrils flared. "Yes." He put his needlework away in his pack and motioned for Finn to let him up.

"My heart, my own, there's something here that should not be." Finn sent the silent warning even as Diego rose from his seat by the window. A soft, muted hum of power gathered at Diego's fingertips, the flows so well controlled Finn couldn't help a surge of pride.

"It's in the last overhead compartment," Diego sent back. *"Keep everyone back, please."*

"Sir?" The trio of human security had spotted Diego's movements and they were hurrying down the aisle. "Everything okay?"

"Stay there, Kurt, please," Diego ordered softly. "We have a stowaway."

Diego paced down the aisle to the last overhead compartment, the larger one with the blankets and medical boxes. He moved slowly, calmly still, so Finn had no qualms about throwing his arm across the aisle to keep the security folks back. Theo, slender and agile, simply ducked under his arm and slid around him. Finn was about to call him back when he finally sifted the strange smell from the cleaning chemicals and scents of the plane.

"Oh, crud," Diego muttered as he obviously came to the same conclusion. He pinched the bridge of his nose between thumb and forefinger, letting out a slow, exasperated breath. He called out to the compartment, "We know you're in there. I'm opening the door now, so don't be startled."

Theo had reached his side, muttered a soft curse in Spanish and sneezed. *Ah, our Nightwalker buck has puzzled it out as well.* A bit of scuffling and a muffled squeak came from the compartment when Diego opened the door.

"Come out, Limpet. You can't possibly be comfortable in there." Diego turned to the security staff. "Did someone check all the overheads before we boarded?"

"Yes, sir." Kurt's face was as scarlet as the horns on Theo's thread dragon. "Checked them myself. I'm s—"

Diego held up a hand to cut him off even as he helped Limpet down with the other. "You couldn't have known. Selkies are good at not being seen, when they wish."

"They can be invisible?" the wide-eyed young woman behind Kurt asked.

"Not precisely, no. They redirect your attention. It doesn't work well in full sun, but it boils down to Limpet thinking *you can't see me* very hard and your brain complying."

"What are you doing here?" Theo asked when Limpet had both feet on the floor.

"Ah, well…" Limpet's eyes were huge, obviously distressed as he took in all the people staring at him. "I fell asleep in there. Didn't realize we were going somewhere."

Finn snorted and leaned back against the nearest seat. "You are perhaps the worst liar in all of the universe. Except perhaps our Zachary, whose face turns interesting pinks and reds. Try another one?"

Limpet hung his head, his blue-gray-green hair obscuring his face a moment. When he lifted his face again, he seized Diego's sleeve and began prattling rapid-fire. "I know you sent word back to my pod. They would come soon to take me home. But I don't wish to go home. I wish to see things. They would keep me by the home shore forever and always since I'm the youngest. But I'm not that young anymore. I'm grown. And I wish to see the human world. And I wanted to come with you rather than stay on the island with the Devourer. He seems nice enough but he's still what he is and I knew if I asked, you would say no. So I crept into the back of the magic carriage with the bags when you left the island and crept into this odd bird-box while the humans brought the bags on. And I hid." He waggled his fingers at the young man at Diego's elbow. "Hello, Theo."

Theo heaved a small, aggrieved sigh. Diego appeared to be fighting a headache.

"It's not as if we can put him back, is it?" Finn asked. This far into a flight, he surmised they weren't able to turn around.

"No, we can't." Diego patted Limpet's hand. "This wasn't a smart move, hon. We're going somewhere dangerous and you'll be an added distraction for my security." He called up the aisle, "Kurt, see if we can cobble together a uniform for him. Jess is probably about his size. I can hide his appearance to a certain extent, but anything to help him blend in."

"Could we leave him with the plane?" Finn suggested.

Theo muttered something that could have been, "If you want baked selkie."

"I'm afraid not. Do you remember sitting in the car for five minutes when I ran into the Sobeys?"

"Ah. Yes." Finn shuddered. It hadn't occurred to him that a plane would heat up like a car, and this would be for several days, in a place that apparently reached temperatures hot enough to bake a selkie *outside* of a vehicle.

His curiosity pricked up when Theo stepped closer to take Limpet's chin in hand, forcing the selkie's head around to meet his gaze. Finn had found that holding Theo's gaze for more than a moment was unnerving, but Limpet held steady, actually concentrating.

"You'll have to be very quiet around the humans here. No questions. No blurting out things," Theo told him, his voice soft but stern.

"No whispering?" Limpet asked.

"No. Whispering."

Finn gaped in astonishment as Limpet nodded mutely against Theo's hand. A selkie, whose nature dictated that he talk, about everything, incessantly, had just agreed to be quiet.

Chapter Five

Vampire
Classification: Magically altered human
Appoquinimink social scale: Varies according to the individual
While many governments still classify vampirism as a kelan structure disease, the Fae Collective recognizes this rare alteration as a unique class of human. The difficulties of a hemovore assimilating into human society have been well documented, but vampires can and do act as respected, contributing members of several communities worldwide, given the proper social and legal support.
The Compendium of the Magically Sensitive, 4th Edition, Dr. Nathan Cooper

The airport resembled every other one set up to receive private jets except for the squad of armed military types waiting for them in formation on the tarmac.

"I'd feel more comfortable if I spoke the language." Diego had expected some sort of official greeting, but with no embassy car or diplomatic delegation in sight, this seemed more threat than welcome. "Kurt?"

"Could just be an honor guard, sir." Kurt didn't sound invested in the idea. "Captain says our translator's on the way. I'd advise we hold off disembarking until we have a visual on him."

"Good advice." Diego turned to the flight attendant on his left. "Elaine, if it's possible to delay, I'd prefer that door remain locked until we know what kind of reception's waiting."

"Yes, sir. Not a problem."

If Elaine was worried, she hid it well. The Fae Collective hired the best and Diego knew this flight crew from before his exile, all seasoned professionals. He hoped he hadn't landed them in an untenable situation.

"Golf cart," Theo called out from his window spot.

Zipping across the tarmac at an impressive clip, a shaded cart brought a driver and a single passenger toward them. Diego just had time for a glimpse of a slender man in a summer-weight suit when his phone buzzed.

"Hello?"

"Mr. Sandoval? This is Anas Bakkal, from the Swiss embassy. Is everything all right?"

"Is that you in the golf cart?"

"Yes, I'm so sorry I'm late for your arrival. The ground crew tells me you've refused to disarm the door?"

"We don't mean to alarm anyone with the delay, Mr. Bakkal, but there are guards with rifles out there. We weren't certain of our welcome."

"Again, my apologies. Shera'alej has implemented new airport security regulations. Charter planes must be searched upon landing. The security guards are here to accomplish the search, nothing more."

"Just between us, Mr. Bakkal, in your estimation, are my staff and I at risk?"

A smile crept into Bakkal's voice. "You and I both know there are always risks. But in this case, they should be minimal."

The voice in Diego's ear was so calm, so civilized and dry, he couldn't help feeling a little ashamed at his reaction. *I'm trusting you, Mr. Bakkal.* "Thank you. Please tell them we're opening the door. I'll see you in a moment." Diego turned to his assigned staff. "The guards are part of customs procedures, here to search the plane. I'm not sure I like the sound of it, but I don't think we have much choice."

Kurt, as senior security, took charge from there, ordering Theo and Jess up front as first out and taking the rear with Matt. Limpet, now in a black security uniform with his hair tucked under a cap and his features under a glamour that made his ears and eyes appear human, fidgeted between Diego and Finn.

Elaine opened the door and heat slammed into them. Even though they'd been forewarned that it was nearly a hundred and twenty degrees on the tarmac, the oppressive, heavy air was a shock to the system. Theo hesitated at the top of the rolling stairs, most likely needing his eyes to adjust despite his wide-brimmed hat and sunglasses. Jess, bless her, waited patiently for him, then at his nod, they descended together, a wall of professional, purposeful black between Diego and the approaching squad of airport security.

At the foot of the stairs, a man in a khaki uniform with more gold than the others pointed to his left and began barking orders at Theo. A few feet away, Mr. Bakkal appeared to be arguing vehemently with another member of the airport detail who held him back. Theo and Jess stood fast, tense and wary, since they couldn't determine what the man wanted.

Unable to reach them, Bakkal called out, "It's all right, Mr. Sandoval! Please have your people move over to the left there! They want you to wait while they do the search."

"All right, everyone," Diego addressed his party, hoping his voice didn't shake too badly. "Let's move. Steadily. With purpose. Hands away from holsters and pockets." He raised his voice to call over, "Luggage, too?"

"Yes, please! So sorry about all this! Please line your bags up on the ground where the sergeant is pointing!"

"Not exactly VIP treatment, sir," Kurt muttered from the back.

"No, but let's remember why we're here and not antagonize anyone, please."

Bakkal finally broke away from the guards and hurried over to them, breathless and nearly wringing his hands in agitation. "I wish we could have briefed you, but the changes were sudden and we weren't informed. There will be a request for weapons permits before they go through the bags and I'm afraid your party will be frisked. I hope that's not an issue."

"Mr. Bakkal, I don't think we have a choice. We do have female personnel with us and I don't see any female guards. Would you ask them, please, how they propose to handle that?"

After more discussion and angry gestures back and forth, two female airport employees hurried from the terminal to separate Jess and Elaine from the group and take them behind a hastily erected screen while the men had to endure being frisked in the open. Diego made no open protest, but the guard was too thorough for his liking.

"Could've bought me dinner first," Matt muttered as his groin was patted down. "Probably won't even call tomorrow."

Diego shot him a sharp look. "Steady, gentlemen. Stay respectful, please. Anyone might be able to understand you."

"What on earth are they looking for?" Finn asked as he raised his arms to have his sides patted down.

"Extra weapons not on the permits. Drugs. Explosives."

Finn's frown darkened. "Will they take your pills?"

The seizure meds had become something of an obsession for Finn. For the past three years, he had been the one to fly back to the *sidhe* court every three months to pick up the refill Zack brought in from Diego's doctor.

"No, *cariño*. They're looking for illegal drugs, not prescriptions. I have that, too, if they need to see it."

Permits checked and rechecked, several cell phone calls and a lot of shouting later, the guards moved on to the bags, pawing through the contents of each one and stuffing everything back in without much care.

Diego pulled at the collar of his dress shirt, beads of sweat sliding down his back. Beside him, Theo's normally straight posture had crumpled, his shoulders hunched, his head down as if he could hide from the sun that way.

"Mr. Bakkal." He waved the translator over again. "Isn't there somewhere out of the sun we could wait? My staff isn't acclimated to this heat."

Another short flurry of short, sharp sentences with the officer in charge and Mr. Bakkal had to apologize again. They would not be permitted to move. "I'm sure it won't be long," he offered, though the anxious darting of his eyes said otherwise.

Diego leaned in closer. "Theo?"

"I'm all right, sir."

"No, you're not. But hang on the best you can."

Twenty-five minutes later, security boarded the plane, presumably to make a mess in the cabin as well. Fifty-five minutes after they had disembarked, they still stood in the blazing sun. Diego mopped at his forehead. *If I'm feeling woozy, I can't imagine –*

In complete silence, without a single word of complaint, Theo toppled. Diego lunged for him, but Finn was faster and caught him before he could hit the hot concrete.

"*Mierda.*" Diego dropped to one knee beside them, patting Theo's cheek. "Theo, *mijo*, can you hear me?"

"He's warm," Finn hissed close to Diego's ear. "Aren't Nightwalkers supposed to be cold?"

"Yes, damn it." Diego stood, brushing off the knees of his dress pants. "Mr. Bakkal, I need to speak to the officer in charge. This is beyond unacceptable."

The officer listened grimly, though he never once looked at Diego and never spoke directly to him. Though this was a terrible breach of diplomatic etiquette, Diego's points apparently hit home about the international press having a field day if American citizens died on the tarmac because of security delays. They were allowed to gather their bags, with Finn carrying Theo, and retreat inside the terminal to wait for clearance. Limpet dogged Finn's steps, clearly concerned about their stricken vampire.

"It's a game." Diego cornered Bakkal in the arrivals lounge while the remaining security staff hovered nearby, their expressions ranging from exhausted to furious. "What game are they playing? Was it to intimidate us? Humiliate us? Both? Were they hoping for some display of power from us so they could arrest us all?"

"All of those things could potentially apply." Anas Bakkal drooped into a nearby seat. He hadn't done much better out there than the Tearmann Island contingent. "We must also concede that this may have been an issue with unfamiliar new procedures."

Diego nodded. Diplomacy meant biting his tongue and pretending certain things were a misunderstanding or an oversight or merely incompetence. "We're not welcome. I understand that."

Bakkal waved a hand. "They know perfectly well who you are, Mr. Sandoval, but they still agreed to meet with you since you have the support of the international community here. You're not here for your own gain. Everyone understands that."

"Right now, my staff has to be my first priority." Diego drew in a steadying breath. "I was born to the heat, but most of them are from places where 'too hot' is a good thirty degrees colder than out there."

"Poor Theo. Finn, how is he doing?"

"Breathing, my heart. Some ice, some rest, he should be well."

"He'd better be, or this isn't going to be a quiet diplomatic incident much longer."

* * * *

Limpet sat by the Nightwalker's bed. The others had gone to a meeting in this strange place where the heat made shimmering pools in the air. Diego said they were safe here with the Swiss. He trusted them, so Limpet resolved to as well. He had no room to complain, of course, since he was here because he had indulged his curiosity without thinking again.

"That's what nearly cost me my ear, you know," he said to the unconscious Nightwalker. *Theo, his name is Theo. He's not a monster. He's Theo.* "Always sticking my nose into hollows and crevices. It was a small kraken, mind you, but still a kraken, and very much determined to take my head off. My pod sent it off with a good thrashing, thank the currents. But that's why I have scars, since it happened when I was a child. Do you have a pod? No, I suppose you were human once. Humans don't have pods, really, do they? Pairings with children, mostly. Like birds. Seems odd. Would be safer with more family."

He readjusted the icepack on Theo's forehead, guzzled some more water and tucked his feet up on the chair. Chairs were outrageously uncomfortable but this odd habit humans had of sleeping up high made it difficult to keep watch from the floor. Theo most likely couldn't hear him, but Limpet kept talking to let him know someone was there. He certainly wasn't babbling because he was frightened.

"These humans are lovely. They left us water and said I could take off those horrid shoes. How do you wear them all the time? Although you're not wearing them now. You look rather handsome in just your small clothes. I like these humans better than the ones on your night patrols. I don't think they liked you. Or me. Or that I was with you. It was difficult to say and you wouldn't let me ask questions. I would have asked you what a vamp fairy is. I suppose if you woke up now, I could ask you questions. So long as no one's about. I do hope you will. Wake up, that is. The humans said it was sunstroke. I suppose that's why they always have you on guard at night."

Limpet took a breath, wriggling on the goddesses-forsaken chair. "I liked walking with you."

Theo shifted on the bed, dislodging his icepack again. His forehead creased as he worried at something in his sleep, but he didn't wake. Carefully, Limpet replaced the ice and took one of Theo's hands in his. The long, pale fingers twitched, then curled tight around Limpet's. That strong hand around his felt lovely but now he was trapped. He didn't want to wake Theo by pulling away. Nothing for it, he would simply have to sit still for a bit and it really was a wonderful hand.

* * * *

"Prince Faisal, thank you for taking time out of your schedule to meet with me on such short notice." Sitting on cushions on the air-conditioned veranda, Diego took a sip of tea from the delicate gold-etched cup.

Beside him, Finn carefully mimicked his mannerisms and kept his mouth shut. Though he had to be careful of the black tea since it gave him raging headaches, he could still go through the motions to be polite. Filigree shadows decorated the tea setting from the pierced-carving arches that led out into lush, manicured gardens with softly laughing fountains. All a bit too controlled for Finn's tastes, but the surroundings did make their point. Here was vast wealth and power, a human privileged to live apart from his fellows.

"It is a delicate situation, Mr. Sandoval." The prince folded manicured hands in front of him, his mocha skin beautiful against the table's white marble. "Laws governing witchcraft are very strict here. Please understand that it is considered a great sin. Some have suggested that perhaps deportation to a more permissive country would be preferable, but my father and his advisors believe that it is better, safer, for the world to contain as many witches and demons as we can."

Demons, indeed. There is only one race of demons in this world. Finn bit his tongue, though. Prince Faisal was the second youngest of King Aziz's sons, considered the most liberal minded of the royal house. The Swiss ambassador had suggested the prince might be their best hope for an ally.

"We haven't come to interfere in your laws or court systems, Your Highness." *"Although I certainly want to,"* Diego sent internally to Finn. "The three young people in question are Canadian citizens, though."

Faisal swept a hand in a half-apologetic gesture. "The crime was committed here. But I appreciate that you wish to resolve this quietly, before it becomes an international media circus."

Diego put his cup down, the exaggerated care a measure of how tightly he held himself in check. "Thank you, Highness. I am authorized by the Fae Collective to offer whatever reparations the law deems necessary, or to otherwise negotiate for their release and subsequent return home."

A bitter smile flitted across the prince's face. "And you are here, rather than a Canadian diplomat, because they cannot be seen negotiating with such a barbarous regime, I suspect."

"I only know that we were asked to mediate, Highness."

With a tiny flick of his fingers, Prince Faisal waved away the attendant trying to pour him more tea. "I know what Westerners think of us but there is so much you don't understand about this region. However, I — "

Another palace employee hurried up on slippered feet to whisper in the prince's ear. His forehead creased as his expression darkened. Then he rose gracefully from his cushion and inclined his head toward them. "My apologies, Mr. Sandoval, Mr. Shannon. I shouldn't be more than a moment."

As the prince hurried out, Diego put a hand to his earpiece, his expression darkening. Kurt, outside with the car and the rest of their security, obviously didn't have anything good to say.

"Local police, you think? Or some government branch?" Diego asked before tilting his head to listen again. "All right. Keep everyone calm, please. The last thing we need is to start a shooting war." He halted again then went on. "No. If that happens, you get back to the embassy and call it in. No heroics, all right?"

Finn waited until Diego glanced up. "Your half of the conversation has not made me feel at all secure, my love."

"I don't think we are." Diego gripped his arm. "Kurt says there's trouble. Armed men in official vehicles pulled up, police of some kind. They have paperwork the prince's men are looking over and they're holding our security at gunpoint. Don't do anything threatening if they come for us. Please."

Finn swallowed hard, memories of previous arrests threatening to bury him. Diego in a past life burning at the stake. Diego being thrown to the ground and cuffed before a seizure hit. No matter that he had several friends who worked security now, he simply couldn't get past his fear of armed guards of any sort. "Diego…"

"I know. Me too." Diego's hand slid down, fingers twining with Finn's. "Terrified. But we'll get through this. They can't simply haul diplomats away. It's just not done."

Booted footsteps rang in the hall. A crowd of uniformed men burst through the doors onto the veranda, their expressions grim and forbidding. Finn's heart sank when he realized neither the prince nor any of his staff were with them. In fact, all the soft-spoken staff who had been attending them through the tea service had suddenly vanished.

"At least their guns aren't drawn," Diego sent in wry bravado.

"Leastwise not yet."

Diego stood slowly, pulling Finn up with him. "Can we help you, gentlemen?"

The man in front hesitated as he looked at a photo in his hand then back at Diego. When he finally spoke, it was in English. "Mr. Sandoval, you will come with us."

"May I ask where and for what purpose?"

"You are under arrest, sir."

Finn fought panic. He wanted to shift, to charge these men, bowl them over and fly Diego away. He forced his voice to remain calm. "He's done nothing wrong."

"What are the charges?" Diego asked in that even, flat tone that told Finn he was frightened.

"Suspicion of being a witch and harboring demons."

Diego ran a hand back through his hair. "Officer, with all due respect, this is absurd. As far as I know, it's legal to be a magic user here if you don't actively use magic. And I certainly don't know any demons."

"The new law mandates arrests for suspicion."

"New law? When?"

"This morning." The man motioned to the guards on either side of him.

Both men moved forward and when Diego stepped back and continued to protest, they pulled out things that looked like pistols from space shows on the picture box. Finn couldn't imagine why they were carrying toy guns, so he could only stand by in stupefied horror as these things suddenly shot out tiny wires that attached themselves to Diego.

"What in all go – "

Diego's thought cut off mid-word when strange clicks came from the wires. He stiffened, eyes wide and terrified, and collapsed. *"Finn! Oh…Dios…it hurts…run! Get to Kurt!"*

Every nerve screamed at Finn to do just that, but the need to protect Diego was far stronger. Rage blossomed around his heart as he whirled on the men with a savage roar. If he startled them enough, he might buy them time for an escape. Whatever terrible thing this weapon was doing, he had to get Diego clear of it, had to get him away from here.

He pulled hard on the flows, preparing to increase his mass. Talons grew from his feet and hands, wings sprouted from his back as he flung himself into the shift to dragon. With one sweep of his mighty tail, he would –

Agony shrieked through him as something heavy and burning cold landed over him. Finn struggled wildly, trying to find some way to break free, but the iron net simply tangled around him further. Stuck mid-shift, unable to move a drop of magic, Finn snarled at his attackers, some of whom appeared frightened, but none ran away.

He heard the word *demon* as several of them pulled out heavy truncheons and proceeded to beat him senseless while he lay trapped beneath the web of iron. Through the terrible pain, his last thought was more irritated than frightened. *You'd think I would get this rescue thing right, just once.*

* * * *

Theo woke in a haze of pain and hunger. The knives stabbing into his head made it harder to think. The sharpness of the blood need frightened him. *This shouldn't happen. I fed before we left the island. I should have a week at least.*

Worse still, they hadn't locked him away. Someone sat beside him, clutching his hand. Steady thrum of pulse beating against his skin. Scent of hot blood near, so very near…

"Go," he managed to whisper, though his throat felt raw and a growl started in his chest. Through the rising, pounding hunger, he latched on to the person's scent. *Limpet.* "Run. Please."

"Why would I do that? You just woke up." Limpet's hissing whisper grated on his frayed nerves. "Humans are shouting downstairs. I think it's safer here with you. They left and came back, and now there's all this ye –"

"Limpet!" Theo slitted his eyes open, grateful for the drawn curtains and dim lamplight. He wrenched his hand from Limpet's, gritting his teeth against the growing need. "Leave the room. Close the door. Or you'll be dinner."

The selkie's black eyes grew huge as he knocked the chair over in his attempt to back away. Theo expected him to flee. Any sensible person would have. He knew how he looked—eyes red and half-mad, fangs extended, hands shaking with need. Like a crazed junkie, that's how. He just needed a few minutes alone to pull himself together.

But Limpet stopped, still within reach, and shook the hair back from his eyes with a lift of his chin that screamed forced bravado. "You've fed from other fae. The humans told me. I could...could help you."

"I'm not in control," Theo grated out as he curled into a ball and buried his face in the pillow. *Your scent is making me crazy.* Comemierda, *selkie.*

"You are." Limpet's soft tenor shook and cracked, but he took a step closer. "You haven't attacked me."

Theo snarled in frustration. "Go get Kurt. *Carajo*, you're an idiot. You think I'm a monster. Why are you still here?"

"You're..." Limpet swallowed hard and Theo fought not to think about his Adam's apple sliding up and down his long, beautiful throat. "You're not a monster. You're Theo."

He heard all the yelling downstairs. Something had gone wrong. He had to find out, but he couldn't leave the room, not like this. Kurt had said he would volunteer in an emergency, but feeding from human males was hard, in too many ways. If it wasn't a violent feeding, the sexual charge lacing it made the process horribly uncomfortable. Sure, if he had someone who loved him, like his friend Jasper did, feeding would have been easy, even wonderful. As a nonhuman, Limpet was actually the better choice.

"Sit," Theo growled. "Don't move from there." He waited until Limpet settled on the edge of the chair as if it were made of eggshells. "Wrist."

"Don't you need a throat to feed from? How will you—"

"Shh. Safer this way."

"Safer if I only offer my wrist or safer if I'm quiet? Will this hurt? How much do you take? Will I bleed all over the floor?"

"Shut up. Please. Just shut up."

Limpet clamped his lips shut and held out his left arm, which shook as badly as Theo's hands. *Great. Nothing like fear to make the predator reactions worse.*

With exaggerated care, Theo turned on his side and slid his hand under Limpet's forearm. Warmth seeped into his fingers, the accelerated thump of a living pulse driving spikes of need through him. He shivered, resting his forehead on his arm and breathing in little sips. None of the clichéd things he wanted to say— *Trust me. I won't hurt you. Just relax*—made it past his clenched teeth. He didn't think he could get any more words out through the scarlet drumbeat in his head.

There was a whimper. He wasn't sure if it was his or Limpet's. Then Limpet moved in closer and stroked his hair. "It's all right. I'm not a fragile human. Let me help you."

Sea, salt, blood, musk—this close, Limpet's scent escalated from maddening to a full-cry assault. Theo dug the fingers of his free hand into the mattress, fighting hard with his bestial side. If he lost his grip, even for an instant, he would become a raving, mindless hunter. Everyone in the building would be at risk. Limpet was wrong. He was a monster.

Forcing himself to move with excruciating deliberation, as if he had to draw each movement anew cell-animation style, he hovered over Limpet's wrist, squeezing his eyes shut as he leaned down to lick over the vein. Now the selkie did whimper, but instead of tensing and trying to pull away, the muscles in his forearm relaxed under Theo's grip. The angle was awkward. Most of his fae feeders preferred to hold him when he fed. Those huge warrior types seemed to have an overwhelming urge to comfort *him* while he took blood from *them*.

"Go on," Limpet whispered, soft and soothing rather than his usual *sotto voce* hiss. "I'm here."

No more slow motion. The bite had to be quick and clean. Theo opened his mouth, positioned his fangs carefully and bit down. The sensation of teeth piercing skin went straight to his groin. That didn't often happen with a fae feeding. He shifted to hide his growing erection. *Damn it, where are the rest of my clothes? Concentrate. Pull the fangs gently so flesh won't tear. Clamp on tight and suck hard.* If he ever did have a lover again, at least he would have the suction part down.

Above him, Limpet drew in a shuddering breath. He squirmed around, slid off the chair to kneel beside the bed, then laid his head on Theo's shoulder. Such a strange thing to do, so trusting, almost tender, the oddness of it helped him stay present and sane. After a few good pulls, enough to ease the pain the sun had caused and before the fae-blood buzz slid over into a disabling high, Theo let go, licking at the little punctures to help close them. It was hardly necessary with the fae, they healed so quickly, but it always felt more polite.

Still draped over him, Limpet asked, "Better?"

Now Theo had to fight the urge to wrap his arms around Limpet. He sat up instead with a hand over his lap. "Yes. I have to get downstairs now."

A little fae drunk, he had to steady himself on the nightstand when he tugged on his pants. It wasn't too bad, though. He wasn't falling over and giggling as he did after a *sidhe* feeding. The yelling had died down to an occasional angry, shouted sentence now, which could be good or bad. Theo yanked on a T-shirt and left his boots and gear, more anxious by the second to know what was happening.

He yanked the door open and was about to rush out when something urged him to glance back. Limpet stood in the middle of the room, eyes just as huge as they had been before, shifting from one foot to the other.

"You better come too." When Limpet didn't budge, Theo grabbed his hand and tugged him along. "You'll probably explode if you have to wait alone."

The unhappy, anxious look persisted and Theo could have smacked himself.

"Ah, thank you. For helping me. You...thank you."

He must have been a touch more drunk than he thought since Limpet's smile made his chest feel tight and strange.

Chapter Six

Phoenix
Classification: Dual-natured fae *shifter*
Appoquinimink social scale: 6
Phoenix sightings are rare due equally to habitat, wariness of
humans and reported numbers. Some sources claim only one
or two phoenixes exist in an eternal cycle of self-immolation
and rebirth.
The Compendium of the Magically Sensitive, 4th Edition,
Dr. Nathan Cooper

"We're going to need a location." Sick with worry and frustration, Zack rubbed at the side of his face and tried to calm the screaming in his brain. "I'll try everything, but it'll be better if we know where."

"Fucking prison's a state secret! Nobody has a clue where the thing is!" Kurt bellowed. "Sorry, sir. I'm just— Damn it. There should've been something we could've done."

"Like what? The ambassador said we could trust the meeting location. We had to trust someone's intel on the ground. Once the police arrived, you couldn't light up the place. Or are you James Bond now?"

"No, sir." Kurt's response was so sullen and defeated Zack knew he had to come up with something.

"Look, you handled it the best way possible. We were set up. Proper authorities handled the arrest. You got four of your original party to safety without casualties and two more remained secure." Zack began typing instructions to Carol, trying to plan his next steps. "Stay low. Stay quiet. No movement unless it's on my say so. But if you or that Bakkal guy can come up with where this senmaj prison is, you call me. I don't care if it's freaking three in the morning."

"Sir."

That's our Kurt. Better.

He hung up and leaned back against Lugh, wishing he could just break down and cry. "I should never have let him talk me into letting him go."

"And make him feel that his help was unwelcome and that he couldn't be trusted?" Lugh smoothed a hand over Zack's hair. "We're all worried, you know. But you couldn't trample Diego's shaken pride that way."

"A real leader has to know when to trample."

"Still, we will find a way, through one means or another. It is merely a prison and not a witch-burning, after all."

"God, I hope so. What if they change the laws again and decide to have bonfires instead of prison sentences? Shit."

"We can't look at what might be, my braveheart. Prince Faisal was very apologetic. He had no idea his father was sending the police and he promises to help in any way he can."

"Yeah, 'cause he's been such a big help so far."

Lugh sighed, his huge hands moving down to knead Zack's shoulders. "Is our Theo all right?"

"He's fine. That selkie kid stowed away on the plane, hell only knows how that happened. But he's the one who fed Theo after that disaster at the airport."

"Good, as far as Theo's concerned. Though I don't look forward to telling Limpet's pod when they arrive searching for him."

Zack completely understood wanting to think about a confrontation they could handle, but he said the obvious anyway, "Somehow, I don't think that's our biggest problem right now."

* * * *

Gray. Something had leached all the color from the world. Had he hit his head and lost his ability to perceive color? Diego curled up on his side, trying to make sense of things before he attempted to move. A gray cinderblock wall four feet away connected to another, shorter wall...

Ah. A cell. Right. We were being arrested. "Finn?"

No answer. He pushed himself up on one arm, sitting up with muscles that felt bruised on the inside. It wasn't the same as the pain after a seizure. Some sort of loose gray pajamas had replaced his clothes. The sleeves were too long and when Diego rolled them up, he found dull gray metal cuffs around his wrists.

This can't be good.

Cuffs encircled his ankles and when he felt a cold weight on his collarbones, he reached up with shaking fingers to find a metal collar around his throat. He got to his feet, trying to make sense of his surroundings. If this was a prison cell, it was an odd one. Both longer walls were solid. Both shorter walls had featureless metal doors. A single, bare bulb burned overhead. A single speaker crouched in one corner of the ceiling.

"Hello? Can someone hear me? Am I allowed a phone call?" As he spoke to the ceiling, the cinderblock walls and concrete floor gave him some hope. If he could gather his magic carefully, he could make a door. He could…nothing.

No. Esta de pinga. Not again.

Diego refocused and reached outward from his center, only to run up against barriers at his throat and limbs. The cuffs and collar contained lead, most likely lead-cored steel from the looks of them. Iron weakened the fae and blocked their magic but one of the only things that kept a human from reaching the flows was lead.

A squawk came from the speaker, followed by a voice speaking what Diego assumed were several Middle Eastern languages in succession. When Mandarin followed, he was certain it was the same repeated message, though he had to wait until the French portion to glean even a sense of what it meant. *Door, exit, now* — those words were ones he could pick out.

Finally, the message repeated in English, "When the door opens, step through immediately. The intake chamber will be chemically cleansed. For your safety, you must vacate the intake chamber now."

The door to his left slid open and closed behind him after he stepped through. He had assumed he was moving into another cell, but a long hallway of the same dimly lit cinderblock walls and concrete floor as the cell stretched before him, though these walls soared at least twenty feet up into the gloom. No further instructions followed, so Diego started walking, his bare feet whispering in the oppressive silence. The anxious emptiness of separation hadn't hit him, so Finn had to be here somewhere. Finding him had to be the first priority.

He pulled at the collar as he went, hoping that its lead core might make it weak, running his hands over it to find a catch or a lock. The thing wouldn't budge and only bit into his neck as he yanked on it. He couldn't even find a seam where it had been fastened.

The hallway led into a cross-corridor, the walls here dotted with recessed, empty rooms. None of these small spaces had doors or bars. No guards appeared at any point to impede his progress or tell him he wasn't allowed to go on. Was he alone in this prison? It was a prison, wasn't it?

Diego continued on, slowing as he passed larger spaces, ominous in their darkness. When the path turned right, he caught movement out of the corner of his eye, a whisper of cloth, but whoever it was had vanished when he spun around. A brighter light shone farther along, so he hurried toward that, suddenly fearful of the darker spaces. When he reached the three rectangles of sunlight on the floor, he followed the shafts to three slits fifteen feet up on the ceiling, openings so narrow they wouldn't have served as arrow slits in a medieval fortress.

If he had been able to access his magic, he might have considered those an escape option. But then, if he could have ripped holes in walls with his magic, he could have simply built a magical door and gone home.

The whispers returned, just at the edge of hearing, the owners nowhere in sight. An odd anticipation hung in the air. A klaxon blared, heart-stopping as it sliced through the silence. Dark rectangles began to drop from the windows and Diego took two involuntary steps back to avoid them. Suddenly the corridor exploded with human activity. People in gray prison pajamas raced toward the rectangles, bulging packets maybe eight inches long. The prisoners shoved each other out of the way, tripping those too far in front. One man, larger than his fellows, tossed people aside as he waded through to claim the majority of the largest pile. Others, furtive and quick, snatched single bundles from the edges and darted away into the gloom.

A group of prisoners with covered heads swooped in, maintaining a tight phalanx to snatch up packets and hand them into the center of the group. They successfully fended off the few prisoners who tried to steal from them and vanished as swiftly as they had arrived. *Men and women in the same prison?*

It was over within moments. Every one of the dropped items had been seized and most of the prisoners had scurried off into the dark. One man lay moaning on the floor a moment before he managed to stagger away empty-handed. Then the only people left in the eerily quiet space were Diego and three young people huddled by the wall with one packet between them. Thoroughly confused, he walked toward them.

"Hurry up! Before someone comes!" the one on the left whispered.

The one on the right twitched and glanced up at Diego. "Fuck. Too late."

"Don't look. Don't pay any attention." The third one with the packet said. "Just do it fast. He can't take what we've already scarfed down."

Apparently, he was a threat. Diego stopped and sat down cross-legged, still a good ten feet from them, with his hands on his knees. The trio huddled close with their heads bent over the packet, scooping things into their mouths. The whole series of events began to make sense in horrible ways.

"You three aren't from here," he said in what he hoped was his gentlest tone.

The triple-headed double-take was almost funny. Almost.

"English. And he sounds American," the middle one whispered, his eyes huge in what might have been hope or sheer terror.

Diego hazarded an educated guess. "My name is Diego Sandoval. I am American but I was here with Tearmann Island staff to try to negotiate the release of three Canadian college students. Could that be you?"

"Oh my God. It's him." The one on the right tugged at the middle one's sleeve. "The guy from...you know, the TV. You're getting us out?"

"I had hoped to get you out." Diego cleared his throat. "But they changed the laws the morning I arrived and arrested me for being a witch."

"Crud."

Diego dragged a hand back through his hair. "Yes. Sorry about that. You are the ones? Ethan? Josh? Gavin?" They each reacted in turn to a name, so Diego was certain he had the middle one pegged as Ethan, the one who seemed most assertive. "Don't think you're abandoned, though, just because my mission failed. There are a lot of people trying to get you out."

For some reason, this reassurance made Josh hide his face in his hands, sniffling.

"Hey. Stop." Ethan cuffed him gently. "The others might be watching. We can't be weak, right?"

Diego waited until Josh wiped at his eyes, pulling himself together, then asked, "Since I just arrived, could you tell me what happened here?"

"Feeding time at the zoo," Gavin muttered bitterly.

"Seemed so. But isn't there enough for everyone? Why the frantic scramble?"

Ethan shrugged. "It's not much. It's once a day. There might be enough for everyone but some jerks take more. Because they can."

"There aren't any guards in here to keep order?"

"No. Just us zoo animals."

"And no one tells them no."

"If you want to get hit, sure." Gavin shook his head. "Ethan tried the first day we were here. We were worried he'd never wake up again."

Diego filed that away, distressed at how quickly humans turned on each other in a bad situation. Though throwing everyone together, regardless of gender, criminal past or state of mental health, was asking for chaos. *The government would probably be happy if we killed each other off.*

So many questions, but only one Diego really wanted answered. "I only saw humans in the scramble. Are there nonhumans here, too? Or are they kept in a different prison?"

All three youngsters blinked at him in confusion.

"My husband was with me when I was arrested. I haven't seen him yet. He's a pooka." *If they arrested him. If nothing worse happened.*

"He might be in the monster cell block," Josh muttered.

Gavin snorted. "Tactful much? It's in the center of this place. We heard other prisoners call the fae 'monsters', but there's only a couple of monster-type things down there."

"You speak Arabic?"

"Yeah, well, some. That's why we came to this damn country. Language exchange students."

"Could you show me?"

"Dunno, Mr. Sandoval. We've got a pretty full schedule today." Ethan furrowed his brow as if he had to consider.

"Just Diego, please." Diego stood and offered him a hand up. "Good to see your sense of humor's intact. We're going to get out of this." *I just don't know how or when yet.*

Ethan tore the now-empty packet into strips and handed them round. "Here. Everybody take some leaf. Mr. – Diego, we don't know what it is, but it's safe to eat."

"Thank you."

The leaf was tough but edible and they all gnawed on their pieces in silence as they walked. The boys stayed close together, eyes darting everywhere as if they expected an ambush any moment. Ethan stopped them at the next turn, checking around the corner before he waved them on. They passed one or two figures huddled against the wall, but most of the prison's occupants had vanished.

After another right-hand turn, it became clear that the prison hallways comprised a rectangle and that along this looping main corridor, there were open rooms with sometimes obvious and sometimes not at all obvious uses, but no cells. They finally arrived at a door, the first one since Diego had left the intake room, and Ethan pushed through. A darker, short hall greeted them, leading into the heart of the prison rectangle. Heavy-looking metal doors with tiny barred windows near the top lined both sides.

"Monster jail," Josh whispered as they crept down the corridor.

Diego pushed tentatively at the first door. Locked. Snuffling came from behind that one and a scrabble of claws. Too short to peek in the window, he moved on. He tried several more on his way down. All locked tight. Finally, he placed himself in the center and bellowed, "Finn! *Mi vida? Dónde estás?*"

Shrieking and howling answered him from some of the cells. The echoing corridor made it difficult to tell how many. But underneath the cacophony, he heard a voice, the one he so needed to hear.

"Diego? I'm here…please…"

Halfway down on the left, a hand waved through the bars of a cell door. Diego moved toward it since it matched the direction of Finn's answer. He stopped short, though. The hand had scales and claws. "Finn? Is that you?"

"The one and only." Finn's voice shook and the clawed hand waved again. "I'm so sorry, my heart. I couldn't—" He broke off on a huge sniff, the sound nearly breaking Diego's heart.

"No apologies, *cariño.* Why do you have claws?" Diego reached up to take the offered hand and knew beyond a doubt that it was Finn when the claws closed around his fingers gently, the thumb claw caressing his knuckles.

"I tried…there was an iron net. If only I'd been a little blasted faster."

Unable to wait for more non-explanations, Diego seized the bars with both hands and dragged himself up so he could look through the window.

Finn blinked at him and offered a watery smile. "There you are. Are you unarrested?"

"No. I just get a bigger cage to wander around in." Diego took in the too-sharp teeth, the start of a crest, the odd color of Finn's eyes, and the collar around his throat. "Finn...*Dios*...they trapped you mid-dragon shift?"

His poor husband nodded, unable to meet Diego's eyes. "The iron net. And with this goddesses-forsaken iron collar, I can't finish and I can't change back."

"How do you feel?" Diego had to let himself down on shaking arms, but he took Finn's offered hand again. "Have they fed you?"

The hand rose and fell and Diego could envision the shrug that went with the movement. "They dropped something through the slit in the ceiling. I think it's meant to be food but with the iron, I can't eat."

Diego swallowed hard, pressing his cheek to the scaled back of Finn's hand. "I wish I could take it off. I can't even take my own off. Does it hurt terribly?"

"Oh, it's not so bad, love. Don't fret about me." Finn gave him a squeeze, his voice full of false bravado. "I'm sure our friends will come for us. Or you'll figure a way out."

"Finn..." Diego kissed each half-scaled finger, trying to blink back the tears.

"Don't you cry, bucko. Then I will and where will we be then? Separated still and wet. I'm sure you have things to plan, my clever Taliesin."

"I don't know what I can do. I can't feel the flows at all." He told Finn about the prison layout and the other inmates at feeding time. "I've never felt so useless. Well, rarely. Even if they do get us out, what about these other poor people?"

"I don't much care about them," Finn grumbled. "Just that you're safe. But listen — you were powerful before. Before you met me. Before your channels unblocked and you could direct the flows again. You're still that man. Without your magic, you're still that man. Use what you have always had. Find out all you can. Perhaps there will be a way."

"I don't want to leave you alone here."

"Oh, I'm not alone. There's a lovely phoenix in the next cell and a Were in the one across the way. He's not much company now, but I expect when he changes back he could be. Go on, Diego. Find out what you can. Come visit me in between. I'll be here."

"I love you."

Finn managed an almost convincing laugh. "I know. I love you, too, but you're embarrassing your young friends. I can feel them rolling their eyes from here."

"All right. Try to rest, *mi vida*. I'll be back soon."

As he walked away, Diego told himself it wasn't like other times they had been separated. He knew exactly where Finn was and could speak to him whenever he needed to. But, damn it, he hated to leave Finn in pain, unable to help him.

And what does he mean, what I was before? How does having once been a failed, starving writer help us now?

A shudder ran up Diego's spine as they left the cellblock. One of the doors stood open, a bundle of cloth indicating there had been an occupant. He could only assume the poor fae had died.

* * * *

A furtive scrape woke Limpet. Not that he'd been sleeping deeply. The news of the arrests had been too disturbing, the shouting, angry humans just a little too unsettling. They weren't upset with him, but that hadn't made his heartbeat any calmer. He cracked an eye open, peeking out from his blanket nest on the floor of Theo's room. *What do I do if someone's here who shouldn't be?*

It was Theo, though, moving about in near silence, an occasional flash of metal catching in the moonlight while he stuffed things into a bag. *He's going somewhere. That's what humans do. They stuff things in bags before they go somewhere.*

Limpet watched a bit longer, careful not to move or make a sound. *And he doesn't want anyone to know. Why?*

He waited until Theo had opened the window and climbed out before he slipped into his human clothes and followed with his human shoes in hand. Boots. These were called boots. He hated having the heavy things on his feet but some of the surfaces humans walked on were too hot or too horrid for bare feet. Leaning out, he just caught the edge of Theo's shadow as he slid along the wall. Eel silent, he moved through the shadows like water and Limpet saw him only because he knew where to look.

Theo had been quietly enraged earlier that evening. The older security people said they didn't know where to find the prison and wouldn't listen when Theo said he could try to find it. The big one, Kurt, had said, "Oh, yeah? What then, kid? You gonna pull a Spartacus and get the prisoners to revolt? Take down all the guards alone? You suddenly immune to a bullet through the heart?"

Perhaps he had a point, but Limpet thought it a cruel way to say it. The older ones disregarded Theo and it seemed simply because he was younger and not because he was a Nightwalker.

There were guards at the gate to this walled human place, ones armed with guns. Theo had explained modern guns on evening patrol. They sounded nasty. But the Nightwalker simply found the darkest spot of shadow on the high wall, leaped straight up to catch the top of it and pulled himself over. Regular humans couldn't do that. Limpet had to follow more slowly, using the cracks in the stones to climb. Despite the delay, he located his quarry as Theo moved down the street.

The hour for humans was late. Most slept and the city was relatively quiet. Limpet threw the hood of his borrowed jacket up to cover his ears and his hair, just in case. His pulse pounded, terrified of being caught and dragged off to prison as Finn had been, equally terrified of what Theo's plans might be. He liked Theo, but what if he only *appeared* good? Limpet had certainly been mistaken about people before.

Theo continued along the wall, heading for the place where their host humans kept all their conveyances. His parents had always told him that horses and oxen pulled humans' coaches and carriages. Clearly, that was no longer the case and he couldn't help but feel smug about already knowing more concerning current human customs than the rest of his pod combined.

He flattened himself against the wall when Theo stopped and crouched low. He seemed to be assessing the guardhouse and the humans manning it. There were three — one in the little house itself, one standing at the metal fence and one pacing the walkway in front. They hadn't spotted Theo, but human eyesight was terrible.

He's going to attack them. Should I warn them? Will he hurt them? Limpet dithered long enough that it was too late. Theo exploded from his crouch and flattened the guard on the walkway with a single punch. He raced to the next guard and took him down in a shadowed blur. By the time the guard seated in the house looked up from his reading, Theo was on him, having leapt over the gate, ripped the door open and subdued him as well. Fangs flashed in the lighted room and Limpet's heart stuttered and thumped in fear. *He's killed them! He didn't get enough from me and he's killed them...*

Before he had finished the thought, Theo had done something to open the gate and moved on, into the corral where the vehicles rested for the night. Trying to keep silent, though he wanted to whimper, Limpet crept forward and checked the first guard. *Still alive. Neck's not even broken.* Limpet frowned and moved on to the next and found a strong pulse still beating. So he only killed the third one? Carefully, Limpet slipped up to the third guard. His heart also beat steadily and he appeared to be simply sleeping, a peaceful smile on his face despite the fang marks on his throat.

Confused, Limpet followed Theo's scent trail out among the vehicles. The trail led to one of the taller vehicles, one with big wheels and the seat compartment set higher off the ground. Theo cursed softly as he fiddled with the set of keys in his hand. The last round of curses seemed more relieved than angry as the vehicle roared to life and Theo began to back it out of its corral spot.

Limpet leaped into the open back of the thing just before Theo made it roar away. Of course this was a foolish, muddleheaded thing to do, but he simply had to find out what Theo intended.

Chapter Seven

Djinn
Classification: Elemental fae
Appoquinimink social scale: 5
Born of wind and fire, djinn are powerful manipulators of
magic. While naturally social, unfortunate contacts with
humans over the centuries have resulted in suspicion and
even open hostility.
The Compendium of the Magically Sensitive, 4th Edition,
Dr. Nathan Cooper

By the second day, Diego understood how the prison worked, more or less. No guards ever entered the prison itself. Apparently, even collared in lead, magical prisoners were considered too dangerous.

Facilities were in one of the cavernous rooms along the hallway nearest the intake chamber. Gavin explained that the group of women left a headscarf hanging on a peg at the entrance when they occupied it, and heaven have mercy on any male who wandered in. Long troughs carved into the floor along two walls with constantly flowing water served as the toilets, relatively sanitary in theory if no one missed, but woefully lacking in privacy.

Showers were without soap, though the nozzles flowed with a combination of water and some sharp-smelling disinfectant. For clean clothes, one simply showered with them on, since there were no changes of clothing. Diego wondered what happened when the prison pajamas wore out.

In between any necessary activities, most of the prisoners vanished into the dark rooms to huddle in some anonymous corner. The women made up the only organized group, ten of them currently, who snatched up any female incarcerated before the males could harass her or worse. For mutual assistance and protection, it seemed to work well, though their presence in any area only heightened the anxiety and antisocial behavior of the male prisoners.

"It's almost feeding time," Josh whispered as they hurried through the corridor.

Furtive shuffling and muffled curses came from close by, the prisoners on the move, but Diego hadn't heard any warning or announcement. "How do you know?"

"You kinda get to know by feel," Ethan said. "But the sun shines directly through those murder hole slits when it's time."

They were barely in position when the klaxon sounded and Diego rushed in with the rest, snatching up a food packet that had bounced and fallen at the periphery of the melee. He backed up to the wall, waiting for his Canadian friends to emerge. Just like the previous day, the frenzied scramble was over in moments. The large man had made off with more than his share, again. The squad of women had taken every packet they could. Ethan was elated that they had managed three packets between them—a good day apparently—and once again, more than one inmate was left sprawled on the floor with nothing.

One of them, a man with graying hair, knelt on the stones with his head in his hands and wept. While Diego wasn't certain, he thought it might have been the same man who had been left lying on the floor the previous day. A hand caught his sleeve when he took a step forward.

"Don't." Gavin shook his head frantically. "He'll just take your food and the others will think you're an easy target."

Diego patted his hand. "I'll probably be desperately hungry in a few days, but right now, I think he's gone without longer than I have."

His young friends still looked at him as if he'd lost his mind, but Diego approached slowly, kneeling on the floor just out of reach when the man flinched away. English probably wasn't a common language between them, but Diego still spoke as he held out the packet, understanding the universality of a gentle voice. "Here. For you. I saw you didn't get any."

The man stared at him, his expression hostile and wary. His hand, scarred and gaunt, shook as he reached across the intervening space, bit by bit, as if certain the food would be yanked back. Finally, he snatched it and scuttled away to put his back to the wall while Diego stayed where he was, making certain no one interrupted him while he wolfed down the meager portion.

The man stared at him with more speculation than fear once he had finished. He tore off little bits of the leaf wrapping, chewing thoughtfully as he got up and scurried away.

The boys waited for Diego just in the shadows. "That was crazy," Josh said. "You're certifiable."

Diego shrugged. "People who are hungry and without hope act like animals. Treat them like people and they act like people."

"Or they turn on you and kill you," Gavin muttered.

"I thought it was decent." Ethan's tone said there wouldn't be any more argument. "Everybody give Diego some of theirs so he doesn't starve."

Despite their horror at him sharing with a stranger, all three gave him a portion without hesitation. *Ah, it's safe to share with friends. Good to have friends in a scary spot.* The contents of the leaf packet turned out to be some sort of bulgur wheat mash. Bland but filling. The leaves themselves, Diego decided, were a variety of grape leaf. Not the most complete diet, but it could keep a body going for some time.

When they turned to make their own way back into the relative safety of the shadows, a man on the other side of the feeding area caught his eye. The man met his stare, without reaction or apparent hostility. Tall, with a regal hooked nose, he simply watched every movement Diego made. A trick of the light made his eyes flash gold, then he was gone.

"Did you see...?"

"What?"

Diego shook his head, wondering if the man had been there at all. "Never mind."

* * * *

At the first traffic signal, Theo let out a slow, irritated breath. "You may as well come out. I know you're back there."

The expected blue-gray-green head of hair popped up from the tarp-covered bed of the truck. "Oh. Hello!"

"Hello yourself. You need to get your annoying butt out of that truck bed and back to the embassy where you're safe."

Limpet frowned as he climbed over the divider to plunk into the passenger seat. "I can't let you do whatever you're doing. It can't be anything good, since you're slinking around in the middle of the night and you hurt those guards. Though you didn't kill them. I checked. But then you drank from one of them. And I thought you said you didn't drink from humans. Wasn't my blood terribly filling? What are you about, anyway? Are you going to find more humans to drink from?" Limpet stopped and blinked at him. "You think my rump is annoying?"

Theo banged his head on the steering wheel. It didn't help and Limpet was still there when he stopped. "I don't usually drink from humans because it's too uncomfortable. Too tangled up with sex, not that it's your business. And I have to find out where they took Finn and Mr. Sandoval. We can't just leave them there and hope someone else will help."

"Oh." Limpet nodded as if arriving at some conclusion. "Good. You're so right. We should find them. But you drank from that human. And you didn't answer the last question."

"You can't come with me," Theo infused his voice with the iron-cold compulsion that he'd found worked on humans. It was an odd, uncomfortable magic that left the taste of old onions in his mouth, but it was effective.

"Of course I can," Limpet said cheerfully, putting his boots up on the dash. "I know how to ride in human vehicles now."

Mierda, mierda, mierda... "Go away! You'll slow me down. I can't feed you. I can't keep you safe. You're a water creature and we're probably going out into the fucking desert!" Theo drove on when the signal changed, taking deep, careful breaths. He hadn't shouted at anyone like that in years. He couldn't lose control. Before the change, it had made him feel wretched and guilty. Now, it couldn't be a choice. He lost control and people died.

Instead of edging away or, more sensible still, jumping out at the next traffic signal and running, Limpet did an odd thing. He put his head on Theo's shoulder with a little sigh. "You're worried. I knew you couldn't be bad. You worry about Diego and Finn. You worry about the people you feed from. You worry about me. I suppose that's nice of you, but it's a bit irritating—"

Theo choked on a breath, trying not to sputter. Limpet paused only to pat his chest.

"Everyone's always worried about me. As if they could wrap me up in a kelp bed and keep me safe forever. But nothing's safe forever, is it? And if you don't let things *not* be safe, they suffocate. I won't slow you down since we're in a conveyance. I can go without food for weeks and I've been doing well without swimming. If you"—Limpet poked a finger at Theo's sternum—"can travel into the sun-parched land when the sun makes you ill, which you shouldn't do alone, it's just not smart, I certainly can. And you never answered the last question."

Theo took a left turn, chewing carefully on his bottom lip. One thing at a time. He had to get to the prince's palace first. There was no guarantee he could even pick up a trail. He couldn't take a chance on heading back now, though, since the guards had most likely woken. *What last question? Oh.* "Fine. You can come as far as the palace, at least. Stay quiet. Don't be a nuisance. If I tell you to do something, you do it. And no, your butt's not annoying. You are."

Limpet snuggled close on the bench seat, which wasn't nearly as irritating as it should have been. As they drove out of the city toward the prince's estate, Theo tried to make plans. He hadn't really expected to get this far.

* * * *

Zack stared into the garden fountain, trying desperately to get his brain to work. He'd put in a call to his friends at the Heersford Institute, but he hadn't heard back yet. If the Silver Adepts couldn't find the prison, he didn't know what to do next. The assumption had been that the prison was in the capitol somewhere, but he'd had word from his staff in Shera'alej that anyone arrested for breaking magic control laws was transported by helicopter. Lugh was still on the phone getting support lined up from certain key international players, but so far no one was willing to commit or so much as issue an official statement.

The buzzing in his pocket interrupted his moment of quiet. *Carol's number. What now?*

"Zack? You might want to get over here." Carol had to raise her voice over the babble in the administrative office.

He was moving even as he asked, "What is it? What in hells is all that noise?"

"Our little selkie stowaway's parents have come looking for him and they brought the family."

"Wonderful. Sorry about all this, Carol."

"Don't apologize. I took this job because I was tired of boring office work, remember?"

Zack managed a strangled laugh and tried to control the tic in his jaw when he walked into the verbal chaos. Quite a mob had crowded into the office, which was roomy for the three or four humans usually working there, but cramped for twelve angry, arm-waving fae. They wore robes from the receiving room at the top of the fae cavern stairs, so selkies apparently lived *au natural* normally. Except for the small ears and the black on black eyes, they appeared human…if maybe they had been a rock band with an odd taste in hair dye. Long hair in various shades of white, blue, gray and green tumbled down their backs, all the colors of the world's ocean waves.

"Hello? Excuse me." He tried to speak politely above the tumult. When that got him nowhere, he bellowed, "Hey! Quiet down in here!"

The selkies turned to him, those big, black eyes conveying surprise. They were beautiful and just a little bit creepy as they all stared at him like they had one brain.

He decided to address the biggest male, since he seemed to have been making the most noise. "Good morning, I'm Zack Morrison, the Fae Collective Consul.

I'm going to take a wild guess here and say you're Limpet's family."

"We are his pod." The big guy's voice shook as he held out a hand to one of the female selkies. "I am his father, Cerith, and this is his mother, Lyonsia. He's our pod's youngest child. We've come to take him home."

"Folks, I'd love to let you do that, but he's not here."

The mom, Lyonsia, wailed and threw herself sobbing into Cerith's arms. "I told you! The Devourer has eaten him!"

"What? No!"

Just like that, Zack lost control of the situation again, and everyone reverted to trying to yell over each other. Flummoxed, Zack leaned against the doorway, rubbing at his forehead. *I really don't need this right now.*

A sharp blare shredded through the yelling and Zack jerked his head up to find Carol standing on her desk in her sensible, proper dress shoes, with an air horn in hand and a scowl on her face. "That's quite enough! Inside voices! If you can't behave like civilized selkies, you'll have to go back down to the caverns. Now, then. Consul Morrison is a Were. We don't like the D-word here and he's a lovely man who would never eat your son. Limpet isn't here because of choices *Limpet* made. I suggest you go out to the garden with the Consul and he'll explain all he can."

"Thanks, Carol. The icing on my day," Zack said, but he waved the selkies after him. "Come on, folks. We'll go have a seat in the garden and hopefully talk instead of yell."

The selkies followed, subdued and unhappy, and managed to settle quietly in the grass by the fountain. Cerith held his sobbing mate, trying to soothe her, so another one of the big ones spoke up. "Simply tell us where Limpet has gone. We won't trouble you any further. One ocean or another, we'll find him."

Zack heard the unspoken *since you managed to lose him*, and ignored it. "Well, that's part of the problem. You can't reach him by ocean and I really don't recommend you going where he is."

He explained, as briefly as he could, about magical laws, Shera'alej, the Canadian college students, Diego's hopes to retrieve them and Limpet's stowaway stunt. The selkies listened attentively, though they seemed to droop more and more through the telling.

"We should have taken him." Lyonsia sniffed miserably. "He was so curious, so angry that we kept him by the home shore. We should have come through the door, all of us, so he could have seen for himself and been safe."

There was a babble of voices then and Zack wondered how any of them ever made themselves understood. The phone buzzed against his thigh again and he excused himself to walk away a few steps and take the call.

"Hey, Sarge!"

"Nate! How's it hanging, bud? Oh, sorry — guess I need to say Dr. Cooper now, huh?"

Nathan laughed, that same low, happy one he'd always had. "Yeah, well, Dr. Cooper's for students, not for our Sergeant Morrison. Jazz says hi and he's sorry we haven't been able to visit. But you know, busy with our first grad students coming in and new research patients."

"Hey, it's okay. I get that. Maybe over the holidays or something. But I'm thinking you didn't call just to catch up."

"Right." All the laughter drained from Nathan's voice. "So we got your message about Mr. S. and Finn. Damn, I'm so sorry."

"Just spit it out. You haven't been able to look?"

"Oh, we tried. Kara's here this week, so we had the full coven. We did the map dowsing, which should have worked, but we could only get so far. All we can tell you is that prison is somewhere in the desert of Shera'alej."

"What's that mean? Only so far?"

"Something was blocking us, Sarge. Either they're using magic to hide the place, and wouldn't that just be the most hypocritical thing ever, or they're using one of the metals that act as a magic insulator for humans. Lead, tin to some extent, something like that. Whatever they're using, we can't get through."

"Damn it. Damn, damn, damn," Zack muttered, kicking at a stone wall on one of the raised flowerbeds. "Sorry. Thanks for trying, Nate. It's just so damn frustrating, sitting here wondering what's happening to them."

"I know. We feel it here, too. You just got them back and now this."

Nate promised they would keep trying and as soon as Zack disconnected, the phone buzzed again.

"Morrison," he snapped without looking at the number.

"Sir, it's Kurt."

"Tell me you have good news." But Zack already knew from the defeated tone that he didn't.

"Wish it was. Theo's run off, sir, and took the selkie kid with him. They knocked out three guards, stole a truck from the embassy motor pool and took off."

Theo? Zack stood frozen for a moment, trying to get his brain to reboot. "Fuck me running."

"Sir?"

But Theo didn't just do things without reason. He was one of the most reasonable people Zack knew. "Wait. When Mr. S. was arrested, did Theo say anything? Suggest anything?"

"I…I think he was saying something about being able to track Mr. Sandoval. But the kid was just out of bed after a sunstroke incident. He wasn't making a lot of sense."

Oh, Kurt, you idiot. "So you told him he was crazy and to shut up."

"Something like that, I guess. You think he… Oh, crap."

"Yeah, crap. They have a connection, those two, and I don't know what the hell a vampire can and can't track, do you?"

"No, sir."

"Next time Theo tells you something like that, you listen. Hear me?"

"Yes, sir."

Zack pinched the bridge of his nose. "Meantime, you see if you can't get a fix on what direction they went. Quietly, damn it. The last thing we need is for the anti-magic police to be looking for a vamp and a selkie. God, they'd probably shoot Theo on the spot if they knew what he is."

He accepted Kurt's chagrined apologies and sat down on the little retaining wall. The whole mess had just gotten a fuck ton messier.

* * * *

At the next feeding, Diego found he had allies. The gray-haired gentleman, who communicated through Ethan that he had been his village's healer before his arrest, brought another man with him. Suddenly, they were a force of six and Diego instructed them to snatch up as many packets as they could.

When the frenzy quieted, they had four extra, which they gave to some of the prisoners who had been knocked to the floor and hadn't grabbed any. The women's rearguard paused to watch them, making the whole phalanx of women halt with her. She pointed and there was arguing, but after much gesticulation and angry whispering, the woman who had stopped took a packet and brought it to another older man crouched by the wall.

She nodded to Diego, rejoined the women, and they hurried off into the shadows.

"That was wild," Josh breathed. "You campaigning for mayor or something?"

"Just trying to get everyone to see that we're all in this together," Diego said between hurried bites of his own food. "Everyone gets fed, no one's scared. No one's scared, people start thinking again."

"What are we supposed to be thinking of?" Ethan asked.

"I'm not sure yet. But I can't help believing there's some way out of this."

"Been in some tight spots before, Mr. Diplomat?" Gavin's question was more teasing than caustic.

"You wouldn't believe the half of it."

The boys stayed at the turn in the corridor as they always did when Diego made his second visit of the day to Finn. He began to dread each visit more and more, but he couldn't bear to stay away. Abandoning

Finn in his increasing deterioration was out of the question.

Before he went to Finn's cell, he checked the others, wondering how many fae the prison held and how bad off they all were. At least he could give the information to Zack if he managed to find a way out. Maybe there would be a way for the Fae Collective to mount a rescue.

Many of the cells were empty, or were from what he could see. It was late afternoon and the little bit of sun that made it into the locked cells cast strange shadows. He couldn't be certain with all of them, and some of the doors had metal plates over the barred windows. Those he couldn't see in at all.

One held a scraggly gray wolf, the werewolf Finn had mentioned. In another there was a phoenix, a beautiful woman with feathers for hair and more running along her arms. She stared at the wall, her eyes dull and listless, her lack of reaction to his presence quite worrisome. The next contained what he presumed was a griffin, curled up and growling in its sleep. The last was occupied by something canine that kept to the shadows, pacing the floor. He thought he spied something in a fifth cell, but there was no movement. *Just another bundle of cloth.*

His inventory complete, Diego hurried over to Finn's.

"*Mi vida*, I'm here," he called softly at the door. Ear pressed against the seam, he tried again. "Finn? Are you all right?"

Nothing. Only silence came from the cell. Diego panicked and banged on the door. "Finn! Please answer me!"

The hallway erupted in snarls and shrieks, all the captive fae disturbed from their iron-induced torpor.

The werewolf across the way howled and the cries bled into someone pleading in Arabic. Desperate, Diego pulled himself up by the window bars to look inside. He could only hold the position for a minute or two, but he had to see.

Finn was just uncurling from his place on the floor. He sat up, eyes dazed and wandering, until he caught sight of Diego in his window. "Hello, my handsome husband. Are you back so soon?"

"I haven't seen you since this morning. Are you..." *Are you all right?* was about the stupidest thing Diego could have asked. "How are you managing?"

Finn leaned against the wall, his charade of nonchalance ruined by how badly his clawed hands shook. "Oh, well enough. I ate a bit today."

"Good. That's good." Diego could see the open food packet from his vantage point. There might have been a tiny dent in the mound of mash, but he didn't have the heart to call Finn on his exaggeration. "Head?"

"Oh, it aches a bit."

"Finn..."

"Fine. It hurts as if my brains were about to leak out of my ears. I don't think I can get up right now, love. I hope you can forgive me."

"Don't say that, *cariño*. I don't want you hurting yourself more." He swallowed hard, trying to blink back the sting at the backs of his eyes. "I wish I could get in there to you. Somehow make it better."

"Wsht. Nothing you can do right now." Finn gave a lethargic wave. "It's always good to see you, though. Might not help the headache, but it makes me feel better. Tell me what you've done today."

Diego had to let himself down, but he still spoke to the window, telling Finn what had happened at the feeding. The other fae had grown quiet again, perhaps listening, perhaps lulled back to sleep by his not-terribly-exciting story. Even Finn had gone silent.

"Finn?"

"I'm here. That's my Diego. The one that wants the best for everyone. I hope you won't mind too much, but I think perhaps I'll go back to sleep now."

"It's all right. You need to rest. I'll...I'll be back in the morning."

"Farewell, my hero." Finn's words were muffled, as if he had already curled into a ball again. "Be careful."

Diego moved away from the door, turned to rejoin his friends and jerked to a startled halt. A man blocked the corridor, the same strange man he had glimpsed on the edge of the feeding area. He stood with his arms crossed over his bare chest, his shirt wound around his head as an improvised keffiyeh.

"Hello," Diego said, still blinking in surprise. Why hadn't the boys told him someone was coming?

"Why do you care about the pooka?" The man's voice was rich and deep, one made for singing. "What is he to you?"

The tone was belligerent and Diego struggled not to bristle. "He's my husband."

"Ha!" The man threw back his head on a bitter laugh. "You've bound him to you, sorcerer, is that it? A bond slave to do your bidding?"

The heated anger puzzled Diego, so he proceeded carefully. "No, I married him. We love each other and pledged our love in front of witnesses just like any married couple. We have a connection, but he's as likely to demand things of me as I am of him."

The man tilted his head, frowning at Diego as if he were a puzzle box he couldn't open. "I've been watching you. You're either the most manipulative man I have ever met or you truly do have a generous heart. It irritates me that I can't tell which."

"It's probably a little of both. I do try to influence people when I think I'm right. No reason to deny that. But I also think that treating people with respect and kindness is the best way to do that." Diego took a step back so he could take in the whole man. Tall, maybe not as tall as Finn, broad-shouldered and gaunt, he had obviously been incarcerated for some time. His eyes were golden and too reflective. "Your English is excellent. And you're not human, are you?"

Finn's voice drifted from his cell, sleep-slurred and faint, "He's a djinn, love."

"Oh."

The djinn narrowed his eyes at the cell door, obviously annoyed at Finn for outing him. "Yes, djinn. I lived in California for many years, hence the English."

Diego nodded, though several inconsistencies occurred to him simultaneously. "I don't mean to be rude, but if you were happy in California, how did you end up here? And since you did, how are you not locked in a cell like Finn?"

"This is how you start a respectful conversation?"

All the stories said djinn were crafty, manipulative bastards. *But then, who wouldn't be if you were locked up in a bottle and made to grant stupid, greedy wishes?* Maybe he couldn't trust this fae yet, but maybe the feeling was mutual.

"Sorry. My apologies." Diego gave him a little bow. "I'm Diego Sandoval, a consular officer for the Fae Collective."

The djinn's stance relaxed, his shoulders slumping. "I thought it might be you. Television isn't always the same as in person. I'm called Nusair."

The phrasing wasn't lost on Diego. Not *my name is* but *I'm called*. Possession of a djinn's true name was supposed to be one of the ways to enslave him, after all. "Nusair. So how did you end up here?"

"I could ask you the same. The most powerful human sorcerer in recent memory."

"Diplomatic mission gone wrong. They tasered me before I could do anything. Threw an iron net over Finn before he could shift to fly us both away."

"Ah. Bad run of luck, there."

"And now the rules of conversation say that you tell me how you got here."

"There are rules? How inconvenient." Nusair's lips twitched up into a half-smile as he took two steps away and slid down the wall to sit with a weary grunt.

"Are you all right?"

Nusair stared at him again, appraising, perhaps. "The iron's not as agonizing for me as it is your husband, but it's still a nuisance. Yes, I feel the need to return to my home sands sometimes. Yes, it was a mistake and they caught me." He raised a hand to cut Diego off. "I know. If they knew I was one of their monsters, why am I out here? Yes, yes. They locked me up. That open door is mine. I got out."

Diego chewed the edge of his thumb for a bit. Sometimes it was a matter of finding the right questions. He settled cross-legged in the middle of the corridor so they were on eye level again. "What did you have to do to get the door open?"

Again, there was the long, scrutinizing look, the hesitation.

"I know you don't have any reason to trust me and you probably don't like humans much in general. But if there's any chance of getting Finn out of that room... I have to ask."

Nusair heaved a dramatic sigh. "You are a foolish man, falling in love with a pooka." He extended a foot and wiggled his toes at Diego. His nails were more reminiscent of talons than toenails and the one on the big toe was missing. "I have talents that have nothing to do with magic, just so you know. I pulled off my nail and used it as a lock pick."

"As easy as that?"

"Easy? It was ridiculously painful and icky."

It shouldn't have been funny, but the emphasis on the *icky* surprised a laugh from Diego and the djinn flashed a beautiful, white-toothed smile. "I'm sorry. It's not funny. It's the stress, probably."

Nusair flicked his fingers in dismissal. "So ask me the question. The real question. That's a bad habit you have there, dancing around the big issues."

"And here I thought I was being polite. Can you get Finn out?"

"Probably. You do know the whole be careful what you wish for thing, don't you?"

"I've heard that. Yes."

"Look, I don't usually do this. Humans ask me for things and I enjoy seeing them hang themselves on their own consequences. But you're not asking for you. You're worried about him. So think a bit. He's protected in there, safe from angry, suspicious humans. They'll see him as weak. As competition for food. Whatever odd thing occurs in the human brain. In there, he's safe. Out here, he's not."

"But you're —"

"Better equipped to deal with the situation and not half dead yet."

Diego ducked his head, unable to stop his reaction to that statement. "How long have you been here?"

"Oh, about a year," Nusair said airily.

A year? And his nail still hasn't grown back? Nusair might pretend that the iron wasn't such a problem for him, but he was obviously suffering. "I'm sorry this happened to you."

"I think you really mean that." Nusair tucked an escaping strand of bright purple hair back under the shirt keffiyeh. "Even if I could get him out, you have no way to relieve his pain. Let him stay where it's quiet and safe."

There was some horrible amount of sense in that, but the refusal still hurt. *I just want to hold him.* "So why aren't you where it's quiet and safe?"

" "Little sorcerer, when you've been shut up in someone's stinking perfume bottle for a couple hundred years, you develop an aversion to being locked away."

"Oh. Of course. Sorry."

Nusair heaved himself up and stood straight again. "You're okay, for a human. Not that it matters. We'll all die here regardless of race."

He strode out and turned the corner where he apparently ran into the Canadian trio guarding the corridor entrance.

"Hey, kids. How's it hanging?"

"Who the hell —"

"Where did he —"

"Hey, Diego! You okay in there?"

When Diego emerged, the boys pounced on him, demanding to know who that was and what had happened.

"That was Nusair. A potential ally. Please be kind to him when you see him. I think he's been in this purgatory for longer than he wants to admit."

* * * *

The trail had been easy to pick up at the edge of Prince Faisal's estate. Limpet had asked what sort and Theo had had trouble describing it. A psychic trail, if he had to give it a name, but it was the remainder of the connection Mr. Sandoval had forged with him in their first days together. Theo had sworn to him and the connection was simply...there, an invisible Ariadne's thread that could always lead him back.

The thread should have been severed, or he thought it should have been, when Mr. Sandoval regained the lost pieces of his soul. That was another thing no one could explain. If those pieces had been misplaced and recovered, where had they gone? He'd found that people who dealt with magic didn't often have sensible explanations for the things they did. They simply *felt* and things just *were*. For Theo, this lackadaisical attitude didn't fly. There had to be explanations, a set of natural laws that applied.

Consul Morrison said there were and that the dragons understood them. For most humans though, magic was still a fairy-tale *poof* kind of thing.

"Mr. Sandoval wouldn't look at it that way. I know he would try to find out more."

"Pardon?" Limpet glanced over from his contemplation of the desert rolling by and Theo realized to his embarrassment that he'd spoken aloud.

"Nothing. Thinking."

"You spend a great deal of time thinking. But I'm sure I haven't *heard* you thinking before. Does that happen often?"

"No. Sometimes. Maybe." Theo adjusted the truck's sun visor. Two hours outside the city, they were still driving on paved road, passing occasional clusters of houses or roadside businesses. He didn't think that would last too much longer. If the prison lay well hidden in the desert, it wouldn't be along a well-maintained road. "I'm alone a lot. Maybe I talk to myself."

"Ah."

That short statement seemed too good to be true, and it was, since a moment later Limpet launched into a long, complicated story about a kelpie who insisted on living alone and couldn't lure humans to her because she always muttered to herself.

Theo managed to tune him out after the first few sentences, worried about the sun and the increasingly flat landscape. No hills and no trees equaled no shade. He could push on for longer than he probably should but not indefinitely. Limpet's cheerful, animated voice was actually becoming less annoying, at least. It was a soft voice, with one of those beautiful fae accents perfect for storytelling, soothing but not necessarily mentally invasive when Limpet rattled on, like having NPR on as Theo drove.

Another hour and all signs of human habitation ended. Theo pulled his hat lower, trying to ignore the tightening bands of pain around his head and chest.

Heat he could deal with, but the damn sun was just merciless. Worse, he started to feel the pull of the trail off to his left. While he hoped for a crossroad or a turn in the highway, if the tugging on his brain got any worse, they would have to head out into open desert.

Six five-gallon bottles of water in the back of the truck. Four full cans of gas strapped to the sides, so we won't run out of fuel. No more than a hundred kilometers of desert to cross. We'll be all right. Probably.

Limpet was still telling his story, chipper and unconcerned that his audience might not be listening. It didn't matter to him. He was so astonishingly *untouched*, despite the violence he'd experienced early in life, as if everything just slid off him somehow. No guilt, no regrets—how would it feel to live like that?

"Theo?"

"Hmm?"

"Your eye is twitching."

"Yes." Theo hoped that would be the end of it. No such luck.

"You're worried about something? That is, of course you are with Finn and Diego locked in some cage. But I mean something new. That makes your eye twitch. And now you're growling."

Theo choked off the low rumble with a cough. It was his own fault for not tossing the selkie out while in the city, but he hadn't been sure that the little guy would make it back to the embassy on his own. Then it would have been Theo's fault when he was detained by the police. "We have to head off road. This truck is made for it, but, yes, it worries me."

"Ah. Out into the waterless wastes. I think that worries me a bit, too. I don't think I've ever seen so much dry."

"It is a lot of dry."

After another mile, Theo couldn't put it **off** any longer. The pull had just started turning to the left and back, so he knew he was in danger of going too far west. He eased the truck **off** the road and started south, out into the ocean of sand. With its wide, knobbed tires, the truck seemed to handle the uneven ground well. Theo just hoped it stayed that way. Did sand get deep in places? Would they sink?

"I've just worried you more," Limpet said with a frown. "That wasn't what I wanted to do. Should I tell you another story? You seemed to like the last one. Although maybe you were trying to be polite and — "

"Yes. Please. A story." Anything to stop the barrage of rambling, ADHD topic-jumping questions and observations Theo knew was coming.

"Happy to oblige. Once there was a water dragon. I suppose you've never met one of them. They're not really like the mountain dragons you probably know, all wise and fierce and strange. Oh, the water dragons are wise in their own way, but they only care about water things…"

Theo allowed himself a little smile, congratulating himself for getting Limpet focused again so he could concentrate on driving into the hell of sand. While he had a direction, he had no sense of distance yet and he couldn't shake an odd, absurd notion that they would drive off the end of the world.

Chapter Eight

The Appoquinimink social scale, named after fae researcher Appoquinimink Jones, attempts to quantify the approachability of fae and altered humans. While the scale takes into account how a class of beings might react to humans, it also reflects that class's willingness and ability to interact with other fae. For a full explanation of data utilized in determining scale values, please see Appendix C.
The Compendium of the Magically Sensitive, 4th Edition, Dr. Nathan Cooper

By mid-afternoon, Theo was beginning the think the end of the world would never come. He had to drive slowly, the way strewn with rocks alternating with patches of sand and small dunes. The sun was killing him. Maybe not literally, but he wished a stray cloud would wander by now and again. It was just so damn bright and there was no escaping it. If the truck had been an open canopy Jeep, he would have passed out hours before.

Limpet had finally run out of words and dozed fitfully, curled up on the bench seat. *Poor little guy, so far from home*. It was ridiculous, thinking of Limpet as younger. He was at least seven times older than Theo. It was also ridiculous feeling sorry for him. Limpet had done all this to himself.

But when he glanced over at that beautiful, delicate face, the mane of sea-colored hair tangled and snarled, Theo did feel bad. He wasn't an idiot. He knew a lot of his need to protect and to shield came from having four little sisters. After their father had died, Mama had needed to work long hours, sometimes two jobs. Theo had gotten the little ones ready in the morning, packed their lunches and made sure they got to school. He had helped them with their homework and started dinner.

Carajo.

He swiped at his suddenly stinging eyes. Even though he talked to his mother regularly now, he couldn't go back to them. From a distance was fine, but he couldn't bear the fear in their eyes, the rejection, the living reminder that he had killed for one of his sisters. But, damn it, he still missed them.

When they topped the next low rise, a high-pitched squeaking from the engine yanked him out of his thoughts. It went away on the downhill and started up again on the next incline. When it became steady and edged up toward a shriek, Theo stopped the truck on relatively even ground.

"Crud."

Limpet, who had somehow managed to sleep through the racket, jerked awake at Theo's voice. "What is it? Are we stuck?"

"I think a belt's come loose. Stay here."

"A belt? Why does this thing need a belt? It doesn't have trousers. What sort..."

Theo let Limpet rattle on while he got out and went around to the back of the truck to search for tools. Whoever maintained the vehicle had been prepared, at least. The compartment under the floorboards held a full toolbox, neatly packed, along with a stash of protein bars. *You have to love Swiss efficiency.*

The sun hammered against his back as he popped the hood and peered into the engine. At least the hood itself provided some shade. Theo sighed as he glanced over the layout—this wasn't a familiar vehicle and he was going to have to run the engine to find the problem. He trudged back to the cab and leaned in.

"Slide over behind the wheel."

"I don't under—"

Theo patted the driver's seat. "Slide over here. I need you to run this, so you need to be quiet and pay attention. Can you do that?"

Limpet nodded with that wide-eyed look he got when he was anxious.

"Not asking you to drive it, okay? Don't get so scared." Theo reached over and shifted the truck into neutral, trying not to brush against Limpet too much. Leaning across his lap and breathing in the musk at his groin didn't do anything to him. Not a thing. Certainly didn't send fireflies on crack whizzing through his stomach. "*Mira.* You turn this to start it. When I say so, you press down with your foot on the long pedal on the right. You see it?"

Limpet nodded mutely, his lips pressed together hard, probably to keep a flood of questions inside.

"Short presses. A couple of seconds long. The engine will rev...it will get louder when you do. Don't get scared. Then when I yell to stop, you turn the key back toward you until it goes quiet. Can you do that?"

Again, he got a silent nod.

"Can you remember all that?"

That got a raised eyebrow. Right. Someone who could remember hour-long stories wouldn't have trouble with a short list of instructions.

"Don't touch anything else or you might run me over." Theo cringed when that got a little gasp. He didn't think the selkie's eyes could actually get wider. "Just do the things I said to, all right?"

Theo returned to the engine, oddly pleased when Limpet managed to start the truck and depress the accelerator as instructed. The selkie was out of his element, but he wasn't stupid. The timing belt was the culprit. That was the easy part. Limpet turned off the engine when Theo bellowed to shut it down, then the fun began, trying to adjust and tighten. Maybe it would've been fine to keep going with the thing squealing, but he couldn't risk it breaking or coming off and being chewed up somewhere. Wasn't exactly a good place to find an auto parts store.

The work went slowly, of course, with dropped tools and lots of cursing. Theo's hands shook harder the longer he was in the sun, which sure as hell didn't help. He thought he had it, twice, but after Limpet revved the engine, the squeal was still there. Someone else might have been content to make sure the belt was secure, but it would nag at Theo and make him crazy.

Once more unto the breach…okay, maybe a little dramatic. But he was cutting it close. His stomach churned with nausea and his skin felt tight. The engine tilted in odd ways when he stood up from it again.

"Try it now!" Theo's voice cracked but he felt a warm slice of triumph when the engine purred without screeching. *Now, just need to get back to the truck. Back in the shade.*

Every movement suddenly took all his concentration. Theo swore and tried to keep moving in a straight line, more or less. Careful, slow sips of breath against the rising nausea. Another step, another. His stomach cramped so painfully it brought him to his knees and he leaned on his elbows, throwing up in the sunbaked sand.

Limpet drummed his fingers on the wheel, waiting for Theo to bellow at him again. After much longer than the other times, he turned the machine off with a frown.

"Theo?"

Then he heard the miserable retching and flung himself out of the truck. Theo had made it to the corner of the truck and no further, on his hands and knees, head hanging low between his shoulders. He didn't have anything solid to heave up, so the sand drank up his sick like a greedy sponge. When Limpet touched his shoulder, he moaned and collapsed sideways.

"Poor Theo. I shouldn't have let you stay out that long." Limpet took him under the arms and heaved, dragging him into the shade beside the truck. "Poor, poor Theo. Are you dead?"

Limpet put his ear to Theo's chest. His heart did beat but much too quickly. Normally, Theo's pulse was slow and strong. This was so weak, rapid like a sparrow's. Worrisome.

"We really must look after you a little better. Travel at night, perhaps." Limpet kept talking as he pulled Theo under the truck. Talking made him less aware that he was afraid. Maybe not less afraid, but less focused on the afraid-ness. "The truck's nice and high off the ground. It makes a good cave. I'm going to take some of your clothes off. You're far too hot. Probably take some of mine off, too. Dreadful things, clothes. Though I suppose they protect one from this horrid sun a bit. It's so dry and dreadfully...dry here. Should get one of the water bottles, I suppose since — "

Theo whispered something while Limpet eased off his boots.

"Pardon? What was that?"

"The hood. The engine cover." Theo coughed and moaned, trying to draw a deep breath. "Close it. Damn sand."

Limpet stopped in the middle of pulling off one of Theo's socks, trying to process. He thought he understood, so he scooted back out into the sun to puzzle out how to close the truck's mouth. He pushed on it, but it wouldn't budge. Then he realized there was some sort of metal stick holding the mouth up, made of iron since it burned when he touched it. After wrapping his sleeve around his hand and tugging and pulling, he managed to extricate it. The stick fell into a groove inside the mouth and the metal maw suddenly slammed shut, catching the edge of Limpet's thumb.

"Ow! Blasted metal beast!" Limpet hissed in pain and sucked on the wound where the truck had ripped away skin and flesh. "Bad thing!"

Cursing the thing roundly, he climbed in the back of the truck, retrieved one of the heavy water bottles and dragged it back with him to Theo, who looked terrible.

"I don't think you're supposed to be gray. Or be breathing that fast. Please don't die, Theo. You're really a very nice Nightwalker."

Limpet went back to stripping Theo, the process hindered by his injured hand. The hat and dark glasses were easy enough to remove, likewise his pants, but when he unbuttoned Theo's shirt and tried to wrestle it off, Theo began to growl. It wasn't the soft rumble that said Theo was annoyed. This was different. A predator in the dark snarl, a hunter about to lunge. Limpet froze, all his instincts screaming at him to run.

The growl deepened and Theo's eyes snapped open, those lovely brown eyes rimmed in red.

"Theo? It's me. I'll give you whatever you need. You know that. Please."

No recognition flickered in that hungry, smoldering gaze. Theo seized Limpet's injured hand by the wrist, dragging the blood-streaked thumb to his mouth. Whimpering, Limpet tried to pull away, but a small selkie was no match for a Nightwalker. Theo's mouth latched on to the torn, bleeding flesh, his teeth scraping once, then gentling. He closed his eyes on a moan that drove a lightning spear through Limpet's heart to his groin.

"You hurt yourself," Theo whispered between licks, his voice thick and rough, not at all his normal soft Theo-voice.

"I...yes. The truck bit me."

"Bit you...Limpet." Theo moaned again as he sucked on the wound. "I need. *Pinche*...so damn bad. This...trailing blood in the water."

"It feels, um, it doesn't hurt anymore with you licking it," Limpet whispered. "It feels good. Wonderful. My whole body thinks so." He glanced over at the erection pressing up against Theo's small clothes. "I think your body thinks so, too."

"Your blood. Different flavor from other fae." Theo shifted restlessly and pressed the wounded hand to his cheek. "I can't want you. I can't."

"But you do," Limpet said gently. He stroked the hair back from Theo's face and kissed his forehead. "Why can't you?"

"You think I'm a monster."

"Not anymore."

"You're not even human."

"Neither are you."

Theo panted through clenched teeth and Limpet watched in fascination as his fangs extended. "Why...why aren't you scared?"

"Because I've watched you. I've walked with you. Drifted off to sleep beside you. If you wanted to give me reason to be frightened, you've done a terrible job."

"But—"

"You've already fed from me. You were careful and controlled even though you were ill. I know you've said that you don't think of sex when you feed from fae, but I think that might be different with me. I find that rather exciting."

"You're like a selkie kid, though. Have you even...?"

Limpet snickered. "Ah, that's it, is it? You think I'm virginal? Sweet Theo, I'm not a child and I'm more than familiar with how this works."

"Do you even...ever..." Even in the shade, the pink was visible in Theo's pale cheeks. "Like other males?"

"I like a person. The tackle doesn't matter much to me, since I find all varieties appealing."

Theo pressed Limpet's palm to his lips, kissing the heated skin tenderly. He closed his eyes on a slow breath, apparently trying for calm. "Get undressed. Please."

Limpet took his hand back slowly to indicate he wasn't going anywhere and stripped out of his clothes as fast as he could in the confined space. The pants tangled around his ankles, so he left them and lay down beside Theo's partially clothed body.

"Can you wait while I get you undressed?"

"No." The growl ended in a whimper. Theo was most likely at the end of his control.

"All right. No need really. We're most of the way there." Limpet stroked down Theo's chest, tracing hard muscles with his fingertips. The hair on Theo's chest fascinated him. He nuzzled at the dark triangle, coarse and infused with Theo's heady spice. "You can drink from any vein, can't you?"

With his eyes squeezed shut, Theo nodded. "Bigger ones are easier."

"This may take a little wriggling." Limpet kicked off his pants and squirmed around to put them nose to tail. "Be patient just a moment longer. Can you turn on your side?"

With Limpet's hand on his hip, Theo managed. He buried his face in Limpet's crotch, let out a soft growl and nosed at Limpet's sac.

"Easy there. I'd rather you didn't feed from that spot." Limpet shifted his bottom leg forward so Theo could use it as a pillow. "There. Try the big vein in the thigh. That should work. I'll take care of other things down here. Food and sex at once. What could be better?"

"Femoral," Theo whispered and licked at the skin over the vein. "You smell so good here. Delicious."

"Don't be shy. Touch whatever you want while you're down there and —" Limpet broke off with a moan when Theo stroked his ass, teasing at the crease.

"Oh, yes. That's lovely. I won't complain about more of the same. I will tell you if I think you're taking too much, hear me? But otherwise, I'm sure you'll be glad to know, I'm going to find other things to do with my mouth than talk right now."

Theo let out a strangled chuckle, though he seemed to be hesitating rather than diving into his feed. He ran his hand up the underside of Limpet's erection, then caressed the head with his palm alone. As he wrapped his fingers around the shaft, he bit down hard, piercing the vein in Limpet's thigh.

"Oh, yes. Oh, sweet goddesses of the deep," Limpet whispered, his eyes crossing from the sharp shock of pain and pleasure, the heavy wave threatening to drag him under.

Riding waves was what he did best, though. Limpet closed his eyes and let the pleasure crash over him while he bent forward to lick at the head of Theo's cock. That got a twitch and a hoarse moan as Theo fastened his mouth on Limpet's thigh, sucking hard.

That will leave an interesting bruise.

Theo's cock tasted sweet and salty, like the best mussels in the shell. Not that Limpet would eat parts of Theo, but he intended to devour *this* lovely part. He pulled his lips in to protect Theo from his sharp teeth and dove all the way down to Theo's base, sucking hard on the way back up. Theo didn't disappoint him, squirming and growling against Limpet's thigh.

Every pull of Theo's mouth sent a jolt through Limpet's balls. Strange warmth washed over him, lulling and exciting at once, as if he drifted on a sun-heated, caressing bed of kelp that had taken a personal interest. He increased his own suction and his movement up and down Theo's shaft, wanting Theo to come with him. Oh, spirits of sea and air, he was close. The teeth and hands on him, the scent, the patient, soothing *presence* that was Theo was such a heady mix. He more than liked this Nightwalker, so much more. Oh, sweet waves and spray, he was in trouble.

The hand on Limpet's cock tightened, rolling his foreskin up and down in excruciatingly pleasurable ways with each hard tug. Limpet lifted his mouth from Theo, afraid he might bite down when he climaxed. He replaced his mouth with his hand, mirroring Theo's rhythm and rolling Theo's heavy balls with impatient fingers.

"Oh, Theo…yes!" Limpet managed those three coherent words before he came in a confused babble of nonsense, the pulses of his orgasm hard enough to steal what sense he had left. Streams of cum hit his face and chest as Theo followed him, moaning and writhing. Limpet lapped greedily at what he could reach, the salty sweet better than any shellfish imaginable.

Theo licked at the feeding punctures before he rolled onto his back, snickering.

"What's funny?" Limpet wiped the cum off with his hand and licked it clean, pleased that Theo watched him hungrily.

"Sorry. I'm flying right now. So fucking delicious and pretty damn potent. About a hundred and eighty fae proof. Yep, buzzed. Hope I don't get a selkie hangover."

Limpet snuggled down beside him and pulled Theo's head onto his shoulder. "Shh, shh, you need to sleep now. Sleep for a bit and we'll see how you feel in a few hours. Hush."

For some reason, this made Theo laugh helplessly. He clung to Limpet, shaking as he tried to muffle his giggles against Limpet's chest.

"What now? What did I say?"

"You... You..." Theo waved a hand, trying to catch his breath. "You telling me to be quiet is pretty fucking hilarious." He stopped laughing abruptly and nuzzled at Limpet's throat. "Thank you. You should sleep, too. You and your hot little not-annoying ass."

"I'll be right here." Limpet wrapped his arms tight around Theo, rocking him and stroking his hair until he fell asleep. At least he felt cooler now and his heartbeat was slow and even again. Maybe he would listen to advice when he woke and they could travel at night. Theo pushed himself too hard, tried to do too much, and Limpet wasn't about to watch him kill himself, no matter what the cause.

* * * *

At the third feeding time, Diego had more allies. Now they were a group of ten, a force to be reckoned with. When the frenzy ended, he communicated through his student interpreters that everyone might stay in the feeding area and share.

With slow, deliberate movements, he spread his shirt, still relatively clean, out on the floor, opened up the two packets he had managed to acquire and combined them on the spread-out leaves. Then he sat down and gestured to the boys that they should do the same. All three were on board with his 'combine and conquer' plan by now, so they didn't hesitate. Ethan added his shirt to Diego's and the four of them made a larger communal pile, leaving plenty of room for others to join them.

Slowly, some with hope in their eyes and some with guarded reluctance, the six men in their impromptu alliance came to sit with them, followed by two more. No one needed words. Those willing to share could join the circle. Diego led by example, taking a thumb-sized portion with his right hand and eating slowly. The others followed suit, scooping up polite portions, obviously trying to rebuild a patch of civilization.

They exchanged names and occupations, talked about family, all the normal things humans did while getting acquainted. It hurt Diego to hear some of the details, though — how the lives of these ordinary people had been ripped apart by fear. Rashid had been a construction worker, his newborn son only a month old when he was arrested. Vadim had been a teacher and had lived with his elderly parents. Hafiz owned a grocery, or had before the government had seized his assets. Tarek had worked at a clinic, in his last year of residency. It seemed to Diego that most of them were surprised to find out how normal their fellow inmates were, rather than the dangerous criminals the government painted them to be. Some spoke English, some didn't, but in their intersection of languages, they managed.

"We're getting somewhere," Diego told his young friends when the group broke up again.

"But where are we getting?" Josh asked with a shake of his head. "It's nice having things less crazy, but where's it going?"

"I don't know yet." Diego wondered if his exercise in kindness was just that. He wanted to get to know the players, to understand what talents they might draw from, but he couldn't put his finger on why.

Maybe Finn could help, if he was awake. Their brains so often worked better together. Just inside the door to the monster prison, Nusair stepped out of the shadows and into his path.

"Did you see it?"

"What should I have seen?" Diego backed up a step, disturbed by the hungry expression on Nusair's face.

"Ah, you didn't then. I had…hoped."

"Nusair, what? What did you see?"

The djinn turned away with an exasperated snort and threw up his hands. His posture screamed, *well, if you don't know, I'm sure as hell not telling you.*

"Please. Anything might end up helping us all, please."

Something flickered in Nusair's eyes. Pain? Anger? Regret? He paced a few slow circles and finally stopped in front of Diego again. "When you had the humans in a circle, sitting close, knees touching, there was a…trickle."

"A trickle?" Diego cast about frantically for what that could mean. From Nusair, he could think of only one thing. "Of magic?"

"No, of maple syrup. Of course magic!"

"You saw it? Felt it? How could you do that?"

Nusair wrinkled his nose. "I'm always amazed at how ignorant even smart humans can be."

"Sorry. You're my first djinn." *Or I would've known how touchy and cagey they are.* "You're a being of fire and air, is that right?"

"More or less."

"And you've already said that the iron doesn't affect you like it does other fae."

"Give the boy a prize. He remembered."

"So, they can separate us from the earth and from water, but unless they just want to kill us, they can't take away the air." Diego narrowed his eyes. "You can still access the flows. *You* still have your magic."

"Easy there, cowboy. I can't access squat. Do you really think I'd stay if I could?" Nusair leaned a shoulder against the wall. "But I still have eyes."

"Damn it. I'm sorry." Diego rubbed at his temples. "It's hard not being suspicious when you answer questions in circles. Okay. You saw a trickle. Do you see it now?"

"No."

"Only when we were all —" Diego cut himself short, his eyes widening. "*Madre de Dios*. The coven effect."

"And the sun breaks through the clouds," Nusair said on a chuckle.

"I never thought it would work through the lead. And I've never —" Diego broke off, processing hard. If he could get the others to listen. If they could concentrate. If he could convince them to use their gifts.

"You've always worked alone, haven't you? The powerful ones always do."

"I've...no. I couldn't manage at all for a while without Finn. It's comfortable with him. Natural. I've never worked with other humans."

"You are a strange little animal."

"Might have heard that before." Diego walked down the corridor to Finn's door. "I'm getting the start of an idea. So many things could go wrong. But I need him out of there. Could you get my Finn out, please?"

"Is that your wish?"

Oh no, I'm not falling into that trap. "No. Not a wish. I don't have any hold over you and I don't want one. It's a request. I'm asking if you'd do this for all of our sakes. And, yes, out of the goodness of your heart."

Nusair stared at him, blinked twice, then doubled over laughing. "The goodness... No, it's too much. Ha! Oh..." He managed after a few false starts to compose himself, swiping at his eyes and gasping. "I think I'll have to help you just because you made me laugh so hard. It's been so long."

"Glad to be of service," Diego said dryly.

"I need a promise, though, because nothing comes free." Nusair reached up and pulled his claw pick from a fold in his keffiyeh. "You need to swear that no being gets left behind if we break out. And I know that's what you're going for, so don't pretend. You don't trust negotiations to work and you're afraid your husband's failing. This is all about a jail break."

"I'm not denying any of it and I have no intention of leaving anyone behind."

"That wasn't a promise, sorcerer."

Right. He's used to dealing with word traps and humans who only want to use him. "I promise. On my soul, I swear. No being, human or otherwise, will be left behind if this works."

Nusair nodded, apparently satisfied, and moved to Finn's door. "Care to tell me? If what works?"

"I would if I knew. Right now, I don't have enough information."

"Is this how you write your novels, too?" Nusair knelt by the door, inserted the claw, and put his ear against the lock plate. "Make it up as you go?"

"No. Though I haven't written one in years. This isn't the same thing, though. With a novel, I know the ending."

"And they lived happily ever after. Now shush." Eyes squeezed shut, Nusair fished around in the lock until he received one click then two more. With a cocky grin, he swung the door wide. "*S'il vous plaît entrer, monsier.*"

"Polite and multinational. I'm impressed."

"You should be."

Diego forced himself to wait until Nusair moved out of the way before rushing in. Probably rude to knock the djinn over to get to Finn. Then he had no more attention to spare. With a strangled sound of dismay, he dropped to his knees beside Finn and gathered him close.

"Finn, *querido, mi amor*, do you hear me?" He kissed Finn's face over and over, needing him to wake with a desperation approaching madness.

The iron combined with the arrested half-shift had obviously exhausted Finn. Purple shadows ringed his eyes, startling against his too-pale skin. He shifted in Diego's arms, banging one of his cuffs fretfully against the floor before his eyes cracked open.

"Well, hello, my handsome prince," he got out in a hoarse murmur. "Are you another nice dream?"

"No, I'm here. It's me." Diego hugged him tighter, trying to get his shaking voice under control. "I had some help getting your door open."

"How lovely. Are we leaving, then?" Finn patted his arm. "No, I expect not, since you're so upset. Why are you so upset?"

"You look terrible."

"Your pardon. If I knew you were popping in for a visit, I would have cleaned up."

Diego kissed his dry lips gently. "Shh, you're perfect. I'm just worried."

"Hmm. It does feel good to have you here." Finn nuzzled at Diego's chest and sneezed. "You smell a bit odd, though."

"Sorry. Chemicals in the water."

A rustle of cloth at the doorway attracted Finn's wandering attention. "And you brought a friend. Rather handsome djinn, isn't he?"

"Very attractive. Now —"

Finn hitched himself up in Diego's arms to address Nusair. "What color is your hair?"

It seemed an odd question to Diego, but Nusair pulled a strand of bright purple free of his keffiyeh and turned into the light for Finn.

"Ah. Arabian djinn."

"You know that by his hair color?" Diego glanced between them, his planned conversation derailed. "Where would you have met a djinn?"

"They like to travel." Finn gave him a dragon-toothed grin. "I think my husband is having a jealous moment."

Behind him, Nusair laughed and Diego resisted the urge to ask whether they had met before. "Maybe. Not much I can do about your past lovers, though. Listen, *mi vida*. I've learned something that gives me some hope. We'll leave the door unlocked but I'd like you to stay here where you're safe until tomorrow. Then when things settle down after the food drop tomorrow, I'd like to ask Nusair to bring you to the feeding area."

"Bring me?"

"I...don't think you can walk there."

"Perhaps not. But why?"

"Nusair says there's a trickle of magic when several humans are together. I'm hoping we can join the trickles into something useful."

"My clever, clever husband," Finn murmured. "Will you come and sleep with me tonight?"

Diego hugged him tight, stroking his hair. *I don't want to leave you for a second, damn it.* "Of course I will. I've missed you, you know."

"Oh, good. I'd hate to have to think of you in the arms of such a beautiful djinn."

"I'm not—"

"Teasing. I was teasing. This is rather tiresome, not being able to hear each other's thoughts."

"Not too much longer, I hope."

He gave Finn a last, lingering kiss and lowered him gently to the floor before he returned to the hallway to ease the door most of the way shut again. Resting his forehead against the cool metal frame kept him anchored, a fixed point in a universe with a sliding center. He had to remain solid even if he wanted to slide into a puddle of anguish. *My poor Finn. Oh, my poor Finn. How many times do you have to suffer because of my mistakes?*

"I think you do love him." Nusair's voice came from behind him, hushed and perplexed.

"Yes. I know that's hard for you to imagine, but I do."

"It's quite easy to *imagine* for me. I can imagine some absurd and surreal things. It was just hard for me to believe."

Diego ignored him, walking back to the door at the end of the corridor.

"I still think you're a fool." Nusair was suddenly beside him without a whisper of sound.

"You can think whatever you want. Just say you'll help me tomorrow."

"Only if you tell me what you're planning. This trust thing is tough if you doubt me as much as I doubt you."

"One thing." Diego turned on him, poking a finger at his chest. "Why do you care whether or not everyone gets out?"

Nusair stood his ground and offered a slow smile. "Oh, that's an easy one. If you promise no one gets left behind, you can't leave me here."

"That makes...sense." There had to be something Nusair wasn't saying, but Diego let it go. "I want to try to combine magical energies to get the iron off Finn."

"Ah, so your motives are selfish."

"Just listen and stop trying to twist everything. If we get Finn loose, he can shift again. If he can shift again, he can become something small and fly through one of the feeding slits. He can tell us what the prison looks like from the outside, how many guards there are and if there's a way out. If we can do this first thing, everything else becomes possible from there, but I don't think we're going to be able to do big, powerful things with the lead still on. Just little things. And maybe not much of them."

"Why not free me instead? I could become smoke and do the same thing."

Diego raised an eyebrow at him. "Because I trust Finn to come back."

Chapter Nine

Dragon
Classification: Elemental fae
Appoquinimink social scale: 6
Living in highly structured, gender-segregated social groups,
dragons strictly limit their contact with outsiders. When
exceptions are made, they are made with the approval and
sometimes instigation of the current Dragon Lord.
The Compendium of the Magically Sensitive, 4th Edition,
Dr. Nathan Cooper

The sun was lounging atop the nearest sand hill when Limpet woke alone. Theo had abandoned the shelter of his arms and, by the furrows in the sand, had slid out from under the truck, taking his clothes with him.

Ah, not really alone. Black boots paced along the edge of the truck, Theo's scent drifting down in their wake. Limpet closed his eyes, pulling in the memory with the lingering traces of Theo on his body. The Nightwalker had fed deeply, but only so much that Limpet felt a bit sleepy still. He had held Limpet tenderly. He had *laughed*, most glorious of all.

With his heart lighter than it had been since he left home, Limpet wriggled out of their truck cave stark naked. He shot Theo a bright smile, which faltered and collapsed when Theo frowned at him, his eyes once again guarded and cold.

"Better get dressed. We need to get moving." Theo reached under the truck and pulled out the water bottle. "Make sure you drink. Replace the fluids I took from you. And here. Found these. You need to eat."

He tossed a shiny rectangle at Limpet that he caught out of reflex. "Theo?"

Theo fussed with something in the truck, slamming the cover on a heavy compartment with a metallic clang. "Thank you. For what you did. It was a kind thing to do and I'm sorry I behaved so badly."

Behaved badly? "Oh." What else was there to say? Limpet hurried to dress in the horrid human clothes, drank the tepid, odd-tasting water from the bottle he could scarcely lift, and tried to bite the shiny thing. "I don't think I can eat this."

Theo let out the sort of sigh that meant he was trying to be patient. With quick, efficient movements, he ripped into the shiny and Limpet realized it was just a covering. The food was inside. It didn't taste much *better* but at least it seemed to be edible. Theo lifted the water bottle in one hand and took it to the back of the truck to secure it while Limpet scrambled into his seat.

They drove on in silence, Theo staring straight ahead, ignoring the inquiring glances Limpet threw his way. It was a puzzle he couldn't unravel, why Theo seemed...what? Angry over the sex? Ashamed?

Disgusted? They had fit so well together and Theo had been so pleased, so relaxed afterward.

"Are you angry with me?" Limpet ventured softly.

"No."

"Are you certain?"

"I'm not mad at you."

"You're upset about something. Your eye is twitching. If I've done something I shouldn't, I wish you'd tell me. We had such a lovely time earlier —"

"Look, it shouldn't have happened. I'm so damn sorry. It won't happen again."

Limpet stared at him, completely baffled. "I thought we both enjoyed it."

"Have you *looked* at the bruise on your thigh?" Theo snapped. He banged his head on the steering wheel several times, something that concerned Limpet enough that he nearly reached over to intervene. When Theo spoke again, his words were soft and artificially calm. "I lost control. I can't do that. It could've been awful."

But it wasn't. It was wonderful. Limpet clamped his lips together to stop more words escaping. All he did was seem to upset Theo more. They drove in silence as the sun sank, darkness covering the landscape like a sudden flood. Something that wasn't wolf or fox yipped in the distance and Limpet shivered, vowing never to come to such a strange, waterless place again. He didn't feel terribly well, but it was likely the heat of the day and the dreadful thing he'd just consumed that the humans thought was food. Theo taking a little blood so he could recover certainly hadn't done any harm.

After the second hour, Limpet decided to try another subject. The quiet was making him squirm. "What work would you have done as a human? Before the change. Humans usually have some work they do, don't they? Fisherman. Boatwright. That sort of thing. Before your change. Did you have a thing you did?"

"An occupation. A job, you mean?"

"Yes, those, I suppose. If those are the proper words. Or did you always wish to be a warrior?"

Theo sighed and for a long moment, Limpet thought he wouldn't answer. But his voice was calmer, more normal again when he finally said, "No. I was going to go to school. To be an engineer."

Thank you, goddesses! We're speaking again! "Oh, yes? What's that? Isn't an engine the thing that makes this truck move?"

"Yes, but it means other things. An engineer designs things. Invents useful things."

"What sorts of things would you have created?"

Theo fell silent again, staring out into the dark. It wasn't anger rolling off him any longer, though, but terrible sorrow. All of Limpet's questions dried and shriveled up in shame. Instead of distracting Theo from his anguish, he had made it worse.

"I've trampled all over things. We can talk about something else. I'd gladly tell you another story."

"Of course you would," Theo said in a dry-as-dust tone. "It's okay. Nothing anyone can do about it. I loved robotics…hmm, machines that act like humans. At least mimic some things we do."

Limpet squinted at the scattered stars peeping out from the purpled evening sky. "These are useful things?"

"Yes."

Again, Theo stopped and Limpet wriggled around on his seat to watch his face, beginning to understand that this was part of Theo's normal speech pattern. He considered. He weighed words, probably throwing some back that he felt were unsuitable before fishing for more.

"Sometimes, humans lose pieces of their bodies. In accidents. Wars. From illness. They can't grow them back like fae."

"Like adult fae," Limpet murmured, fingering his scarred ear.

"Sorry. Right." With a quick glance over, Theo cleared his throat but forged on, "I wanted to build better prosthetics. Mechanical replacement limbs. Ones that worked like real ones."

"Please don't be angry with me if I ask this. Human cities and groups are complicated and strange. But I see the hunger in your eyes. I feel it from you. This was something you truly wish to do. Why did you become something else?"

"*Pequeñas ironías de la vida.* Funny thing. The university wouldn't let me attend after I'd been declared dead."

"But you're not dead. Most definitely not."

"I'm not. But when vampirism hits, you get sick. You *feel* like you're dying. I was in the hospital. Doctors thought it was some kind of leukemia. When the change happened it looked like my heart stopped beating and that my brain had shut down."

"But your heart had simply slowed. Like a sea turtle hibernating in the mud."

Theo snorted a little laugh. "*Lo mismo.* Exactly like. It was early. Before they knew about vamps. So the doctors said I was dead."

"So they wouldn't let you go to school because someone had *thought* you were dead?"

"Yes."

"But…that's stupid! You could just go there and show them you aren't dead. Did they think you were a shade or spirit?"

"It's complicated." Theo let out a slow breath, not quite a sigh. "Human legal things. Worse was I lost the scholarship, the way to pay for the school, by being dead. And then my mother tossed me out of the house so I didn't have an address… Like I said, it's complicated."

"Your mother exiled you? From your family?" Surely, he must have misunderstood. How could a mother do such a thing? How could the rest of Theo's pod…family accept it? No wonder he was so prickly and silent.

Theo nodded, the tight misery back in his eyes, and Limpet couldn't stand it another moment. He hurled himself across the seat and wrapped his arms around Theo's neck, careful not to jostle him as he drove.

"*Qué madres?* What are you doing?"

"Hugging you."

"You're making it hard to drive." Theo snarled, then asked quietly, "Why?"

"Because you need someone to. Because you carry your hurt around like a knife, just waiting for someone who deserves it to come along so you can slice them into little strips."

"I'm sorry I hurt you."

Limpet swatted Theo's shoulder. "You didn't hurt me, you barnacled lout! You made me feel like everything inside was tail dancing, like waves were leaping and singing in my belly. It was wonderful. It was glorious." He squirmed around on his knees on the seat to murmur right in Theo's ear. "You didn't hurt me. But I hate how your family hurt you."

Theo's shoulders relaxed a hair. "Thank you. I think. Don't you ever say anything bad about my mother, though. Hear me?"

"Promise." *I have plenty of things I will make an effort not to say about your mother. But it's good to know where the sharp edges are.* Limpet slid down onto the seat and rested his head on Theo's shoulder. For his part, Theo didn't tense up and didn't ask him to move away. Small gains against a strong current were still gains.

* * * *

While the night spent with Finn in his arms couldn't have been classified as relaxing, Diego still woke with the sun, resolve firmly in place, feeling stronger than he had since their imprisonment.

With his head nestled on Diego's shoulder, Finn stirred, grunting and hiding his face from the light. "Good morning, my hero."

Diego kissed the top of his head, stroking Finn's back to settle him. "You do know you've been the one to save me the last few times, right?"

"I'd rather not think about some of those things."

"But you are my hero. For so many reasons."

"Hmm. I rather like that. Finn the hero." He tried to slide an arm over Diego's chest and pulled it back with a hiss of pain. "Finn the bloody useless hero right this moment."

"We'll try to fix that today. If this works, I'll be asking a lot of you."

"You may ask the moon and stars of me, love. You know that."

A snort came from the doorway. Diego glanced up in time to see Nusair rolling his eyes. "How revoltingly sweet. Are you sure this human hasn't bewitched you, pooka?"

"Oh, I'm fairly certain," Finn drawled. "Though I can't say I care much one way or the other. The mating is spectacular."

Nusair pretended to gag and, despite his cynicism, Diego was grateful. He'd managed to make Finn laugh.

"I'll stay with him, Diego. Gather your soldiers."

Diego sat up slowly, keeping hold of Finn so as not to dump him on the hard floor. "That's...kind of you. Finn? Are you all right with that?"

"Oh, yes. I'm sure we can amuse each other with stories of past misdeeds."

Diego left them with a kiss for Finn and a request to Nusair to be kind. He didn't intend simply to spring Finn on his fellow inmates later. No, this would take some careful nudging and feeling out. Simply because these people had been jailed for magic use, that didn't mean they would be sympathetic to fae.

With Tarek as his translator, since the doctor in training was much better in both English and Arabic than the college kids were, Diego sought out the prisoners who had joined him in his campaign to civilize feedings. Some were shocked that he would want to free a demon. Diego allowed a little coloring of the truth when Tarek suggested that this 'demon' was under Diego's control. Some wanted to know what he proposed long term. Even if they escaped, they were in the middle of the desert without transport.

"Please let Vadim know that if we can summon enough power to escape, I have the means to get us to safety. But please be clear that it would be to Tearmann Island, far from home. The Fae Collective will classify all prisoners as political refugees and will assist in relocation and in attempting to reunite families whenever possible."

Vadim pursed his lips, his eyes measuring Diego even as Tarek spoke. Then he said something in his soft, polite way that made Tarek's eyebrows quirk up.

"I don't mean to be rude." Tarek cleared his throat. "I'm only translating. But he asks if you really have the authority to make these promises."

Diego nodded. "It's a sensible question. These are standing orders from their majesties, established policies of the Collective."

The teacher seemed satisfied and, though he expressed doubts that any of it would work, he agreed to try.

Saeed, the elderly healer, was the biggest surprise. He agreed to help but with tears in his eyes.

"If it's not rude, could we ask why he's so upset?" Diego asked as Saeed reached out to take his hand.

The old man spoke for some time, shaking his head, his voice breaking. Finally, Tarek began to translate, his own speech wavering as he did. "He says that he always thought his healing was a gift from God. That since he helped others, since what he did was good, it had to be. But now they try to tell us that simply because we feel the world in a different way, we are evil. They tell our neighbors we are dangerous. They lock us away."

Tarek took a deep breath. "I'm sorry, Diego. Some of this is difficult to say, only because we all have suffered. But what Saeed says is that our gifts can't be evil. This is how we were born. To call it evil is to say that God has made mistakes."

Diego gripped both the old man's hands, his heart aching for his anguish. "You're right. You're so right.

You know there's no evil in your intentions or in what you accomplish. The government has made a mistake."

It was hard to swallow his anger as Saeed walked off, still wiping at his eyes. There were laws that could be attributed to cultural differences, of course. Diego knew that, but this was simple inhumanity. No one had that right, to cage another because of how he was born. Maybe he never was the diplomat he had pretended to be. *Advocate, I suppose, activist, and now civil rights terrorist. Couldn't even keep my hands out of things for a whole week after coming back, could I? Finn would be annoyed at me for thinking such things.*

Three years ago, the thought of leading any group of people, ever again, even through suggestion, would have terrified him. It still frightened him, but he knew now that he couldn't change the foundation of his being. He was, as Taliesin had always been, a meddler.

"Mediator," Hssetassk, the dragon lord, had rumbled while Diego sat beside him on a rock ledge, the sunset staining the mountain's teeth purple. "Certainly meddler, sometimes. You are interrogative, Light Wielder. Perhaps the need to intervene has brought you grief from time to time. But you ended feuds. Stopped wars. Brokered trade. The one between. You have ever been so."

His time with the dragons had been early in his exile, while he was still raw and, he could be honest about it now, clinically depressed. Hssetassk and his younglings had kept his mind occupied, showing him magical theory and why human covens worked. Certain fae could work in conjunction with each other, adding to or layering magic one atop another, but only humans worked in concert, melding their abilities, combining their individual strengths into one symphony. The *kelan* of magically sensitive humans called to each other. When they harmonized, covens worked.

The dragons hypothesized that if a human could hear the *kelan* song, adjustments could be made regardless of natural compatibility. Of course, song was just a convenient way to describe something that had no word in human languages. Diego hoped for a successful field test of dragon theory.

At feeding time, Diego and his allies — now fifteen — stood at the edge of the sunlight in a tight group. The women's phalanx hurried in, spotted them and stopped. A strange and eerie battle of manners ensued with the few unattached individuals scuttling in, snatching a packet and hurrying away while the two large groups stared at each other across the patch of light. Even the largest man, who had exhibited the most aggressive behavior, hesitated, head swiveling from one group to the other. He finally strode to the pile, snatched up seven packets, then took two more. Again, he hesitated, glaring suspiciously at everyone watching him without interference. With a snarl, he put the extra two back before shoving through Diego's group to disappear into the shadows.

Once his footsteps had faded, Diego came forward slowly. He took a packet, handed it back to the nearest man in his group, who happened to be Ethan, and motioned for him to go sit down. The next one went to Vadim, who immediately joined Ethan by the wall. When Diego turned his head, he was pleased to see the men had formed an orderly line.

"Please," Diego said to the woman in front. He gestured to the food, then to her. "You as well."

He waited until the woman reached the pile and snatched up a packet. She kept it but made room for the next woman to take her turn. Diego ducked his head to hide his smile. The last thing he wanted was to have his actions misinterpreted as rude or, worse yet, as a sexual advance. His distribution halted until the women caught up in number of packets, then he started handing them back into waiting hands again. Rather than vanish down the corridor, the women took the opposite end of the feeding area to have their meal, sitting close in a wary half-circle so they could watch the men.

When only Diego and the last woman remained, there were still five packets left. He took two, stood back and gestured for her to take the last three. She kept an eye on him, picking them up slowly, apparently still puzzling over his motives. An older woman, taller than the others, she struck him as suspicious but not afraid for herself. *This one, she's the mother of the group, the one to make decisions.*

Filing that away for later, Diego joined his circle to add to the ever-growing pile. Again, the conversation was quiet, the meal peaceful, as if everyone was relieved to feel safe and human again. None of the ones who had scurried away returned, Diego was disappointed to see, but he would address that the next day. If they were getting out, he couldn't bear the thought of leaving anyone behind, which would be unavoidable if there were still people in hiding.

He asked everyone to stay when the leaves had all been claimed, and noted with satisfaction that the women remained as well, though they didn't venture any closer. *You're curious. Stay curious. Stay with me.*

Obviously, Nusair had been watching since he arrived with Finn in his arms less than five breaths later. As Diego had requested, Finn kept his mouth closed and his eyes squeezed shut so at least the dragon teeth and pupils would remain hidden. He appeared convincingly pitiful with his head lolling against Nusair's shoulder and one arm dangling listlessly. If it had been an act, Diego would have been laughing instead of fighting tears.

"Gentlemen, this is Finn," Diego began softly, pausing between sentences to let Tarek translate. "Finn is a pooka, an Irish shapeshifter. He's been my companion for several years." *My love, my husband, but that might cause issues I don't have time for.* "He's seen me through dangerous moments and saved my life several times. I trust him as I do no other being alive. What I hope is that together, we can combine the tiny bits of magic that leaks past our lead dampeners. If we concentrate on breaking his iron bindings, he'll be able to help us gather information. Help us find a way to leave this place. Once freed, he can become any creature we need — a sparrow, a mouse, a snake if that works best."

Many of them had heard this before, but he repeated his plea for the newcomers. So far, they all listened with varied expressions of hope and jaded wariness, but they were still attentive.

"All I ask is that you try. Join hands and concentrate with me on breaking the collar first. We've done no harm if we can't manage, but if we succeed, we may see the outside world again."

Diego paused to look at the men in turn, waiting until he received a nod from each. "Good. Thank you. Nusair, please set him down in the middle of the circle."

Some of the men startled, as if they hadn't really noticed Nusair before that moment. The djinn might not have been able to access his full potential, but he obviously could still manage basic magic such as shifting people's perception just enough to go unnoticed. *I only saw him because he wanted me to. Sneaky bastard.*

Nusair must have seen the realization on Diego's face since he shot him a wink and a smug grin as he set Finn down. Surprised or not, the men in the circle still joined hands, obviously determined to try anything.

"*Coraje, mi vida,*" Diego whispered, placing his right hand on Finn's collar.

Finn placed a shaking hand over Diego's and managed a little squeeze. If the coven effect didn't work, Diego was determined to find a way to pry the damn collar off with his bare hands and sheer desperation.

Saeed, on Diego's right, placed a hand on his shoulder to complete the circle. There was no shock of connection as he'd heard others describe, but when he closed his eyes and felt for it, there was a low *thrum*, a sensation just maddeningly out of reach.

"Concentrate," Diego murmured, aware in a distant way that Tarek still translated. "Think hard about that collar breaking. Only that. About the iron weakening. Letting go."

Saaed's hand tightened on his shoulder and it was as if he had suddenly shoved Diego under a streetlamp, a small circle of light against the oppressive murk. He latched on to the tiny stream of magic, gasping. Sweat dripped from his forehead, but he ignored it. The trickle kept sliding through his grip, the lead numbing his magical senses and making him clumsy.

Like being in frigid water. But not deep enough to drown. Though he was panting with the effort, soon there was enough to gather a small puddle, just enough to begin feeding the flows into the collar. He concentrated on the collar's structure, imagining a seam forming under his hand, encouraging the iron to break its bonds on a molecular level along that seam. *Yes...come on...come on...*

Beside him, Saeed began to chant softly, or maybe it was a prayer. Another man joined him, then another. The growing number of voices distracted Diego for a moment, and his little pool of magic slipped. Frustrated, he was about to ask them to stop when a frisson of power shot through him, the sharpness of that sudden, concentrated stream nearly pitching him forward atop Finn.

Focal point. The chant. Dear God...it's not much but it's so bright, so beautiful. Liquid sunlight.

Working the magic didn't become easier, but there was *more*. Teeth gritted, Diego redoubled his efforts. The men around him faded as all his focus pulled inward again. There was only him and the iron. Small cracks sprouted under his hand. Finn might have whimpered but all Diego felt was the vibration as he poured the shaft of magic sun into the cracks, creating a wedge to open them wider. His vision began to darken, but other hands still held him steady. With a shrieking groan, the iron finally gave up and the collar split. He broke the circle for a moment to put both hands on the collar, though Tarek grabbed for his arm and soon made the circle whole again.

Prying his fingers into the seam, Diego heaved, using both magical and physical strength. The loud snap nearly deafened him as he sat down hard, staring blankly at the two pieces of broken collar.

Gasps and cheers broke out around him while Diego panted, waiting for his lungs to stop burning before he could speak.

"*Cariño,* I don't..." Diego gulped another breath. "I don't think I can do it again today. Can you shift with the cuffs still on?"

Finn shook his head. "It does feel ever so much better, my hero. Thank you for that. But I still can't manage."

Damn. "I suppose another day won't make much difference. We'll try the wrist cuffs tomorrow. Maybe that will be enough."

"I may be able to help." Nusair bulled his way into the circle and took Finn in his arms. "Don't give me that look, little sorcerer. You have your kumbaya circle. I have mine. Back off."

"But—"

"Let him try." Finn patted Diego's knee. "If we can connect as you did with the others...I know it's not the same. But perhaps Nusair can lend me a bit of strength."

Nusair cradled Finn's head in the crook of his neck, the position far too intimate for Diego's taste, but he clamped his mouth shut on any protests. He understood human magic, not djinn. Finn whimpered and thrashed, clutching tight to Nusair, but soon the familiar blue glow began to spark and spread along Finn's body. His arms and legs shrank just enough that he was able to shake the cuffs free and the transformation swept over him in a sudden cerulean wave.

Finn vanished from Nusair's arms and a tiny black bird replaced him, perched on Nusair's knee.

"Better, little cousin?"

The bird cheeped and answered, "Yes, so much better. Epically better. Does one say that?" Finn's deep voice sounded absurd coming from such a tiny creature, but at least he seemed stronger.

"You're handsome enough to say whatever you please," Nusair said with a chuckle.

"I think I might have a bit of a fly. With perhaps several flies along the way. Would that be all right, love?"

Diego waved a hand in a shooing motion toward the ceiling slits. "More than all right. I'm so relieved that you're free. Just don't tire yourself, please."

The bird hopped from Nusair's knee to Diego's. "Thank you, love. I would say the same to you, but I fear it's too late. I won't be long."

Finn ruffled his feathers. Close up, Diego decided he was a black wren, though he didn't think such a thing existed outside pooka wrens. Then with a flip of his wings, Finn took flight, fluttering around one of the arrow slits a moment before he slipped through to the outside world.

A bittersweet ache lodged in Diego's heart, part of him overjoyed that Finn had made it out, part of him wishing he could tell Finn to keep going, just to fly away instead of returning to the dark.

"Diego." Tarek caught his elbow. "Perhaps you should lie down."

"I think... I think I will." Using Finn's shirt as a pillow, he curled up on the concrete floor as the room tilted. "Fair warning. I do have a seizure disorder and they didn't send any of my meds with me."

"We'll watch over you. I was nearly a doctor, you know."

With the world steadying, Diego managed a little chuckle, resolving to rest until Finn came back. He wasn't at all shocked that Nusair had vanished again.

Chapter Ten

Altered humans: for the purposes of this reference, magically altered humans are those whose kelan structures have undergone sufficient changes to alter key human characteristics. While altered humans such as vampires (Nightwalkers or Bloodstalkers in fae terminology) may or may not have other magical abilities, they have gained certain magical attributes not present at birth.
Definitions, *The Compendium of the Magically Sensitive*, 4th Edition, Dr. Nathan Cooper

We have to get to the damn prison soon. Theo slowed the truck and leaned his head out into the moonlight, taking a deep breath of night air. *It's not that far but we're moving too damn slow.*

Their third night of travel, he was feeling steadier. Limpet had fussed and harried him after that first disaster until Theo had agreed to rest during the heat of the day. The selkie snuggled up with him under the truck, but Theo hadn't touched him in anything more than a brotherly way since his feeding. Limpet was probably still alive because of it.

Now, though, his traveling companion wasn't looking too great. Pale and restless, Limpet ate less every day and hardly drank much more. He shifted on the seat again, obviously uncomfortable, though whenever Theo asked, he said he was fine.

Uncomfortable. What sorry doctor ever thought that was a good way to describe pain? "You need to get out and walk around?"

"No. Thank you. We need to kee —" Limpet stopped mid-word and shot up in his seat.

At first, Theo thought he'd spotted something, but his eyes weren't tracking on anything. He hung his head out the window, sniffing much as Theo had just done.

"You okay, little bit?"

"I...I...Theo!" Limpet pointed out the windshield to the left. "You have to go that way! Please, please, that way!"

"It's not the way we need to go." Theo frowned when Limpet clutched his arm, black eyes huge in distress. "At least tell me why. Suddenly you can't talk?"

"Water," Limpet choked on the word. "I smell it. Big water for swimming. Theo, please. I know...I..."

"Hey. Easy." That Limpet could barely put three sentences together disturbed Theo profoundly. *I guess a seal in the desert isn't a good thing, right?* "How far, do you think?"

"Close." Limpet was practically climbing into Theo's lap in his desperation. "I can *smell* it."

Right. Selkie does not equal GPS. "Settle so I can drive. We'll have to stop for the day soon, anyway. If it ends up not being too far, we'll look, okay?"

"Look?" Limpet trembled as he sat back down next to Theo, nestled into him as if he would shiver apart without the contact.

"Yes." Theo put an arm around him and let him lean in. "There might be people. Lots of them."

"People. I suppose that could be bad," Limpet murmured. He seemed to rally a bit tucked under Theo's arm, since he rattled on, "It won't be salt water, of course. That would be best. But it's not an ocean, I can tell that from here. Something small. A pool, a pond, a lake, but water. Clean water for swimming."

"We'll see." Theo pulled him closer when the shakes returned. "Relax. Just relax."

"Even if there are people, I don't *have* to be seal. Swimming. Like this. I could do that."

Theo didn't quite suppress the sigh. "We might be able to explain the hair. But your ears, your eyes—you can't pass. And we'd end up in monster jail, too." *Because they'd arrest you and I'd try to stop them.*

"Oh. Yes. Of course." Limpet sounded so dejected Theo felt like he'd kicked a teacup Maltese puppy. "Do humans find me so ugly, then?"

If it had been anyone else, Theo would have ignored the question as blatant fishing. But Limpet had no real frame of reference with humans. He just knew he looked different. "No." He rubbed his palms over the steering wheel, searching for a less abrupt answer. "Some humans might be...startled. But, no, you're beautiful."

"Thank you. Though I doubt you're like most humans." Limpet glanced up at him. "It's so lovely when you blush."

Theo snorted. "Vampires don't blush."

"You do. Just a little pink, right here." Limpet stroked a line across Theo's cheekbone.

"Great."

"I've made you uncomfortable."

Everyone makes me uncomfortable. "One of those Limpet-practices-how-to-be-quiet times would be good now."

Whether he was following instructions or whether it was hard to talk through his trembling was hard to say. Limpet pointed when he needed an adjustment in heading, but otherwise clammed up. Normally, Theo would have welcomed the silence, but watching Limpet this close to falling to pieces wasn't doing anything for his own nerves.

The dunes had gradually increased in height over the past few miles, some of them monsters that Theo was sure would capsize the truck if he attempted them. One of these giants loomed in front of the truck when Limpet pointed him to the left. Rather than risk upending them like an unlucky turtle, Theo drove around the near end of the dune, hoping there wasn't another one just behind it.

Gray had just crept into the sky on the edges of the black desert night, the first hint of approaching morning, when they rounded the dune. Theo stomped on the brake, stunned, wondering if the landscape was an elaborate mirage.

No, that only happens in movies, idiot.

Hidden between mountainous dunes, an oasis spread out before them. Palms and tall ferns swayed in the night breeze. Flowering vines clambered in joyous riot over exposed rocks. Through the sudden violent explosion of plant life, the moonlight glanced off the water, though it was tough to see how large a body of water through the leaves.

Limpet surged toward the door, but Theo grabbed his arm. "No. Wait. Let me look first."

"But it's quiet. There's no one —"

"Stay. Here. No argument. I'll be back in a minute."

Theo held up a finger when Limpet opened his mouth again and the selkie subsided. He slid out of the truck, checked his gun and left the door open in case anyone was nearby to hear it slam. Scent first on the hunt, always scent first. He picked up citrus, dirt and water, some sort of small rodent. He clung to the deepest shadows, analyzing, categorizing as he went. A few small birds, yes, something canine had come to the water to drink. Jackal? Not a threat. Finally, he stood at the edge of the trees, the toes of his boots touching the water, and he smiled.

No humans.

Only the faintest lingering trace, so they might have come here, but not for a long while. Theo holstered his sidearm and jogged back to the truck.

"We're clear. Come on out." Theo frowned as Limpet slid down, clinging to the side of the truck. "Can you walk?"

Limpet righted himself, chin lifting in defiance, though his eyes were distressingly huge. "Of course I can."

His steps were far from steady, but Theo kept his distance. Even a selkie had his pride. Limpet snagged the hem of his shirt and yanked it over his head as he walked. He dropped it and started unlacing his right boot on every other step. Shaking his head, Theo stayed a few feet behind to keep an eye on him, picking up articles of clothing as they hit the sand. So far, Limpet seemed all right, if a little dazed.

Selkies can't drown, can they?

Barefoot now, Limpet pushed through the leaves and vines then stopped with a gasp. "Oh, Theo. It's beautiful."

The pool wasn't huge, maybe five hundred meters long and a hundred wide, but obviously spring fed, clean and clear enough to see the sandy bottom. Theo imagined it was probably a stunning blue in the sunlight.

"Yes. Beautiful. Did you just need to stare at it?"

Limpet shot him a reproachful look that melted into a smile. "You were teasing. Now I know you're not as serious and dark as you pretend. I need to swim."

"Go on. I'll keep watch."

Toes splashing in the water, Limpet seemed hesitant, almost embarrassed. "I have to do something first. I'm not sure you'll want to watch."

He runs around naked whenever he can. What could he be embarrassed about? "You were having some kind of fit. Not taking my eyes off you."

"Ah. Well, then. Nothing for it." Limpet reached over to the side of his right thigh. Theo's jaw dropped when he reached *inside* his thigh and pulled something out.

Inside. But there's no blood. Dios... Theo's brain reconnected a moment later and he realized there was a pouch there, like a kangaroo's or an opossum's. The seam-like opening was nearly invisible unless one knew it was there. Limpet took the gray rectangle and shook it out until it looked like a...rug? Blanket?

Limpet put one end of it on the ground, the part that seemed to have a tail attached, and Theo began to understand. He leaned against a date palm, keeping silent so he wouldn't disturb Limpet, who now stepped into the tail as if it were a garment. Carefully stretching the hide — since hide it was — out so the darker gray spots became visible against the lighter gray fur, Limpet pulled the other end up so it fitted over his head like a hood.

He pulled his arms in and he *shrank* into the sealskin as it closed over his smooth fae skin, his taut abdomen vanishing last before Limpet thumped to the ground onto his front flippers. Black eyes turned to regard Theo, the only part of him unchanged.

"You're still beautiful," Theo whispered. "Go swim."

With a joyous bark, Limpet galumphed the few feet to the water and slid in, his clumsy body suddenly transformed into a sleek, swift missile hurtling through the pool. He was beautiful, incredibly so, turning and twisting in seemingly impossible ways, breaking the surface every now and then to search out Theo before he submerged again.

Soon Limpet broke the water near Theo's feet. He snorted and barked at Theo, splashing him with a flipper.

"You want me to come in?"

Limpet barked in obvious approval.

"I don't swim. Not really."

Theo would never have thought a seal could appear incredulous. This one did. He barked again and stood on his tail in the shallow water, his front flippers resting atop the surface to show Theo it wasn't deep.

"Wading. Okay."

The oasis still hadn't shown any signs of recent humans, not even a hint of old exhaust fumes or ancient camel dung. It wasn't large enough to support an actual settlement. Desert nomads may have used the oasis in the past, but apparently they no longer had a need for it in the modern world. This morning might be the only one in hell knew how long that Theo would be able to let his guard down.

A flat rock presented a good place for him to set things out of the sand. Limpet barked impatiently, but Theo took the time to fold first Limpet's clothes then his own as he stripped. He wrapped his sidearm in his shirt, holster and all, just in case Limpet decided to splash in that direction. *No need to be careless.*

Limpet surfaced and submerged several times, finally settling on floating with just his eyes and nose showing, watching Theo's every move. It was a little disconcerting, those black eyes practically devouring him, but it wasn't anything Limpet hadn't already seen and Theo knew he had nothing to be ashamed of, all lean muscles and long legs.

The warm waves lapped over his toes when he approached the pool. Not hot, but city pool in the summer warm, without all the nasty, eye-stinging chemicals and the kids peeing in the water. Limpet let out a series of noisy barks and flipped backward to splash Theo with his tail.

"Working on it. Shh."

Living on the island, Theo had tried to learn to improve his swimming. Problem was, vampire bones were quite dense and he had become even less buoyant after the change. *Water is not my friend.* Slowly, cautious of sudden drop-offs, he waded in to his waist. It did feel soothing against his skin. The delicious badness of skinny-dipping with the water gently caressing his balls did send a little thrill through him.

"Not half bad," Theo murmured, staring through the glass-clear water at his feet. "Not bad at—whoa!"

A black torpedo shot around him and slammed into the backs of his knees, taking him down before he could react. He sputtered and swore when his head broke the surface again, trying to clear water and hair from his eyes and find Limpet to glare at all at once.

"*Cabrón!*" Theo bellowed at the black head bobbing ten feet to his right. "Do you want me to drown?"

The seal let out a sad little squeak and approached more slowly. The black nose nudged at Theo's shoulder, whiskers tickling him. Limpet ducked underneath and nosed under Theo's arm so that it rested across his back. He surfaced just far enough to take some of Theo's weight in the water.

"I see. You'd rescue me after drowning me. Nice of you."

Limpet nuzzled at his throat and jaw, making little chipping sounds in what had to be an apology. He swam slowly around Theo's torso, the leathery texture of the skin surprising him, though the coarse fur gave another feeling entirely when Limpet rubbed back instead of forward. Strangely sensual, having a sentient seal pay court. Theo was certain he blushed when he realized how incredibly wrong that sounded.

He's not a seal, though. Not really. That brain in there's still Limpet, with all his quirks and weird thoughts.

Careful of his footing, Theo ventured in to midchest when Limpet nudged him from behind. With his anxiety subsiding, Theo had to admit that the clean water felt wonderful after days of hot sand and grit in every fold of clothing and in places he didn't think about ever having sand. He dunked his head back to straighten out his hair, scrubbing at his scalp to ease the feeling of days without a shower.

When Limpet left him again to zoom through the water, gyrating and somersaulting under the surface, Theo had to laugh. It was good to see him showing off, having fun. He obviously felt much better than he had an hour before. Theo decided the limit for keeping a selkie from water was about three days. God help them if they still had a longer stretch to go without an oasis in between.

This time when he returned, Limpet rested his head on Theo's shoulder with a soft sigh. Theo put his arms around the barrel body, guessing correctly that Limpet wanted to be held since he snuggled closer.

Theo cleared his throat. "Might be better in your other shape? Not cutting your swim short. Swim as long as you need to. But this is getting strange for me." *Really strange.*

Limpet-seal made an odd rattling sound that might have been a laugh before he flipped away from Theo, did one more circuit of the pool and flopped out onto the sand. The reverse transformation was more disturbing than fae to seal, as the seal pelt split and Limpet started to struggle out. Theo swallowed back nausea when fingers reached through the seal chest, the process too much like John Hurt's death in *Alien*.

Probably should stop watching old school sci-fi with Morrigan on my nights off.

The shocking part didn't last long, though, and once Limpet freed his head from his seal hood, it just looked like he was struggling out of a kid-sized sleeping bag. When he had wriggled out, Limpet rinsed the pelt and shook it out before folding it in half, then in half again. He kept folding until it was impossibly small, a roughly rectangular packet the size of his palm that he tucked into his neat little thigh pouch. Now that he knew it was there, Theo could see the slight bulge, as if something had been implanted under the skin.

"There. Is that better?" Limpet asked with a little grin.

"Better," Theo growled, taking in the rest of Limpet, his first leisurely, unobstructed, undistracted view.

He really wasn't that little. Maybe five foot ten or so. His sleek, compact body made him seem smaller somehow, muscular but without the hard definitions of an athletic human. The lovely, delicate features would have been strange on a human male, but they still left no doubt that he was male in the turn of the jaw and the breadth of the nose. His glorious hair, gray, green and blue seeming to shift as colors on an ocean would, hung down to the top curve of his ass. That tight little bubble butt, one of Theo's great weaknesses and something that had gotten him into trouble when he was younger. He found out the hard way that staring goggle-eyed at a beautiful male backside could get one beaten into the dirt.

He didn't have any business looking at this one, either, even though owner of said ass was about to set Theo on fire with his eyes. "I can't, little bit. I can't. You're wonderful. You're beautiful. But I'm...it's dangerous."

Limpet frowned and sat on the rock next to their clothes. "You say that, but I haven't seen it. Why do you think this? What has you so terribly afraid?"

"I'm not—" *Liar. Yes, you are. You're scared out of your mind.* "I've killed. I lost control once and I killed."

"Did you do it for the pleasure of killing?"

"No."

"Did you do it because you have no care for anything but yourself?"

"No!"

"Then tell me, Theo the Nightwalker, terrible and vicious hunter, scourge of the living, why you did this thing."

Theo waded back toward shore, wanting more solid footing. He stopped when he was waist deep again, plenty of room between them still. "I...have little sisters."

Limpet pulled in a shocked breath. "You killed your sisters?"

"What? No! Just...shut up so I can tell you."

"Your pardon."

"Okay." Theo closed his eyes, trying to stop the shiver that crept up his spine. Only Mr. Sandoval knew the whole story. Even Luz didn't know everything, since she would never speak to him again. "The oldest of my sisters, Luz, she was fourteen then. I don't know why she was out so late. Probably coming back from a friend's house later than she'd promised. We lived in a neighborhood that maybe wasn't that bad, but a young girl late at night, alone in the city? No. Just no."

Limpet gave him a slow nod. He might not really understand, but he was following.

"Luz was maybe two blocks from home. This bunch of *Sureño* punks must've started following her. I was living on the rooftops already then."

"After your mother banished you."

"Yes. They...cornered her and forced her into an alley. Those *chingasos*... Four of them against a ninety-pound girl. They ripped her clothes off. I heard her scream and ran there, roof to roof. They never saw me coming."

Limpet pulled his legs up onto the rock, his eyes widening. "Theo..."

"The big one, they held her down and he took her from behind. I couldn't…all I heard after that was the blood pounding in my ears. Blood. Blood, everywhere. So much and more and in my rage, I couldn't stop. I broke their spines and drank until the last one fell lifeless from my hands. When I looked up, Luz was staring at me, all that blood and horror in her eyes. She had watched while her older brother, her protector, the one to read her stories at night, became a vicious monster in front of her."

Theo swallowed hard and sat down in the shallow water. Somehow, he had drifted up to where it was only ankle deep. "Sounds came back then and I heard her screaming."

"You saved her but you feel you frightened her more than those terrible humans," Limpet said gently.

"Yes. She ran home. I made sure she made it but didn't let her see me. Never again. You understand now. Understand I'm a killer. I have to keep hold of it. So tight. That can't ever happen again."

"But you feed."

"Under controlled conditions. Yes. With a spotter, just in case. There are always two fae warriors in the room when I feed. And fae feedings make me drunk, all happy and sleepy, which helps."

Limpet tipped his head to the side. "My blood makes you happy and sleepy."

"Yes, but I *want* you!" Theo choked out and buried his head in his hands. "And I can't keep having feedings from you so close together. It's not good for you."

"So." Limpet shifted off the rock, crawling over the sand until he could put his hand on Theo's knee. "So.

You have fed recently. You are uninjured and well again and should not need to."

Theo nodded cautiously.

"Easy enough, then. We can just mate." Limpet's guileless, blinding smile almost made Theo believe it was that easy.

"But the sex…and the feeding…I've never…"

Limpet's blue-gray eyebrows rose to try to meet his hairline. "From what you say, you've fed many times without sex. Which means the other should be possible. And now you tell me you never have? You've gone *without* since your change, what, four or five years ago?"

Theo nodded again, though this time with a miserable ache in his chest.

"My dear Theo the Nightwalker, you are honorable and courageous and strong. But you are an idiot."

"No, I'm—"

"You are. You wish to keep control of your urges and yet you deny yourself the most basic one. How can you maintain control if you dam all that desire up inside, waiting for it to explode? Despite the temperature of your skin, you are not cold. Your passion burns hotter than the sands hereabouts. You can't simply deny what is in your nature and hope that all will magically be well."

"I can. And I have. I don't see why I should change that."

Limpet moved in close to whisper in Theo's ear. "Because you are lonely. And, I'd wager, unhappy. One day your carefully made levee will break in some storm, and goddesses help the world when it does." He leaned closer, dragging his tongue against Theo's jaw. "Because by then you will have stored an ocean's worth behind that wall and the world will both burn and drown."

A sound stuck in Theo's throat, embarrassingly close to a whimper. His muscles had locked. Unable to pull away or surge forward, he couldn't figure out which he wanted more. "I don't want to hurt you. Please."

"I could tell you that you won't," Limpet murmured against Theo's throat, "but it seems you won't believe me. We should play a game. Mating is more fun with games."

"You've got to—"

"Tsk, you haven't even heard the rules yet. You must keep your hands to yourself. While you may touch me with anything else you please, lips, tongue, your cock that wants nothing more than to touch me—"

Theo moaned as his erection swelled from half-hard to concrete pillar.

"—anything but your hands."

"What happens if I touch you?"

Limpet chuckled as he nibbled on Theo's collarbone. "I win, of course."

"And if I don't?"

The nibbling stopped as Limpet jerked his head up, staring into Theo's eyes with equal shares of heat and amusement. "I still win."

Hands balled into fists, Theo leaned forward to press a gentle, searching kiss on the selkie's lips. "Hardly seems fair," he breathed against Limpet's cheek.

"Oh, I think your notion of fair will be served before the end." Limpet tangled his fingers in Theo's hair and crashed their mouths together, his predatory hunger sparking a primal need in Theo's belly.

His canines ached, begging to distend. Limpet's pulse beat a war-drum tattoo against his brain. He broke the kiss, leaning his head back to distance his teeth but that only gave Limpet better access to this throat. "I can't. It's too hard."

"A challenge. I know you do well with one." Limpet pressed his hands against Theo's chest. "Lie back. Head out of the water. That's it."

Theo swallowed hard, staring over Limpet's head as clever hands stroked his arms and chest. The sun sat just atop the largest dune opposite, rising just in time to play voyeur as it peeked through the leaves. They had plenty of shade here by the pool and it did mean they had to stop traveling for the day—

"Ah!" Theo arched up into Limpet's grabby hand, fingers fastened tight around his cock. *Too much, too soon.* "Damn it, Limpet."

Fine. You want it like that? He might have been reserved and reticent, but passive acceptance wasn't something he managed well. With a low growl, Theo wrapped his legs around Limpet and yanked him forward hard so he tumbled on top. That was a completely different set of pleasurable agonies, but at least Theo had reasserted some control.

"Clever." Limpet nuzzled under Theo's jaw, his hard cock pressing against Theo's hip. "Is this what you intended?"

"No. Damn it. Move over." Theo shoved with his right thigh, putting Limpet more squarely between his legs as he hitched further out of the water.

Now it was Limpet's turn to moan as their erections pressed alongside each other. His hair spilled over Theo's skin, a silken curtain to torment him even more, but he had the satisfaction of watching Limpet's eyes cross, his body squirming in delight. His movements became desperate and frustrated as he tried to find the right angle.

"Hey." Theo waited until Limpet stilled. "You can still use your hands."

Limpet reached between them, tearing a groan from both of them when he wrapped his long fingers around both cocks, stroking slowly. "So, so clever. One of the things I find most attractive about you. And how patient and heart-strong you are. And—"

"Hey."

Again Limpet froze, waiting for Theo to speak.

"Quiet time. Kiss me."

"So demanding, too," Limpet whispered before he brought his lips down on Theo's, the kiss searching and gentle at first, then catching desperate fire as he sped up his stroking.

Theo tightened his hold, locking his ankles over Limpet's ass and humping up hard against him. *Feels so good, oh, fuck, it feels so good.* It wasn't just the physical, which was incredible, but to have a heart beating next to his, to have *this* heart beating with his, this free-spirited, sometimes reckless, beautiful heart who saw the fangs and the peril and ran into his arms at full speed anyway.

Shivers ran the length of Limpet's body as he whimpered and writhed against Theo, his tongue plundering Theo's mouth, laying claim to every inch, sharp teeth meeting sharp teeth as Theo's fangs came down fully.

"You can bite, you know," Limpet whispered against his lips. "Bite without feeding. Your teeth ache to sink in, don't they? Mine do."

Theo cried out in shock when Limpet broke their kiss and bit down where shoulder met neck. The pain was sharp and exquisite, shooting heated sparks through his balls. That was it. He couldn't hold out any longer. With a roar, Theo reared up far enough to sink his fangs into Limpet's biceps, the trickle of blood and Limpet's sweet skin giving him that last shove, his bellows muffled against Limpet's arm as he came harder than he could ever remember.

Finally, they both lay still, panting. Theo moved first, removing his fangs carefully, licking the little punctures and wrapping his arms around Limpet. "You win."

Limpet smiled down at him and kissed him sweetly before he slid to the side, nestling against Theo. "So do you."

Chapter Eleven

Kelan structures: Most human researchers have adopted the dragon terminology for what may be roughly described as magical DNA. While kelan, which can be viewed through magical means as attachments to DNA, exist in every living organism, the concentration and distribution of kelan take on unique patterns in every species. Only in humans are there wide variations in concentration and pattern, resulting in wild variations in human sensitivity to and ability to manipulate magic.
Definitions, *The Compendium of the Magically Sensitive*, 4th Edition, Dr. Nathan Cooper

"How do you fare, love?"

Diego opened his eyes to find a tiny black eye staring back at him. The black wren hopped back a step to let him sit up. "Sorry. I must have gone to sleep. I'll be fine. You?"

Finn hopped up on Diego's knee. "A mite tired. Perhaps more than a mite. I would shift back, but I don't want to shock these nice gentlemen."

"Ah. Very considerate." Diego cradled Finn in his hand while he climbed to his feet. Wren-Finn's eyes were closing when Diego had his prison pajamas gathered off the floor, confirmation that *a mite tired* translated into *completely exhausted.* "I'm so sorry, Tarek, but I do need to let Finn rest a bit. Is it all right if I come back and tell you what he's said?"

"I wouldn't have believed it, that demons are modest." Tarek shot him a wry smile, since he had indicated he didn't believe in demons any more than Diego did. "I'll wait here. It's as good a place as any."

The Canadian boys trailed Diego, as had become their habit, and waited outside the door to the monster cell corridor as they always did.

"It's just us, *mi vida*, if you want to shift. You want to go back to your, ah, private room, or would you rather stay out here?"

Finn snorted and half fell, half flew to the floor. "I'm quite content never to see the inside of my prison again, thank you." Wren-Finn glowed blue a moment before he began to gain mass and elongate. Soon Finn reclined on the floor in the wren's place, beautiful in his nakedness and grinning at his ability to shift successfully again. "Mostly, though, I'm grateful to no longer be stuck as a pooka collage."

Diego lowered himself to the floor so he could hand Finn his pants. "You weren't precisely a collage, you know. Just a...hybrid."

"Mixed media of some sort," Finn grumbled as he dressed. Then he flung his arms around Diego and pulled him close. "Thank you. So very much, husband of mine, for freeing me. I wish I could do the same for you."

"We'll get there, don't worry." Diego indulged himself, leaning into the embrace. "With that in mind, what did you see on your flight?"

"Yes, what did you see?"

Diego jerked around to find Nusair standing behind him. "I wish you wouldn't do that."

"I didn't even try for stealthy this time." Nusair waved a hand in an airy gesture. "You two were just so *involved*."

"Come sit and I'll tell you," Finn said on a chuckle. "I do wish I had something or other to draw with."

Nusair tipped his head sideways as if considering. Then he got up and slipped inside Finn's old cell, returning with the most recent food packet.

"Oh, thank you! Just the thing." Finn took it from him and spread the leaf out on the floor, his long fingers beginning to push the mash into shapes as he spoke. "We are, as they say on the picture box, at the ass end of nowhere. There truly is nothing at all interesting for miles, unless you are particularly fond of sand. I've never seen a place so frighteningly dry. The nearest water I could sense is a day's travel away."

Diego had suspected they were in the middle of the desert but he hadn't considered logistics. "Where does the water come from for the prison?"

"Oh, that." Finn flicked his fingers in dismissal. "There's certainly water underground here and there. I expect they've done something with machines to reach it."

"Sorry, *mi vida*, I'll stop interrupting."

Finn planted a swift kiss on Diego's cheek and continued as he shaped his model. "The prison is, I must say, a singularly ugly design. Someone certainly could have done better. It's simply one clumsy block, roughly so..." He evened out the sides of his roughly rectangular model and began to add a little square on one side. "With a little protrusion over here on the southern side."

"Any idea what the protrusion is?" Diego watched in fascination as Finn recreated what appeared to be vents and ductwork on the roof of the prison.

"Seems to be where the only door lies. I thought there might be an entrance on the roof, since someone must stand there to drop these goddess-forsaken packets through the slits. But no. I found only the one door. There are ladders up the outside." Finn paused to indicate where, one on each side of the prison. "They are the only way up. The guards who walk the walls use them."

Nusair leaned closer to the model. "How many guards?"

Finn shrugged. "There were six that I could see on the walls. How many more were in the little box room, I can't say."

"Why do you think there are more inside?" Diego asked, though he was certain Finn was right.

"I saw one come out of there through the only door. He climbed the ladder and spoke with another guard. That one went down and back inside."

Diego drummed his fingers on his knee. "Were there any vehicles? Any way for the guards to get to the prison or does it seem they live here?"

"There were no vehicles with wheels. But there was one of those things that flies with the spinning blades. Heliochopper?"

"Helicopter," Diego corrected, half-distracted. The reconnaissance was incomplete, but a picture was starting to form. The prison was so remote that unconscious prisoners were transferred in by helicopter. None of the human inmates he had asked recalled the trip to the prison, but they all remembered the same experience of waking up and having to leave the intake cell. Finn didn't recall his trip, either, but he had woken in his prison cell.

"All right. So we're in a block with no real windows, no real ventilation system besides small holes in the ceiling and only one door leading in from the outside. We know where the interior door to the intake cell is and I'd wager that the opposite door leads into this blockhouse at the base of the prison. With guards coming in and out of there, I'd venture further and say that's the communications and command center."

"But we've no notion of how many guards." Nusair rested his chin on his fist. "Or whether there are more or less at night."

"Or how they placed you in your cells," Diego said cautiously.

Nusair narrowed his eyes at Diego. "What are you saying, little sorcerer? Or what are you not saying?"

"That you're withholding information. You remember being brought to your cell, don't you?"

Finn looked from one to the other, his eyebrows climbing. "Do you?"

"I'm not going to sit here and listen to this." Nusair started to get up but Diego grabbed his wrist.

"It's hard to trust us. We know that. But keeping something back out of habit, because you've needed contingency plans before, probably isn't going to help here. Unless you have a way out of this other entrance, whatever it is, knowing about it won't help you. And you don't have a way out."

"You don't know that."

"It's a good guess. You're still here."

Nusair snorted and sat down again. "Your human's too smart for his own good, Finn. Bet it gets him in plenty of trouble."

"From time to time," Finn murmured, though he was staring down at his model in glum fascination. "We could have come through the intake door as well, I suppose. Though guards would have needed to carry us to our cells and the human prisoners would have seen that. But they've never seen anyone brought to the monster cells, have they?"

"No. They claim they've never seen guards inside for any reason." Diego let go of Nusair, hoping this wouldn't escalate into something ugly. "So there has to be a way to get into this corridor directly, without going through the prison."

Nusair sat back, lips pressed in a hard line. He let out a sudden bark of laughter, one that rang of despair. "It won't make any difference. Finn says there's no other way out. The damn door just leads back to the same command post."

"You know that?"

"No, I—" Nusair broke off with a grimace and went on in a less belligerent tone. "No, I don't. There's no way to know that."

Finn tried to stifle a huge yawn, rubbing at his eyes. "Oh, such little faith. You can show me in a bit. This door. Not just this moment, though."

"Typical." Nusair snorted as he stomped off.

Diego would have asked Finn what he had in mind, but his husband had fallen fast asleep with his head cradled on Diego's thigh. He stroked a hank of snarled black hair back from Finn's cheek and leaned against the corridor wall, content to watch Finn taking his first real rest in days.

* * * *

Finn burrowed further into Diego's arms. There was nothing more lovely than those nights when Diego stopped work early and they could have dinner with a movie in the common room. Others might have been there at the beginning, but they seemed to have drifted out at some point.

The movie, he was nearly certain, had begun as My Neighbor Totoro, *but had morphed somewhere in the middle into a strange mix of* Alice in Wonderland *and* The Italian Job, *with the Mad Hatter driving a very small car along the stems of monstrous flowers. Finn was about to ask Diego what was happening, since he had lost the plot entirely, when he realized his husband was missing. His arm slid through the empty hole in the sofa and he was falling…*

"Shh, hey, it's all right."

Finn jerked awake with Diego's voice in his ear. *Not home. Not on the sofa. At least he's actually here and hasn't vanished.* "I dreamt…I don't recall much now. Something unpleasant."

"I wish I could say these past few days have all been a dream, *corazón.*" Diego hugged him tight, his warmth steadying Finn as nothing else could.

"Ah, well, if wishes had wings. How do you feel?" Finn reached up to stroke Diego's face, warmed even further when he leaned into the touch. Diego's seizures came when he was under too much physical or mental duress but he hadn't suffered one yet.

"A little tired. Much better now that I'm not so worried about you. I do need to find Nusair to see if he'll show us his door."

Ah. Too busy scheming to wallow in worry. Good. Finn planted a tender kiss on Diego's lips as he sat up. "He's not far. I have his scent if you'd like me to find him for you."

"Such a relief to see you feeling better. I was starting to —" Diego broke off on a strangled laugh and pulled him into a fierce embrace. "No. I won't even say that. You're all right now. Even if it takes years to get out of here, you're here with me and you're well again."

"He still loves me after all this time." Finn leaned back to shoot his husband a grin as he stood and pulled Diego up with him. "That alone gives me strength for conspiring. Onward, shall we?"

Diego's smile was like the sun after a winter storm, the smile Finn had thought lost for a time. The things he had done while soul-shattered had been the actions of another man, but of course, Diego hadn't seen it that way. He still didn't and had whispered to Finn one night that he would never be able to atone for those things. He blamed himself too much, in Finn's opinion, but Diego had always felt responsible for everyone he touched, for the whole world sometimes.

He was better, oh, so very much better, than he'd been those first dark days after his rescue, but it had been a long road. It had required a journeyman's travels, as Diego had used every moment of his exile to learn from any fae who would teach him — dragon, bane sidhe, trolde, spriggan, selkie. Awareness that he was often his own enemy and a deeper connection to the world had allowed Diego to find his balance again, to become this steadier, well-grounded man. But Finn still woke sometimes to find him staring into the night, the sorrow in his eyes quieter but still as deep as the Salmon's Well.

It will always be there, Fionnachd. Accept his happiness as a gift and accept that there must be sorrow as well. He had nearly lost track of his surroundings while he scolded himself, so he only had time to turn Diego and nod at the door at the end of the corridor before Nusair wandered through it.

"Finally. I was just coming to ask if Diego needed to perform some convoluted sexual act to wake you. True love's reverse cowboy or something." Nusair's snide comments would have been more convincing if the anxious scent hadn't rolled off him so strongly.

"Ah, and you were coming to watch? I don't mind onlookers but it makes Diego rather uncomfortable."

Diego rolled his eyes at them both. "No exhibitionism for me, thank you. Nusair? The door?"

The djinn shrugged. "Come on, then. Though I don't see how it can help."

He led the way to one of the closed cell doors. Finn had assumed they were all locked, but this one opened easily. Nusair waved at them to follow and once they were all inside, Finn stared about in confusion.

"But it's simply another cell."

"It's meant to look like one, yes." Nusair nodded to the far wall. "But you have your collar off, pooka-boy. Is it really just another cell?"

Finn stared hard at the far wall. While he knew something was off, he wasn't certain what, exactly. "It's as if it's not a wall. Clearly it is, but something…" He paced around the room, placed his hand against the stones and yanked them back in shock. "It's a burrow! That is, it's hollow. Water goddesses help me, I swear there's a great bloody hole back there."

"If it's a door, it's a well-camouflaged one." Diego approached, examining the stones with narrowed eyes.

He ran his hands along the blocks from one side of the wall to the other, tapping on the stone from time to time. "It's veneer. Right here in the middle. Not real stone but plastic or composite made to look like it. The light's bad in the cell, or we'd probably be able to see the difference right away."

"So now you've seen it." Nusair gave a weary shrug. "Wonderful. Fat lot of good it does us."

"Faith." Finn gave Diego a wink. "Patience."

"*Faith is not something to grasp, it is a state to grow into,*" Diego said with a laugh. "Or sometimes to shrink into, I think."

"Shakespeare?"

"No, *caro*, Gandhi."

"What are you two idiots babbling about?"

"Give him a moment, please." Diego held out his hand. "Maybe give me your clothes, Finn, while you decide."

"So thoughtful." Finn yanked his shirt over his head, slipped out of his pants, and handed them to Diego. "Would have taken me a few moments to find my way out of the pants, I expect."

He concentrated on thoughts both small and flat, packing away the large portion of his mass for later. Diego and Nusair grew taller until even Diego's foot looked enormous. Finn waved one of his new legs experimentally. Good, good. Not too difficult to maneuver.

"Stinkbug's sort of an odd choice, isn't it?" Even Diego's voice seemed huge and distant.

"Not a bit of it." Finn gesticulated with a front leg, knowing his voice coming from a bug would seem incredibly odd. "Now I'm quite flat. I doubt the door's so well sealed that there are no cracks. As a stinkbug, I will find them. I'll return as soon as I can, but be patient."

He tried to fly a bit to the door, but gave it up after wobbling clumsily a half-inch off the ground. It was far too much like attaching wings to a luggage cart. Grateful that both his companions stood carefully still so they wouldn't squash him, Finn trundled to the door and began poking about the bottom edge. Sure enough, he found a little indentation in the concrete floor where he could slip underneath. Even as a stink bug, it was a tight fit, but the ungainly trolley cart of the bug world was far better suited for slipping between than for flying.

When he reached the other side, he stopped and shifted to badger — safer in case he ran into something that liked bugs for supper — and found himself in another corridor. This one seemed more tunnel-like, though, since it immediately sloped downward, quite badger-appropriate. He had expected, since Nusair was certain the door would lead to the same part of the prison the human ingress door did, that the passage would turn and turn again. It did not. There was a gradual curve and after the tunnel descended perhaps fifteen feet underground, the slope began to rise again.

Not through the prison at all — under. Why would it go under?

He finally reached the end of the tunnel-corridor at a metal ladder leading to a round door in the ceiling. A quick shift to raven to hop up the ladder, then back to stink bug got him through the odd round door where he emerged...

Outside.

That was strange. After a moment's thought, he shifted to jackal, an animal that was unlikely to arouse suspicion for the brief time he needed the shape to see more clearly. Yes, outside the prison. The round door came out not far from the square room Diego called the command center, perhaps a hundred yards from it. Between the door and the room sat the helicopter's concrete roost, though the flying vehicle was nowhere in sight.

Finn believed he understood. The helicopter brought prisoners. The humans were taken through the square room and into the prison, there to be set loose to survive or not among the other prisoners. Nonhumans were taken through the tunnel directly to the corridor with the locked cells. The transferring guards would have no contact with the human prisoners and the human prisoners would never see the 'monsters' who were brought to the locked cages.

Most likely, a human could make sense of such things. Finn surely couldn't. One of the guards atop the wall turned to watch him, so he snuffled at the round door like a curious jackal would and loped off behind the square protruding room. He rested in the shade of the building, panting, heart pounding. *More careful. Need to be more careful.*

Still, he wanted to remain a bit longer, to glean all the information he could. He took a deep jackal breath and quickly shifted to scorpion. Not his favorite shape, but not something anyone would question. He shifted right and left and moved his poisonous tail carefully. Creatures with more than six appendages were difficult at first. He always felt he wouldn't be able to keep track of all the legs to walk correctly.

As usual, it took a few false starts, but once he stopped thinking about all the legs, his body moved easily. Quickly, before some bored guard decided target practice using scorpions would be fun, he scuttled under a rock near the building and settled in to watch. Evening was closing in but he would be able to observe the guards for a while longer.

His patience was rewarded when the *thup-thup-thup* of a helicopter became audible, heading directly for the prison. From his vantage point, Finn had a clear view of the roost. The helicopter landed and eight humans in guard uniforms leaped out and entered the building. Perhaps twenty minutes later, eight different guards came out and boarded the helicopter, which started its engines up with a whine and a windstorm of blades. It rose back into the air and took the guards away.

So many interesting things I have to tell. Once the sun had set, he scuttled back to the round door on scorpion legs, changed quickly to stinkbug and squeezed back inside through the seam in the door. An unexpected feeling in the flows stopped him halfway through. Stinkbug-Finn held still, feelers testing the nearby flows. *Oh, yes, so many things to tell.*

* * * *

"Brandon, good to see you, kid." Zack stood just outside the magical doorway that had opened between the Heersford Institute and the consulate's garden. The only one of the coven who overtopped Zack by a couple of inches, Brandon took Zack's offered hand and they did the manly awkward handshake while one-armed hugging thing.

"Hey, Sarge. You look tired."

Zack snorted as he let Brandon step aside. "Gosh, thanks. Any problems?"

Brandon shook his head. "Mink's got this. We don't even have to be touching anymore to do the coven thing."

"I thought she couldn't do the doorway thing? Her pooka bloodline and all that?"

"Ha! She found a way around it. Does it her own way. Let the dragon lord chew on that the next time we see him."

The next young man through couldn't have been less like Brandon if they were different species. By some accounts, they were. Slender and on the short side, frost pale and auburn haired, Jasper's smaller frame hid a vampire's strength and a huge heart. Even with the wide-brimmed hat pulled down and sunglasses on, the twinkle in those eyes was apparent. He broke into a huge grin when he stepped through and nearly took Zack down with the force of his greeting.

"Sarge!" He thrust a plastic container into Zack's hands. "I brought you beignets."

"You made them?"

"Yep. Think I finally got them right this time."

"I thought you had it right the first six times, but I'll play guinea pig for your baking any day." Zack shifted the container to his left hand so he could catch Kara in a one-armed bear hug when she came through. "Hey, feisty, how're things?"

"Just coming to pull your bits out of the fire again, Sarge. Same old, same old."

It felt damn good to laugh. The situation wasn't funny, but somehow, having the coven there in person made everything less grim. William came next, always quiet, but more confident with each passing year, then Nate, who seized Zack in a back-thumping embrace.

"Dr. Cooper, I presume?" Zack matched Nate's mad grin with one of his own. "You behaving for Jasper?"

"Never. Jazz wouldn't have it any other way."

Finally, Minky stepped through and let the magical door snap shut behind her. She shook her raven-dark hair out of her eyes and tilted her head back to meet Zack's gaze head on. "Ready to get them home, Sarge?"

While she wouldn't touch him — and wasn't comfortable with touch in general — the difference between this self-assured young woman and the painfully awkward girl he had met three years ago was astounding. "More than ready. You don't know how glad I am that you're all here."

"Any new information?"

Zack shook his head. "Not a whisper. Let's go inside and get Jasper out of the sun."

They all piled into the kitchen, the Silver Adepts coven plus Jasper the vampire, and took seats around the table. Zack had to turn away and busy himself pulling drinks out of the fridge. All his kids had grown up while he wasn't looking and damn if it didn't make his heart ache.

"So, here's the little bit we do know." Zack cleared his throat as he plunked sodas and water bottles on the table then pulled up an extra chair. "Diego and Finn went to negotiate the release of the three Canadian students. They went to Prince Faisal's palace near the capital to see if he'd help. The parliament made nasty changes to their laws on magical beings and someone, for whatever reason, tipped off the police."

"Lots of disagreements within the royal family there, from what I've read," Nate said as he leaned back in his chair.

"Yeah. We've seen it firsthand. The official government line is that they have no idea what happened to our guys. But our security confirms the arrests and Prince Faisal has apologized, unofficially, for their imprisonment. He's furious. Sure that his dad engineered the whole thing as a lesson to him."

"Good that it wasn't a deliberate trap," Will offered, staring at his hands on the table. "But he can't help, I'm guessing."

"Right. So we've been able to confirm that the prison is out in the desert somewhere and that prisoners are taken there by helicopter. We also know that Theo went to find them. He may have taken a young selkie named Limpet with him or, more likely, Limpet followed Theo."

"What're the odds of Theo finding Diego?" Brandon asked.

"I don't really know. There are a couple of things that Lugh pointed out. One, that Theo's an amazing hunter. And two, he seems to have some locating sense for people he's connected to that most magical beings don't have. What kind of range he has on that is anyone's guess."

Jasper laced his fingers with Nate's, a frown creasing his forehead. "Why would he take a selkie into the desert?"

"He wouldn't. Theo's the most responsible person I know. That's why I'm sure Limpet followed him. He tagged along with Theo on his patrols for three nights running and I think he stowed away on their plane because Theo was part of the security force. It's either a curiosity fascination or a major crush, but he just had to be where Theo was."

"Anyone try the easy route and call Theo?" Kara asked.

Zack nodded. "Yeah. We keep trying. He either has his phone off or he ditched it, not wanting the signal tracked."

Minky was drawing meandering shapes on the table with her index finger, the gesture so like her many-times great-grandfather Finn that Zack had to smile. She looked up and everyone fell silent, waiting for whatever idea had struck her to find its way into words. "We can't find the prison because it's lead-shielded and we're so far away. Theo may be able to find it because he's following a local magical trail. So we don't need to find the prison. We need to find Theo."

"Well, Mink does it again," Kara said drily. "Remind me why I listen to any of the rest of you?"

"Because you love us," Nate said with a grin. "We have anything personal of Theo's we can focus on, Sarge?"

Zack got up from the table. "I don't like invading his space without permission. But this is an emergency. Let me see what he has in his room."

God, I hope this works. They're both too nice for prison and who the hell knows what's happening in there.

Chapter Twelve

Magically sensitive humans: While all humans possess kelan structures, only a small percentage exhibit abilities, large or small, that indicate a sensitivity to magical flows. These abilities may never manifest beyond moments of strong déjà vu or they may, in rare cases, manifest with enough strength to rival most fae.
Definitions, *The Compendium of the Magically Sensitive*, 4th Edition, Dr. Nathan Cooper

Midafternoon, Theo woke to splashing. He jerked awake, disoriented by the gentle breeze on his naked skin and the dappled quality of the light, both things one didn't get sleeping under a truck. Palm fronds waved above him. *Right. Oasis pit stop.*

A black head broke the water briefly before dunking under again. Apparently, Limpet was going to get every moment of enjoyment out of the pool that he could. Soon, the sun would make its way down toward the dunes. Theo could wait another hour. He tugged his pack toward him, settled cross-legged under the palms and pulled out his needlework while he waited. Maybe it would've been more sensible to leave it behind, but he couldn't stand the thought of someone pawing through his things and carelessly damaging the work.

Maybe it was stupid to keep working on it at all. He made things to satisfy the ache in his fingers, the itch he couldn't scratch from the things he could never make. Most of the needlework, no one ever saw. The other security personnel, most of them, made fun of him — or worse — when they had.

"Why do I have to patrol opposite that sissy fag vamp?" one of them had hissed at Kevin over the assignment board. "Does fucking embroidery like my granny."

Of course, Kevin had reprimanded the man and he hadn't lasted long with Fae Collective security. But Theo had heard from outside the command center. He knew most of them would have agreed even if they didn't say it.

The split stitch for the fine dragon scales soothed him, eased the trembling that had settled into his fingers. Something about the precision necessary for that particular stitch made it the perfect meditation exercise. In the filtered light under the palms, the dragon's scales seemed to shimmer and move with the shadows, as if it were alive. The world around him vanished — until a shadow crept over the cloth and a drop of water plopped onto the edge of the mountains.

"Back up an inch," Theo murmured. "Please don't get it wetter."

Limpet sat back on his butt, still clutching his sealskin to his chest. "You're making a picture with colored skeins. That's awfully clever of you. Do all humans do this? I've made pictures out of seaweed but it never looks like the actual thing and then it washes away. Is this something to wear? One of the human girls at the consulate had a shirt with bright blue and green birds on it. It was so wonderful and soft. She laughed when I asked to touch it. Humans laugh at odd things. Is it something like that?"

Theo carefully folded the needle into the cloth and packed everything away in the double plastic bags, waiting to see if Limpet had actually run down. "Do you care if I answer your questions?"

"Pardon? Of course I care. Why would I ask, otherwise?"

"Maybe ask them one at a time." Theo stood to brush sand off before he started dressing. "There was a first question in there. Hell if I know what after all that."

Limpet seemed both puzzled and entranced as he watched Theo pulling on his pants. "You have such lovely, strong thighs. I don't recall what the question was, either."

"Works for me. Get your things. We need to get rolling."

Limpet nodded, head down as he folded up his sealskin and returned it to its pouch.

Damn it, I'm not good at this. Theo zipped up his pack, trying to figure out what he had said, or maybe how he had said it. Or maybe what he hadn't said. "Hey." He took Limpet under the chin and forced his head up for a sweet, lingering kiss. "I loved this day. This beautiful spot in the middle of all this misery."

Ah, that did it. Limpet beamed at him and bounced up, hurrying into his clothes so he could race after Theo to the truck. He couldn't help a little smile. Damn it, but he liked Limpet way too much, every hyper, loquacious, overcurious inch of him. If things had been different…

Stupid, stupid to think along those lines. They weren't and they wouldn't ever be. He had to treasure the time they had because once they got home, and they would get home, Limpet's family would claim him. A human monster had no place with people as bright and lively as selkies. Limpet's pod would make sure of that.

And I'll go back to being a glorified rent-a-cop. That's all right. If I can help get them out and back home, at least I've done something good.

Not that he was so simple-minded that he thought an equal number of good things would cancel out the bad ones. He would always be a murderer, no matter how much good he did. It wasn't really atonement, redemption or karma. Redemption was a fairy tale for children. Grown people just tried to do better.

The truck coughed and sputtered, irritated at having to leave, but it rolled off without complaint once they were moving. The trail had grown colder but the feeling of an end point approaching had intensified. Theo drove carefully around or over each dune. The last thing he wanted was to have the prison suddenly appear in front of them and the two of them go down in a hail of gunfire from the walls.

A couple of hours after full dark, Limpet tugged on his sleeve. "Over there. I don't think that's normal."

Theo followed where he pointed. The top of one of the dunes to the right was glowing, not so much the top of the dune itself but behind it. "That's it. Has to be."

Unless it's a refinery. Can't be anything else out here en casa del culo.

Theo parked the truck at the bottom of the dune, took his binoculars and hiked up. He didn't bother to tell

Limpet to stay in the truck, but he did pull the selkie down as they reached the summit, showing him how to low crawl the last few feet. More than happy to squirm along in the sand, Limpet's eyes shone as if this were some wonderful game.

"No noise," Theo whispered. "Stay still."

Limpet wriggled close, head on his hands as they peered over the crest of the dune. Spotlights lit the ground around an almost featureless rectangular building. That was no refinery. Through the binoculars, Theo scanned for movement, for entrances, for something to tell him how to proceed. There were armed guards on the roof, pacing off short distances, their attentions focused outside the walls. Clearly, they weren't concerned over what happened inside, but they were ready to shoot anything that made it out.

"Three guards visible from here. Probably that many more on the other side."

Limpet only nodded, taking Theo's admonishment to be quiet seriously. Theo scanned the building itself, the walls unbroken by doors or windows. *What kind of a prison is this? Do they lower prisoners in through the roof?*

"Stay here with the truck, little bit. I need to scout around, see the whole building."

Limpet grabbed his arm before he could go. "This is the prison, then? This horrid place?"

"Has to be." This was where the trail led. All his instincts screamed toward this one point. "I'll be back. Stay put and stay down."

Theo slipped the binoculars into his jacket and raced off into the dark. The desert might not have been his element, but the night sure as hell was. *I am the night and all that shit. Maybe Batman was really a vampire.*

* * * *

"Then the helicopter flew off again." Finn's grin grew wider with each sentence. "I'm sorry I worried you, but I had to stay and watch a bit."

"No, I'm glad you did. It's frustrating not being able to hear your thoughts, so I can't help being concerned." Diego took Finn's hand, gripping those long fingers tight. Damn right, he'd been sick with worry. Finn had been gone for hours and now his shit-eating grin was threatening to swallow his face. "So what aren't you telling us?"

"I haven't been able to keep a secret from you in so long. Can't I enjoy it a moment longer?" Finn wheedled.

"If you want to give me an aneurysm on top of the stroke you nearly gave me this afternoon, certainly."

Finn shot Nusair a sidelong look and said in a conspiratorial whisper, "Sometimes humans are no fun at all."

"There's always divorce." Nusair gave him a nudge with one clawed foot. "Spill, pooka, or you'll have us both trying to rip it out of you."

"So violent." Finn nestled closer to rest his head on Diego's shoulder. "Theo's here."

Diego startled, accidentally bumping Finn's chin. "Sorry. What do you mean *Theo's here*?"

"I mean he's here. Nearby. I caught his scent."

"Huh." Diego tried to process that. A rescue squad? But what could they hope to accomplish if they couldn't get inside? "Who's with him? How many of our folks?"

Finn sat up, rubbing at his face, as his smile evaporated. "That's the odd thing. I smelled no other humans or altered humans. There was only one other scent and it was selkie."

"Really? Oh...dear. Limpet?"

"That was my thought, yes."

"*Dios.* What was Theo thinking?" Since he was still trying to piece together something sensible out of Finn's reconnaissance, this new development threw all of Diego's thoughts askew. He believed it might be possible, with all the prisoners working together, to open the doors to the outside. If they— "Damn it."

"What?" Nusair sat forward, chin on his knees, his unsettling golden eyes unguarded in a moment of anguished hope.

"Cameras. I've forgotten about cameras. They must be watching everything we do."

Nusair's cagey smirk returned. "Oh, not quite everything."

"Which means what, exactly?"

"Ha! Come here. I'll show you." Nusair leaped up and left the false cell. When Diego joined him, he was pointing to the camera above the door inside the monster corridor. "I broke that one when I first escaped. I hid for a few days since I was sure they would send someone to fix it. No one ever came."

He waved to Diego to follow and went out into the main corridor, where he slid to the right and pointed up to the camera immediately outside the door. "That one I left in place, but I turned it. If you approach the door from this side, they can't see you."

"And you were going to share this, when?" Diego arched a brow at him.

"Oh, not the supercilious single eyebrow!" Nusair clutched his chest and fell against the wall dramatically. Then he straightened and shrugged. "I wasn't sure of you. I'm still not, but you seem to be getting farther than anyone else."

"Good to see you feeling more chipper," Diego grumbled. "But thank you, for the trust you're willing to give. Do you know if they have sound?"

"Pretty certain not. I've yelled things about bombs and about being able to tunnel out, and no one's come to investigate."

"Why haven't they at least realized you're out of your cell? They must have seen you on one camera or another?"

Nusair's ebullient mood abruptly vanished. "I don't look the same as I did."

"Fair enough," Finn said with a nod. "So, my love, where were you going with your scheming before you thought of cameras?"

"We need to get the prisoners to cooperate. As many as possible. I think we're nearly there on that count. We need to get the doors open. I'm assuming you couldn't pick the locks on those doors?"

Nusair smacked his forehead. "Oh, my gracious! Why didn't I think of that? I could've just picked the locks and been merrily on my way!"

"The sarcasm doesn't really help."

"Use your eyes then, oh great sorcerer. The lock mechanism's internal. Probably activated from the control room or whatever we're calling it."

"Sorry. We may be able to force them open magically with everyone's help. But then what? We'll be shot once we clear the outside door." Diego banged his head back against the wall.

"It's not that hard. The pooka can get outside and you just heard that you have allies out there. Assuming they are allies? Or are they weak, useless allies?"

A low growl rumbled in Finn's chest. "The *pooka* can take care of a few slow human guards and Theo is a vampire, neither weak nor useless."

"*Caro*, I don't want to put you or Theo in danger. The guards may be human but they have guns. Remember the last time you were shot?"

"Yes, well, those humans surprised us and I was a bit too upset to think clearly. It will have to be at night, when both Theo and I have the advantage. There are eight of them. Only eight. Surely, we can manage."

Nusair stood with his arms crossed, tapping a sharp nail on his forearm. "You have a vampire outside and you're hesitating? Let me explain something. Dithering is not the same as planning. Just in case you weren't sure."

On the verge of telling Nusair to shut the hell up, Diego stopped when Finn took both of his hands. "My hero, my own, we may only have this one chance."

"It's so frustrating," Diego whispered. "If I had my magic, this would be over in seconds. I'd be able to keep you safe. Get everyone safe."

"Let us all do the things we do best. You can't always do everything, much as you'd like to." Finn kissed the back of one hand, then the other, his smile tinged with sorrow. "I love you so, the way you care about every being you meet. But for all the waters' sakes, Diego, stop thinking you have to save the world on your own. You have a small army at your disposal. Use us."

Shrieks and the rumble of falling masonry haunted Diego's memories, a girl dead because of his scheming. Those kids had been his soldiers, too, his army.

"And don't you dare." Finn gave him a little shake. "I don't need to hear your thoughts to know what you're thinking. Don't you go back there, because it's not the same thing, not a bit of it."

"We could wait. Hope a diplomatic resolution comes soon. It's not as if —"

"No! Damn it, no!" Nusair's bellow shocked him into silence. "You have everything in place now. Everything aligning for this to work. You wait for diplomats and you get out" — he pointed a shaking finger at Finn — "and maybe he gets out. And that's it! Don't you fucking dare think about leaving the rest of us, not after everything I've done!"

Nusair stood there glaring with his chest heaving, his breaths nearly sobs.

Oh, my friend, what haven't you told me still? "You're right. You're both right. I'm getting all tangled and confused. Let's go back inside our more private space and hash this out. Finn, I'm afraid you may have to make the trip back outside again tonight to talk to Theo."

Finn caught him up in a brief hug. "I thought you'd never ask."

* * * *

Zack rubbed both hands over his eyes. The moon was waxing toward full, which made him irritable and tired as it was. The timing just couldn't be any worse. "What do you mean, *he's gone again?*"

"It's not like a building, Sarge." Nate flung himself into one of the chairs on the other side of the desk. "Buildings stay still. Theo's on the move. We think we've got him, then he's not there anymore. He's got a truck, from what you said. It must still be running. And every time he goes off again, we're back at start."

"You can't be back at start. We know the general area he's in."

"Okay, fine. Teensy exaggeration. But we still can't pin him down." Nate bounced his leg, looking more worried than Zack could ever remember. "I figure when Theo finds the prison, he'll stop moving for more than a few hours. So when he finds Diego and Finn, we find them."

"Or something's gone wrong and he can't keep going."

"Not a bad time to find him, either, don't you think?"

"Damn it, I'm sorry, Nate. I don't mean to be so snarly with you."

Nate reached across and patted his arm. "You're worried. Not much you can do about that until we have them home. Doesn't help that it's that time of the month, huh? They really should make werewolf Midol or something."

"Jerk." Zack balled up a piece of scratch paper and threw it at Nate's head. Nate didn't move, but the paper mysteriously changed trajectory. "You could at least be all contrite and let it hit you. How do you still have a sense of humor, awful as it is, in all this?"

"Helps when you're part of the world's prickliest coven." Nate shrugged, his smile faltering. "It's how I've always been, I guess. I laugh to stay calm."

"Does it rub off?"

"Not as much as it should. And sometimes it just causes unsolicited projectiles to start flying."

Despite the lead weight in his stomach, Zack managed a little chuckle. "Thanks, Nate. Yell for me when you know something definite?"

"You got it. We have coffee and we'll keep at it until we do." Nate left with a little wave, in many ways still the gangly, easygoing kid Zack had first met, but the years had scoured away the awkwardness, the naïve, wide-eyed simplicity.

Dr. Nathan Cooper. Freaking head of a new research institute. *Why do they have to make me feel so old?*

* * * *

"All quiet here?" Theo whispered as he slid into position next to Limpet again.

Limpet nodded, his trembling telegraphing through his clothes. "They shine huge lights sometimes. Searching the ground nearby. But the light doesn't reach here."

"Good. Searchlights cycle every five minutes. Easy to avoid. You cold?"

"Anxious. I was worried when you didn't return."

Theo threw an arm around him, pulling him close as he took out the field glasses again. "Was trying to get closer. Damn searchlights are a pain."

Limpet's shivers subsided as he snuggled under Theo's arm. Six guards paced the roof, he'd confirmed that, but there was a bunker stuck on one side of the windowless prison. Impossible to say how many might be in there. The only entrance appeared to be through the bunker, unless his roof access theory was correct. But one guard or another would climb down to the bunker every now and then. They used ladders bolted into the outside walls, which seemed ill advised security-wise, too exposed, if there was a roof entrance.

"What's that?" Limpet pointed at the base of the wall.

A quick lift of his head confirmed movement where Limpet pointed and Theo scanned through the binoculars until he had it in sight. "Some kind of dog maybe?"

He handed the glasses to Limpet for a look but the selkie shrugged. "Perhaps. Odd sort of dog. More of a large fox."

Now that Theo had a good bead on it, he didn't need the binoculars and kept watching because the strange canine behaved so oddly. It seemed to be afraid of the searchlight but instead of just cowering in the shadow, it watched carefully with its bat-like ears swiveling. When the searchlight had passed for the second time, the animal dashed out into the desert, heading straight for them.

The jackal — Theo had finally been able to identify it — raced toward them with single-minded intent, tongue lolling out. While he didn't think jackals were usually dangerous except in packs, Theo certainly wasn't an expert. He pushed Limpet behind him, edging down the dune, just in case.

When the jackal cleared the searchlight's perimeter, it slowed to an easy lope, still heading unerringly toward their position. Theo shook his head to clear it. He thought he heard a voice calling him. "*Theo... Theo...*"

It had to be inside his head. No one knew his name out here except Limpet, who was still doing his damnedest to stay quiet.

Suddenly, the jackal popped its head over the dune and said, "Hi!"

Theo jerked back and tumbled down the hill a few feet before he caught himself, spitting sand and irritation. "Finn?"

"Why, yes. Do you often talk to other jackals?"

"Hilarious. Aren't you in jail?"

"I suppose officially, I am. Hello, Limpet. Diego's going to be upset with you for being here."

"Not as if I can go back now," Limpet said with a defiant lift of his chin.

"Ah. Too right, there." Jackal-Finn flopped down in the sand between them. "I found a way out, but I'm certainly not leaving without my Diego. So, he sent me to brief you. We're, as they say, planning an outbreak."

"You mean planning to break out." Theo holstered his handgun. *Finn's found a way out. Maybe things aren't hopeless. And Diego's planning.* Suddenly, it wasn't just him and an unarmed selkie alone against the bad guys.

"That's what I said." Finn huffed and gave Limpet's face a lick. "Poor thing. This is no place for a seal."

"Not the best place for a pooka, either." Limpet snickered, shoving the jackal's head away.

"Granted. But this is serious business." Finn straightened out, forepaws in front, head up in imitation of an Anubis statue. "There has just been a changing of the guards today. Diego says this is significant, because helicopter fuel is expensive and they would not use it to bring new guards in every day. He estimates every third day would even be excessive. So we know they will be without the helicopter and without reinforcements for at least the next day or so."

"Do we know how many guards? Beside the ones on the roof?" The helipad had caused Theo some concern, but not if it wasn't used every day.

"At least eight. I counted eight new ones coming in today and eight different ones going out. The command center" — the way Finn said this implied that he was proud of himself for remembering the phrase — "can't be overly large since it has the, ah, intake room inside it as well."

"Eight at a minimum, then. Maybe ten or twelve. That's not bad." Theo glanced reflexively at the prison. "So he wants me to take them down? Tonight?"

Finn shook his jackal head, his ears twitching to catch the desert night sounds. "He needs time to prepare. Tomorrow night, at moonrise, Diego will begin the work to get the doors open."

"What doors?"

While Finn explained the tunnel and hatch and the internal layout of the prison, Theo crept back to the top of the dune with the binoculars. Yes. There it was. The portal near the helipad looked like something from a submarine. "Tomorrow. Moonrise. He wants me to take down the guards."

Finn bristled. "Not on your own, bucko. I'll come help you."

"You?" Theo blinked back at him. He had a hard time picturing such a kind soul taking anyone down, bad guys or not.

"Two words. Dragon-squashed vampire."

"*A huevo*. Not something I can forget." Theo managed a little smile. "Better we're on the same side."

"I don't even understand what language you two are speaking anymore," Limpet huffed. "And I will have questions. So many, many of them. But I'll save them for later."

Small favors.

Chapter Thirteen

Slattenpatte
Classification: Elemental fae
Appoquinimink social scale: 5
Shy and generally solitary, these Nordic water fae receive their social scale rating largely due to one exception: their insatiable hunger for the company of young human males.
Compendium of the Magically Sensitive, 4th Edition, Dr. Nathan Cooper

Diego stood in the center of the feeding area a few minutes before the normal food drop time. Most of the prisoners, the ones he already knew, stood along the perimeter of the sunlit area singly or in small groups. The women stood to his right, together, but not in the tightly packed defensive group they had used previously. The few outliers, those who had not joined in communal meals, were most likely nearby. He was counting on it.

"Ready?" Tarek murmured nearby, prepared to translate.

"Yes. Thank you, for all your help."

Tarek laughed softly. "You're the closest thing to hope I've seen in this forsaken place. I'd be a fool not to help."

Diego spread his hands and took a deep breath. Public speaking was familiar territory, but it had been a few years.

"Magic is no more an abomination than water is. It can be used for evil or good, but then water can also be used to cleanse or to drown. Magic simply is and because you, all of you, are able to feel it, each in your own way, you have been condemned without process or trial. We have no sentences, no contact with the outside world. As far as we know, we have been left in this terrible place to die."

He waited for the murmurs of anger and assent to die down after Tarek translated, the young doctor's voice breaking on the last words.

"Perhaps some of you committed actual crimes, rather than simply being condemned for who you are. If that's true, you should have been prosecuted for those crimes, not sentenced to life in this giant sarcophagus, denied the opportunity to defend yourselves. What was done to us was done out of fear. The government of Shera'alej fears you and so you suffer."

Again, he paused, waiting for his audience to catch up. There was anger on many faces, resentment and sorrow, but every person he could see still leaned toward him, attentive and curious.

"Their intent is that we should also fear each other, pitting us against each other, taking steps to ensure that we live in enough darkness and uncertainty to breed that fear. *Separate* and alone, each of us is doomed.

Separated into small, warring groups, we have no hope and violence is inevitable. As a community, we may have a way out."

Now there were gasps and questions shouted. Diego waited, turning to Tarek, who explained, "They want to know if you mean a way to escape. Some are saying you are mad, since once out, we would be in the desert without water, so what good is escaping the prison?"

Diego nodded, keeping his expression and his voice calm. "You're right. To leave these walls without a plan would be madness. But we each have abilities beyond normal human skills. Vadim can find lost objects. Saeed can help someone heal. I can make doorways between places. Because of the lead in these walls" — he waved a hand at the stones around them — "I'm unable to do this here. Once outside, with everyone's help, I believe I could, or call to someone who can."

The tall woman spoke up, her voice clear and sharp. Tarek winced before he translated. "She says you are still a great fool because there is no way out and if there was, we would still be shot when we emerge."

Diego turned to her and nodded, acknowledging her comment. "I thought both of these things true, as well. If you will all stay with me, share this next meal with me, I'll explain how we may be able to overcome both obstacles and arrive somewhere safe for us."

Four more figures had edged out of the shadows as he spoke. Diego thought this might be all the prisoners except for the big man with the antisocial tendencies. That one, he would have to deal with separately. The tall woman still regarded him with skepticism, but she inclined her head at his response. He took it as a good sign.

The communal meal, somewhat expanded, was a more boisterous affair than before. The big man had snatched up his multiple packets, his eyes wild in alarm at the gathering watching him, but Diego got his first good look at him and thought he might understand.

When everyone had settled, Diego explained and outlined the plans already in place. Questions and objections flew from all sides, poor Tarek hard-pressed to keep up. The Canadian students helped with translation as well as they could to the people on either side when it became clear that one person couldn't manage.

Finally, all the issues had been resolved except a last, glaring one. "Why should we free monsters?"

Diego took the time for a few bites of lunch before answering. He had to since the query sent shivers of rage through him and if he reacted with anger, he would undo everything. "Why wouldn't we?" he asked the man who had spoken.

Through his translators, Diego understood the man had sputtered, "Because they're monsters! They're dangerous!"

Hesitating deliberately, Diego finally said, "So you fear them. As we are feared by some humans. It was the same fear that locked us all within these same walls."

"But that's not the same at all!"

"One of those monsters, as you call them, has lived among you all this time and hasn't done you any harm. Another is someone I love and won't abandon. Without them, we don't stand a chance of getting out safely."

"We are all from the same creator's hands," Saeed admonished softly.

"Everyone will go," the tall woman called over. "The monsters are probably less dangerous than human males."

Angry muttering from the circle of women and some shamefaced looks among the men made Diego wonder what had happened before the women had banded together. It wasn't a happy thought and he was glad he wouldn't be trying to keep peace too much longer. He ended his recital of plans with the instructions to meet back in the feeding area just after dark. Everyone began to wander away, to find some rest, or to talk in small groups, but Diego stayed until both Finn and Nusair drifted out of the shadows to sit with him.

"I thought that went well," Finn said, though his fingers twitched in an anxious way.

"Thought I'd piss myself laughing at what that woman said," Nusair added with an evil grin. "Maybe we should leave the human males behind. Present company excepted, of course."

"Of course," Diego said with a dry laugh. "But no one gets left if we can help it. Everyone goes. You made me promise."

"So I did." Nusair regarded him with narrowed eyes. "Trust you to remember."

"Yes. Now stop trying so hard to trip me up and work with me here. I have one more prisoner who hasn't come to these meetings."

"That oversized lout with the appetite to match?"

"Yes." Diego watched Nusair carefully when he went on, "I think there's something off about him, don't you?"

Nusair shrugged. "Humans are all odd. Are you asking if I can find him?"

"That would be helpful."

With the djinn leading, they strode down the corridor, past the first left turning, back toward the intake room. Finn slipped his hand into Diego's while they walked and Diego bumped shoulders with him, drawing strength and courage from his presence. Several yards before the intake room, Nusair stopped at one of the cave-like openings dotting the wall. The low-level lighting didn't reach more than a foot or so inside, the black room too much like a monstrous, open mouth for comfort.

Diego was shocked when Nusair shouted into the room in English, "Come out of there, you brute! Someone wants to talk to you!"

There was a snuffle and a rustle of cloth, but no one emerged.

"Maybe yelling at him wasn't the best way to go about it?" Finn said as he peered into the gloom. "I do see him back there, though."

"Your eyes are better than mine, *mi vida*." Diego squeezed Finn's hand. "Could you take me in there?"

Finn sighed. "If he hits you, I do *not* promise to stay polite."

"Fair enough."

Nusair stayed, leaning against the wall, while Diego shuffled after Finn into the darkness. A few steps in, he began to speak, "I guess since Nusair was yelling in English that you can understand me. I haven't come to take anything from you or to hurt you. I just want to talk."

"Go away." The voice sounded like gravel in a blender.

"I will if you want me to. But I need to ask you one question. Do you like being trapped in here?"

"No. Stupid little man. Now leave."

"What if I could get you out?"

There was a long silence and something that sounded like a sob before the big man bellowed, "Go away!"

"How far away is he?" Diego whispered in Finn's ear.

"About ten feet. Directly in front of you."

Diego settled to the floor, even though he didn't like the thought of sitting where he couldn't see and possibly putting his hand on a large spider or worse. "I'm not going away. Not yet. You see, I think I've realized something about you and I think it's something that's made you frightened."

"You don't know shit. If you don't leave me the fuck alone, I'll tear your arms off and feed them to you."

He patted Finn's arm to stop his growling and leaned forward into the darkness. "Your long hair hides your ears. Your eyes are a shade no human's should be. I think, though I can't be sure, that you're hiding a tail. You're afraid the others will see."

"I'm not afraid of those punks!"

"You're afraid and that's why you're so focused on making them afraid of you. Why you take all the food you can and hide."

"Go away," he repeated, though this time it was a hoarse whisper.

"My name is Diego Sandoval and I'm here to help. The Fae Collective sent me."

"They wouldn't want me either. Fuck. Leave me alone, please."

Diego's heart ached at the anguish in that voice. If anyone needed to be rescued, it was this man. "They have a werewolf as their human consul and a vampire on staff. I'd say they're pretty accepting. What's your name?"

"They...do?" Another long silence drummed out in heartbeats, then finally the man said, "Asif."

"It's good to meet you, Asif. Why would you think they would reject you?"

"You just don't give up, do you?"

Finn laughed. "He most assuredly does not. The most incredibly bloody stubborn human I've ever met, thank all the spirits."

"And what the fuck are you? You're not human. I can smell it."

"Goddesses forbid." Finn snorted. "I'm a pooka. Finn Shannon, at your service."

"Why don't you have a collar?" Asif's voice rose to a snarl again. "Why isn't the damn *pooka* collared?"

"We were able to remove it," Diego said quietly. "A dozen or so human magic users pooling the little bits of magic that get past the lead and one djinn to help Finn shift. We think we can use the same methods to break out."

"You're a crazy motherfucker."

"Probably. So what are you, Asif who hides his ears and knows nonhumans by scent?"

"Pushy little twit," Asif mumbled. "I'm a half-breed, all right? My mother was a slattenpatte. She dragged my dad into a stream when he was in college, got knocked up, then dumped me with him."

"Where did your father go to college?" Diego asked, trying desperately to recall what a slattenpatte was.

"Norway, you idiot."

Oh, yes. Water fae. "Sorry. Of course. You sound like you grew up in the Northeast somewhere, though. And somehow you ended up here?"

"Really? You're writing a biography or something? Dad was from here. We came back when he had to take care of the family business. Then he died. Okay? All fucking clear now?"

Too clear. Dios, I'm sorry. "You couldn't go home? Wherever home was?"

"Not like I'm a US citizen, and no way in hell I'd get through security here hiding that damn tail."

"How did you get into the country?"

"My dad protected me." Asif's voice was softer now, tinged with sorrow. "He could do that shit. Hiding stuff so you couldn't see it. I never learned how."

"I'm so sorry you lost him."

"Yeah, well, he's the one who left me stuck in this hellhole. Didn't even get arrested for being a freak. Not at first. Got caught lifting electronics. Then the fucking police didn't know what to do with a perp with a tail and human ID."

"So they classified you as human and sent you here with the rest of us abominations."

"Pretty much." Asif's sigh carried his exasperation through the darkness. "How the fuck did you do that?"

"Do what?"

"Get me to tell you every damn thing. Just like that."

Diego shook his head, not certain if Asif could see him. "I don't think I did anything. I think you needed to tell someone and I asked."

Asif snorted, still not entirely friendly, but at least he had stopped yelling.

"Come with us, Asif. Please. I don't want to leave you here."

"I don't get it. Why do you care? Did the Fae Collective tell you to collect nonhumans or something? That why you have a pooka?"

Finn sniffed in offense. "No one ever *has* a pooka."

"Except in the Biblical sense," Diego said on a chuckle. "I married Finn several years ago, though, so I suppose I have *this* pooka more than most would." He kissed Finn's fingers and sobered. "I care because I can't help it."

"It's his superpower," Finn said deadpan. "If he could, Diego would save everyone."

"You're both idiots," Asif muttered, but the insult lacked conviction.

"Tonight. Before moonrise. Please come to the feeding area. We're starting from there. I can't guarantee that this will work but it's better than doing nothing."

"Go away, little man," Asif said one more time, his voice quiet and broken now. "Leave me alone. The others would tear you apart if I showed up. Just go away."

Diego rose reluctantly. "Please think about what I've said. If you're not there, and I can manage it, I'll come back for you."

Silence was Asif's only answer, so Diego left him in peace with a heavy heart. Finn threw an arm around him as they returned to the monster cellblock.

"You truly can't save everyone, love. If he doesn't want to come with us, what can we do?"

"You're right. I just wish—"

"Whst. Don't say such things where Nusair will hear."

"Right."

* * * *

"So the Theo has landed?" Zack peered down at the map on the table, computer printouts from satellite imaging.

"Looks that way," Minky said. "His position's been stable for the last eight hours."

Kara still clutched the pillowcase from Theo's room, her face white from the effort of so much dowsing. "You think it's time to move, Sarge?"

"I think we better muster some reinforcements," Zack said, patting Brandon on the shoulder where he slumped on the sofa. "You, all of you, go grab something from the kitchen and go rest. Let's give it a few hours or you'll never be able to hold a doorway. Jasper can tell me when you're ready. I trust him to have the sense to know when it's actually true."

He hurried down to the ambassador's office, pleased to see that Lugh was wrapping up a phone call. His prince replaced the phone in its cradle and buried his head in his hands.

"Hey? All right there?"

Lugh mustered a smile for him. "Oh. Yes. Frustrated. The Americans refuse to help. They say that the region was listed as hazardous for the magically sensitive and we should never have sent a mission in."

"Yeah, well, there're probably a lot of things they're not saying. Deals and trade agreements. I have better news. You up for it?"

"Always." Lugh finally lifted his head. "Zachary, we've found them?"

"Sort of. Things could get hairy. But we've found Theo out in the desert. He's stopped moving so he's either in trouble and needs extraction or he's found the prison."

"My instincts say the latter." Lugh sat back in his chair, dark eyes weary and troubled. "If we go in with force, there will be bloodshed."

"If we don't go in with force, we lose more people." Zack came around the desk to knead those broad shoulders, Lugh leaning back gratefully against him.

"Perhaps if Grandfather goes as well. His eye could disable rather than kill if he's careful. We might avoid the worst of it that way."

"Now you're thinking. Want me to go talk to him? Gather the troops?"

"Yes, if you would, please. He likes you and is more liable to listen to you than to me." Lugh moaned as Zack hit a hard knot of muscle.

"Keep making noises like that, babe, and I won't be able to do anything except crawl on my knees under your desk."

Lugh turned his head to kiss Zack's wrist. "Any other time, I would gladly succumb. If you speak to Grandfather, I'll go speak to Kevin and gather our human battle group."

"Rain check on the blow job. Got it." Zack gave him a quick hug. "Back in a few. I told the kids — the coven — to rest. As soon as they're ready, we're good to go."

"You should remain here."

"Not on your life, Your Highness. Don't worry. I'll grab the Kevlar."

* * * *

"Can we get the cells open and make sure all the nonhuman folks understand what's happening?" Diego had caught up with Nusair again in the monster cellblock.

Nusair gave him that evil half-smile. "We?"

"Would you please, Nusair? So they're briefed before we have a human invasion in here." Diego paced the corridor, counting doors, ten on each side. One had been Nusair's. One was the false cell. "Do all these other closed cells hold prisoners?"

"Closed doesn't mean locked," Nusair said curtly as he went down on one knee in front of the phoenix's door to start working on her lock.

"It's good that I like you," Diego said in exasperation. "Or you might be a little hard to take sometimes. Finn? Would you check the doors on the right, please? Let's see how many we have."

Finn tugged on the doors on his side and Diego on the left-hand ones. Several of them opened without a problem, leaving six still locked, including the phoenix's. Nusair soon had hers open, revealing a once-beautiful woman with flame-colored feathers for hair curled up on her side. Her limbs were pitifully thin, the skin on her face stretched tight with starvation. Someone would need to carry her out.

Nusair had moved to the cell beside hers, the tip of his tongue protruding as he concentrated on picking the lock. Finn went from one locked cell to the next, checking on occupants.

"Werewolf…griffin…oh, my love, best not look in this one…there's a poor little ghoul…" Finn peeked into the cell Nusair was just opening. With a cry, he hurled his full weight against the door and slammed it shut again. "Are you mad, Nusair? You can't let that out!"

"What?" Diego hurried over to them in alarm. "What's in there?"

"No one gets left behind," Nusair said through clenched teeth. "You promised."

Finn waved his arms in agitation, though he still leaned on the door. "The griffin and the ghoul I can reason with. The werewolf is harmless as a human. But this?"

"Nusair." Diego drew in a slow breath. "What's in there?"

"Basilisk," Finn hissed.

"You made me a promise, sorcerer."

Diego rubbed both hands over his face. "I did. Yes. But isn't it counterproductive to release something that's going to turn your best chance of escape to stone the minute it gets out?"

"It only does that when it's frightened." Nusair pulled himself straight, golden eyes flashing with anger. "The basilisk is a creature of the desert, like me. It can't survive in here much longer."

"We have hours still before we'll be attempting to open the door. I'm not saying leave it behind. I'm asking that we please delay letting it — him, her?"

"Her."

"Letting her out. Maybe we could cover her eyes when we do?"

"I—I could." Nusair's voice cracked, his naked anguish so out of character Diego had to wonder.

"You feel responsible for her. I won't ask why or how. But you do. Nusair, it's all right. If we get the doors open, she comes with us. But if she's free too much before and a sudden influx of humans invades this space, I'm pretty sure we're asking for a disaster."

Finn still seemed wary and unhappy even when Nusair relocked the door. "If you were so upset about her, why didn't you let her out before?"

"Oh, I have," Nusair said with a ghost of his usual smile. "I open the door every night for her so she can come out and see me. Sometimes I bring her spiders I've found. She's been with me since she was a little fingerling lizard."

A pet. Madre de Dios, who knew djinns had pets? "All right. When we're closer to the time, she won't get left behind." Diego even dared to pat Nusair's shoulder before he went to the cell Finn said he shouldn't see. "And this one, *mi vida*? What's in here?"

Finn hesitated, his pale complexion edging a few shades whiter, so Diego grabbed the bars and pulled himself up. He was expecting some horrible monster, maybe something gelatinous or insect-like, so he wasn't at all prepared.

For a moment, he couldn't find anything in the cell until he spotted a lump of cloth in one of the far corners. He squinted into the gloom, caught his breath on a choked exclamation and let himself down with a thud. Huddled in the corner were the remains of a little girl. Hard to say how old she had been since she was so thin and desiccated—maybe eight or ten years old. Her sunken eyes were open and staring. Her little fangs still protruded from her mouth.

"Oh, God…" Diego sank to the floor to put his head on his knees.

"I told you not to look, love."

"She was a vampire and they let her *starve*," Diego said, wiping at his streaming eyes. "What a horrible way to die. She was just a baby." He lifted his head to glare across the room at Nusair. "Why didn't you let her out? How could you let a *child* die like that?"

"Don't get all righteous and bitchy with me." Nusair lifted both hands as if warding off the accusation. "By the time I got out, she was already dead."

"Diego?" Finn's voice was small and uncertain. "I don't think we can take her with us."

"Why?"

"I think she's likely to crumble the moment we pick her up."

"Oh." *Damn it, what about her family? Someone should mourn her.* Diego heaved a breath, trying for control, but he knew the image from that cell would haunt him forever. "Every detail of this place goes to the UN when we're back home. Everything, hear me?"

"Of course, love. I'll help all I can. You know that."

The gentle reproach in Finn's voice brought his head up. "I'm not angry at you, *cariño.*"

Finn bent to kiss his temple before he strode over to speak to the ghoul and the griffin in some language Diego didn't recognize. The griffin dragged himself out into the hallway as soon as his door was open and flopped onto the corridor floor. He looked just like pictures of griffins, with his eagle head and wings and lion's body, but his fur was patchy and his feathers broken and dull. The ghoul was more surprising. Diego had expected someone humanlike, but what emerged was on four feet. *It's a dog? No, a hyena.*

The ghoul, too, lay on the cool concrete floor, tongue lolling, seeming far too much like a canine just rescued from a badly run shelter. Nusair freed the werewolf last, speaking to him in terse, irritated Arabic. The man, who was perhaps in better shape than the rest of the inmates of the cellblock, was still too thin and babbled at Nusair nonstop as he emerged. Nusair barked out something angry and the man ceased.

"Scorpion-brained fool," Nusair muttered. "He thanks us. Profusely. And says he turned a few days ago only because of the terrible stress of his arrest."

"Did he give you a name?"

"Ask him yourself. Moneychanger. Usurer," Nusair snarled and spat at the man's feet.

"All right, leave him alone, please." Diego patted the man's shoulder and indicated that he should sit down as well. Nusair's obvious hatred for bankers would only be a problem if the man got in his way.

"It's almost dark, love," Finn said as he peered up at the ceiling slits in one of the open cells.

"Finn." Diego pulled him into a bone-creaking hug. "Be extra careful. Please don't get shot this time."

"I'll do my very best." Finn lowered his head for a sweet, searching kiss. "Remember that I love you and I'll always do my best to come back to you. So don't shout at me if I do get shot."

Diego hid his face for two quick, steadying breaths against Finn's shoulder. "I'll do my best."

Finn laughed and gave them all a jaunty wave as he disappeared into the false cell. Without the damn collar, Diego would have known each shift Finn underwent and what he became. As it was, when he glanced at the door, all he knew was Finn had gone.

* * * *

Before Theo's change, he would have only seen darkness when night fell. The dark had frightened him, his night vision so bad they had barely allowed him to have an unrestricted driver's license. After? The night opened up in strange and glorious colors, in deep purples and silvers, in sinuous curves and softened lines.

Half an hour before moonrise, the sky was a bright colander of stars and the dunes spread out in silver waves on all sides. He could see where the old cliché of the desert being a sea of sand came from. The shadows transforming the shifting sands into restless water took little imagination. It would have been incredibly peaceful except for one thing.

"Theo? Theo, are you listening?"

Limpet had been going on for the last hour about this and that and Theo had completely lost track. He didn't tune out so much as he found Limpet's voice soothing and his brain stopped interpreting the meaning of the words after a while.

"Listening but not paying attention."

"Wonderful. I could have told you I had the pearl of all wisdom and you wouldn't know."

"Pretty sure you don't."

Limpet made a strange whistling sound through his nose. Theo decided it was an annoyed sound.

"Sorry. What did you say?"

"I'm not staying behind and watching you go down in a hail of musket fire."

Theo turned on his side and put an arm around Limpet's waist to pull him close. "I won't be alone. I'll be fine even if I take a couple of bullets. And you're not going anywhere near the shooting."

"You can't—"

With a quick tug even closer, Theo seized Limpet's soft lips in a kiss to silence him. "No. I can't stop you from doing what you want to do. But I'll be happier if you stay here. Less distracted."

"Oh, distracted," Limpet murmured against his lips. "I love your kisses."

Theo sighed, stroking a hand along Limpet's hip. His body wanted nothing more than to rip his clothes off and rut against Limpet until they both had sand in places they'd never imagined. But now was about the worst time to give in to raging, often-ignored hormones.

"Just think about it. Stay here and I can focus better."

"Hmm," Limpet said as he snuggled deeper into Theo's arms. It might have been agreement or that might have been wishful thinking.

Light, drumming footsteps on the other side of the dune brought Theo up to his knees, with his hand on his sidearm. The running steps belonged to a jackal and the purposeful trajectory meant it could only be Finn.

"Hey." Theo withdrew his hand from his jacket and flopped back down on the sand. "They about ready?"

"Diego is gathering everyone now. They'll start at moonrise." Jackal-Finn shifted to shaggy black dog, then to panther.

"Might want something that can get up the ladder to start."

"True." Finn backed up and shifted to gleaming, black dragon.

"Not really funny."

The dragon flattened his wings against his back and lay down to make himself the smallest possible target atop the dune. "I don't mean it to be amusing. Your pardon. I know it's not your favorite shape, Theo, but consider. Those big, swinging lights look at the ground. I can take you by air and we can drop on them before they even know they've been attacked."

"Makes sense. Is it…safe?"

"You do know that first dragon incident was an accident, don't you?" Finn said in a hurt tone. "I won't drop you and I certainly won't squash you a second time."

Theo waved a hand in dismissal. "The squashing was my fault. Just never flown Dragon Air before." He stared out at the blight of the prison block on the serene landscape. "Moonrise. We better start. Get those guards and weapons secured before they get the doors open."

"Climb up then. I'll drop you on the roof and shift smaller. Please don't shoot any black tigers or lions or wolves you may come across."

"No bears?" Theo asked as he climbed onto Finn's reptilian neck.

"Ah, you do have a sense of humor. I worried that you'd lost it somewhere."

"Theo!" Limpet stood at Finn's shoulder, his hand on Theo's ankle. He opened his mouth a couple of times, uncharacteristically at a loss for words.

"Hey. It's all right. Just stay here."

"Don't die, Theo. Just…don't. Please." Limpet stroked his leg, his black eyes huge and glistening with worry.

"Do my best since you asked nicely. Hang tight, little bit. I won't be long."

Theo wrapped his arms and legs tight around Finn and squeezed his eyes shut when Finn leaped skyward with a sickening lurch. Planes were bad enough. The prince's Sikorski made him queasy. But he wasn't about to tell Finn about flying discomfort now and the flight was a short one. He squinted past Finn's draconian head, watching the prison grow as they approached. If he timed it right, he could drop directly on top of a guard and let Finn get to shifting before someone could shoot him out of the sky.

Finn gained altitude, getting them above the walls and out of the guards' immediate line of sight. As a battle steed, Theo couldn't have asked for a shrewder one. His handgun stayed in its holster. If he didn't have to fire a shot, he wouldn't, but he wasn't optimistic about being able to take down eight men without raising an alarm. He shifted to the right as they crested the wall, right over top one guard. As if they had choreographed it, Finn back winged and Theo dropped, taking the guard down with the force of his fall and a swift punch to the head.

Silently, he pulled zip ties from one of his inside jacket pockets and secured the guard's hands and feet before dragging him out of the central walkway. When he looked up, Finn had already vanished. Theo crouched, listening for his next nearest target. The man was just rounding the southeast corner of the elevated walkway that circled the roof.

Theo faded back into the shadows between the lights and let the man march past. Just as he pulled up short, probably realizing his counterpart on this section of wall was missing, Theo pounced. One hand over the man's mouth to silence him, the other struck in a quick jab behind the man's ear. Two down.

He secured the second man as he had the first. Staying low, he crept farther along the walkway and came across a third man then a fourth sprawled on their faces. He zip tied and dragged them out of immediate sight as well. He was just about to congratulate Finn on being such a swift, silent hunter when a frightened cry went up from directly ahead and a shot rang out.

Shoving caution and silence rudely aside, Theo raced to the sounds of struggle. A huge black panther had a still-screaming man on the ground. Their last wall guard stood fifteen feet down the walkway with his rifle aimed directly at Finn. Theo gauged the distance, took a running leap onto the railing between the walkway and the roof below and launched. Though he was moving fast, the man with the rifle spotted him and got off a shot. Pain tore through Theo's shoulder. He ignored it. A single bullet wound wouldn't slow him down.

Fear ruined the guard's second shot as Theo came down on him, fangs bared and snarling. He ripped the rifle from the man's hands and snapped it in two before he raised his fist to put the man out. Theo held his blow, panting. The man had fainted.

"Finn? All right?" he called softly.

"Well enough." Finn padded over while Theo secured his unconscious victim. "Your pardon for all the fuss, though. We nearly had it done in silence."

"Didn't hear any radio noise. Don't think they got to warn anyone." Theo trussed the last one and took a quick turn around the perimeter walkway. "All accounted for up here. We need to crack into that security bunker."

A sliver of moon had just peeked over the edge of the dunes. Plenty of time.

Chapter Fourteen

Beings of multi-race heritage: While most magically sensitive races are unable to produce children together, certain races have proven to be genetically compatible. There are documented cases of children from sidhe and Fomorian pairings as well as cases of children born from several human/fae pairings such as pookas and several other water fae.

Definitions, *The Compendium of the Magically Sensitive*, 4th Edition, Dr. Nathan Cooper

Diego led his human contingent around the prison to the correct side of the monster cellblock door. He had waited as long as he could. But the moon shone through the ceiling slits and waiting any longer might put Finn and Theo in jeopardy if they were trying to stall an untenable situation alone. His heart ached. Asif hadn't come.

Door open. Get everyone out. I'll go back for him after.

"Nusair, if you'd like to get your, ah, friend ready? We'll need to carry the phoenix, but let's get this door open first." Diego grasped the hands offered to him and waited until every human magic user had a place in the circle—men, women, foreigners, local citizens. He gave Ethan's hand an encouraging squeeze and nodded to Tarek. "There is a lock mechanism inside this door. We must think about it opening. All of us together. Concentrate hard. Think about any lock you have ever seen and how the mechanism turns to open. Think of turning it. Of opening it."

That moment of panic bubbled up again when nothing happened. Again, Saeed made himself the central focus as he began to chant. Everyone but Diego joined in, since everyone else understood the language, but that didn't distress him. Diego was their lightning rod, the conduit for their combined magic. He moved Ethan's hand to his shoulder and set his palm against the door.

A slow trickle caressed his nerves, like a tiny stream of cool water. Panting, a bead of sweat edging down his temple, Diego reached into the stream and fought to channel it. Saeed's chanting grew louder and the trickle increased to a rivulet, to a faucet with the taps opened wide, to a small spring chuckling down the side of a mountain. The jolt of magic he had waited for didn't come. All the people involved must have acted as transformers, but the stream grew wider and wider until he wasn't sure his stunted channels could hold it.

Forehead against the door, Diego fought the ever-increasing pain, blinking spots from his eyes. *Turn, damn you, turn. Disengage. Open...open...*

Down the line, someone sobbed. Beside him, Ethan moaned in obvious distress. Diego was about to tell everyone to stop when metal clicked on metal inside the door. He pulled at the stream, forcing it into the lock, white-hot agony searing through him. The door clicked again and a hard *thunk* echoed inside the metal shell as the bolt shot back. With Diego leaning his weight against it, the door swung open and he would've fallen flat on the floor if hands on either side hadn't supported him.

"Damn...oh, damn...give me a minute." He panted, Ethan patting his back. "All right...okay...careful everyone. The hallway's dark but there's a ladder on the other end with the second door at the top. We're almost there."

Still hand in hand, the circle shuffled down the pitch-black hallway. There were some soft cries of fear but no one panicked, the large group most likely keeping the fear at bay.

"Nusair? Still back there?" Diego called out. "You have her?"

"I'm here, yes, and with the ghoul and griffin. I have the phoenix, too," Nusair's voice came from far back, less cocksure and sardonic than usual.

"Are you all right to keep going?" Tarek asked beside him.

"Yes. We have to keep going. One more door. This is going to get a little clumsy though. You and Ethan are going to have to keep hold of me on the ladder to keep the circle complete."

"We've got you, Diego. Just yell if you need a break," Ethan said close to his ear.

Up the ladder, six rungs, seven, then the metal portal was close enough to put his palms flat on the underside. One more door.

* * * *

One small window, one door, a ventilation shaft not big enough for a fat rat to squeeze into. Theo stood hipshot, eyeing the command center critically. Finn had scouted the roof of this shorter section of the prison while he'd taken the ground level. No easy entrance revealed itself.

"We do it the hard way." Theo glanced up at Finn, currently a raven sitting on his uninjured shoulder. "Door, you think?"

"I could get in and open the door for you."

"You'd be alone and exposed. They'd shoot you."

"They've already shot you."

"I'm fine. I think we can force the door. Gives us a field of fire."

"That's one of those Kevin terms, I'd wager, since there are no fields here and I don't think starting a fire would be wise. But I can get the door down."

Finn hopped off Theo's shoulder. Once he hit the ground, he began to glow blue. "You may want to take a few steps back."

Curious and a little alarmed, Theo backed off while Finn's raven shape melted and expanded, then kept on expanding. He had to fight to keep his jaw from dropping as four thick legs emerged from the shifting mess, a body the size of a dump truck and a trunk.

"One way to do it," Theo said to the elephant now standing beside him.

"Perhaps it will confuse them enough to keep them from shooting for a few moments, as well." Elephant-Finn flapped his huge ears as he lined up with the door. "Stand well back. This may take a try or two."

Theo nodded as he stepped away and drew his gun, the Smith & Wesson comfortably heavy in his hand. The moment Finn needed cover fire, he would have it.

The guards up on the walls might not have had a chance for radio contact, but with a shot fired, the men inside the bunker most likely knew something was wrong.

Finn shifted his huge flat feet, swinging his tusks side to side. He huffed an elephant breath, kicking up a miniature sand devil, and charged with his head lowered. The first blow echoed off the surrounding dunes in eerie repetition, leaving a sizeable dent in the metal door. Finn backed up and tried again. His hard skull bent the door inward on his second attempt and now voices raised in babbling alarm came from inside the bunker.

"Make sure you step aside after the next one!" Theo shouted over as Finn prepared to charge again.

Finn's head connected with a thundering crash and a squeal of tortured metal as the door separated from its hinges and flew into the room. He stumbled to the side as best he could, though shots already rang out. Theo ignored the bullets zipping past him. *Breathe in, breathe out, find the target's center mass.* He fired at the one man foolish enough to be standing in sight of the open doorway. That one flew back with the force of the .44 connecting with his chest, blood spraying the wall behind him. Theo didn't have time to think about what he'd done.

The firing from inside the bunker continued from two distinct trajectories. He laid down cover fire, forcing the remaining guards to keep their heads down, giving Finn time to shift into a smaller target. A quick glance to the left confirmed that the elephant had vanished. The dark shape hidden in the building's shadow was feline, most likely the panther again.

The distraction cost Theo as a bullet creased his right thigh. He dropped and rolled out to the side, telling himself he'd have to deal with the pain later. A quick crawl across the concrete got him to the wall on the side of the door opposite Finn. The men inside still fired, just wasting ammunition.

"Three count. Stay low," Theo murmured. When Finn nodded, Theo held up a hand and counted back on his fingers. *Three...two...one...*

Together, they burst through the doorway, Theo racing along the wall to the right behind a desk, Finn slinking under a counter to the left. Their targets had taken shelter behind a bank of monitors. Speed was their greatest ally, before the guards had a chance to figure out they were being outflanked.

Crouched low, Theo stopped at the counter where the monitors hissed and hummed. It abutted the wall on his side, so no going around it. Under would tangle him in a disorganized collection of wires. One of the guards crouched not four feet from him, rifle barrel supported on the countertop between monitor banks, still aimed toward the empty doorway.

If he and Finn had worked together more often, Theo might have thought of a signal to coordinate their attacks. He realized this too late when Finn struck first, leaping at the target on his side from under the counter. The man went down with a shriek. His rifle fired, destroying one of the monitors in a shower of glass shards and sparks. The second man shot at Finn before Theo could hurl himself over the counter to stop him.

Theo slammed into him, snarling in the man's face as he yanked the rifle from his hands and used it as a club to knock the guard out. The second guard, Finn's target, lay still too, blood welling from claw marks on his shoulders. Theo's heart slowed on a painful thud when he looked beyond to where Finn sprawled in panther form on the floor.

"Finn?" Theo called as he secured the guards. "Finn!"

A quick crawl while he prayed to any god that might be listening got him to Finn. A wet line of blood seeped up behind his feline ear, difficult to see against the sleek, black fur, but the scent hit Theo like a jackhammer to the gut. No bone showed. Finn's chest still rose and fell evenly. The bullet appeared to have creased his head and knocked him senseless.

"Good thing," Theo said as he cradled Finn's head and forequarters gently to drag him out of the bunker. "How would I tell your husband if I got you killed?" He arranged Finn in the shadow outside the bunker, slipped off his jacket and placed it under Finn's head as a pillow. "Back in a second. Stay there."

Which was a stupid thing to say to someone who was unconscious, but he felt like he had to say something. The guards might have had time to send a distress call. There might be reinforcements on the way and if there was any way to determine how far off they were, Theo would feel more confident about their chances.

He settled his shoulder holster more comfortably, the gun a familiar weight against his side now, and strode back through the bent and mangled doorway. A man popped up behind the last desk at the back of the room, screamed out something in Arabic and shot Theo in the chest. The force of the blow knocked Theo back outside onto the concrete beside the helipad. White-hot searing pain let him know it was a silver tipped bullet.

Stupid. Got too cocky. Didn't even bother to listen for other heartbeats. He lay on his back in a storm swell of agony, staring up at the cold, uncaring stars, and realized he wasn't going to be able to get back to Limpet. Odd how that hurt more than the bullet through his heart.

* * * *

Almost, almost... Diego's arms ached from holding them at such an awkward angle over his head. His head throbbed from trying to direct the constricted, intermittent streams of magic. Every one of the humans in his extended coven circle was necessary to produce even this tiny amount. One less, if anyone faltered, and they might not get out after all. He wasn't sure if it was his own magic resonances or Saeed's, or a combination of both that allowed them all to work in tandem, but he didn't care right then.

Finally, the clang of a bolt releasing rang hollow through the port door above him. He nearly sobbed in relief and let his arms down for a moment, rubbing at them to try to coax them into one more effort.

"Diego?" Ethan whispered at the bottom rung of the ladder.

"Just a moment. It's unlocked. I heard it. There's a wheel to turn, though."

Gritting his teeth, Diego lifted his arms and found the wheel again with both hands. *To the left. Everything loosens to the left.* Tired muscles straining, he pulled against the wheel, pleased when it started to move — then it stuck.

Tarek called up, "Diego, what's happening?"

"It's stuck. I'm trying to turn it...*carajo*. It won't budge."

"Are you sure it's unlocked?"

"It's unlocked! It started to turn." Frustration made his voice shake. "Ethan, you're younger. Come up and try."

Careful of the heads below him, Diego felt his way back down the ladder. Ethan had kept hold of him and was able to make his way around and up without incident. Grunts and groans came from above as Ethan evidently tried his best without success as well.

After a few minutes, Ethan called down, panting, "Josh! You're small enough to fit up here with me. Get your bony butt up here and help me."

Gavin handed Josh up the line and Diego guided him to the ladder. If they had a light, any light, this might have been easier, but the dark pressed in on them without mercy. The grunts from above soon started again, but no screech or squeak of the stubborn wheel giving any ground.

Someone toward the back began to wail, babbling something that made Tarek snap at whoever it was. Soft mutters followed, the growing tension just shy of turning ugly.

"Damn it!" Ethan bit out. "It won't fucking move!"

A panicked surge toward the ladder knocked Diego over. "Tarek! Tell them to stop! It won't do any good to trample each other!"

He crouched on the floor, unable to hear Tarek any longer over the frightened babble. Someone stomped on his leg and he curled up tighter, hoping the prisoners would calm once they realized the way out was still blocked rather than turn on each other.

Yes, and the last time we checked pigs still didn't have wings, did they?

"Out of the way!" a gravel-in-a-cement-mixer voice bellowed from behind the crowd. "Move, you jackasses!"

Despite the tightly packed corridor, the voice drew nearer.

"Jesus H. Christ on fucking burnt toast! Move! Diego! Are you in this clusterfuck?"

"Asif! Yes! I'm here by the ladder. The door is stuck and they panicked."

"Idiots. Clear the way! I'll get the damn door!"

Tarek was shouting now, too, and whatever he said caused enough people to scramble back out of Asif's way.

"It's at the top of the ladder?" Asif asked, closer to Diego's spot on the floor.

"Yes. It's like a submarine portal, Finn said. There's a wheel to turn, probably to the left. But none of us are strong enough."

"That's what you get for being fragile full-blood humans."

The ladder creaked, presumably under Asif's weight. His deeper, bass grunts came from above, but with a critical difference. Metallic squealing accompanied his efforts.

After a moment the noise stopped. "All of you morons down there better not rush me when this opens, or you get a fist in the face."

"Tarek, please ask everyone to return to their places in the circle. We'll go up in an orderly fashion and everyone will get out."

There were still some angry murmurs as Tarek translated, but the press of bodies receded and Diego was able to regain his feet.

"I think everything's back under control down here, Asif. Can you open it?"

"The fuck kind of question's that? I got this. You handle your angry mob."

The metallic squealing resumed and with a final grunt and pained exhalation, Asif heaved the portal up. It fell on its back with a clang, moonlight suddenly washing him in silver and spilling down the ladder rungs.

Diego was about to start moving people up the ladder when a scuffle from behind the crowd stopped him. He tried to peer back toward the prison, but the moonlight didn't reach far enough. There seemed to be shoving and someone shouting. Then Nusair yelled back.

"Nusair! Are you all right?"

Instead of Nusair answering, there was a chilling hiss and a scream. The subsequent heavy silence was finally broken by Nusair swearing softly.

"Nusair? What's happening back there?"

"Gamila didn't mean it! It wasn't her fault!"

Diego's tired brain tried to connect that sentence with anything logical. "Gamila? Your...pet? What happened?"

"He panicked. Shoved the ghoul out of the way. Tried to shove me. He said he had to get out first. That you would leave and shut the door behind you. The werewolf." Nusair's voice wavered, either in shock or in profound distress. "He knocked into Gamila and yanked my shirt off her eyes. He scared her."

Traveling back through the corridor by feel, from one person's shoulder to the next, Diego made his way back to the first door where Nusair still stood.

"It's not her fault," Nusair repeated softly.

"Where is he? The werewolf?" Diego patted the djinn's arm, trying to indicate he wasn't angry.

"To your right."

Dreading what he would find, Diego reached a shaking hand out and connected with stone. It wasn't the smooth stone of the prison walls or even the rougher blocks of the monster cells, but something far more complex. The ledge his hand rested on curved up into a smooth column, then to planes and ridges...a face. *Dios, no.*

"He's stone," Diego whispered.

"She didn't mean it. There was just enough light and he scared her," Nusair hissed close to his ear.

Diego shook his head. "Stop, Nusair. We're not leaving her behind. Is this...fixable?"

Nusair didn't answer, though Diego could hear his accelerated breathing.

"Asif!" Diego called desperately.

Grumbling and muttered cursing indicated Asif's passage through to the back. "What's all this?"

"Thank you for getting the door open. I'm so glad you decided to come with us."

"But you need something else."

"Yes. I'm sorry. But we have someone who's been turned to stone. Do you think you could carry him out?"

A grinding noise and a grunt answered him. Then Asif growled, "I've got him. Let's get the hell out of here."

"*Allons-y,*" Nusair said, his voice finally steadier.

"What?" Asif growled.

"Never mind. Lead the way, little sorcerer."

* * * *

Theo drifted in and out of the starlight, not certain why he wasn't dead yet. Something in his vampire constitution kept fighting, so Kevin had been wrong. He could take a shot to the heart and not be quite as dead as anyone else, or at least not as dead quite as fast.

I'm not sure that made sense.

In one of his drifts back to the points of light above him, Limpet leaned over him. That was a nice last hallucination to have.

"Theo? Theo, you promised not to get shot," Limpet said in a broken whisper.

"Don't…think I did," Theo croaked, pleased he could still speak.

Limpet had an arm under him, cradling him against his delicious-smelling chest. Theo nuzzled at his shirt, happy that he wasn't dying alone, but at this angle, he could see into the bunker again. The final guard, the one he'd missed, was on the radio. Yelling into the radio, actually.

"*Cabrón*. That one…shot me. Last one." Theo grabbed Limpet's arm. "Need…make things…safe."

Limpet stared down at him with a worried frown. "The prisoners will be out soon. The moon's up. It's not safe, not at all." He seemed to think for a moment. "Oh! You need me to make it safe for them. I need to take care of this last one."

Theo patted his arm and nodded. He gulped a breath. "My gun."

"I don't know what to do with your strange musket, Theo. I don't even know how to shoot a regular one with gunpowder."

"Club."

Again, the realization came quickly. Theo thanked the universe that Limpet was so clever.

"Ah. Not to shoot, but as a club. I'm not certain I can do this. I've never hit anyone to do them harm like this. It's not as if he's something to eat. I suppose I could pretend he was a large fish or some — "

"Please. My little...*cabrón*."

"Isn't that what you just called the guard? Did you just call me something nasty?"

"For you...badass. Little...selkie badass."

Limpet's snicker was strangled as he gave Theo a quick kiss before laying him down gently. "Don't die while I'm gone."

I'll try my best. Theo turned his head far enough to watch as Limpet approached the bunker and faded from sight. The *you-can't-see-me* trick worked well even on dying vampires, apparently. He waited until he heard the distinctive thump of pistol-butt meeting skull, followed by the thud of a body hitting the floor.

Theo closed his eyes when Limpet cleared the doorway, telling himself he could rest now that his selkie was safe and the area secure.

A moment later, he was jostled awake again, Limpet talking a mile a minute. "...and I tied him up with his own belt. I saw that you'd tied the others up with those white things but I didn't have any of those. And I smashed the thing he was speaking into since there were others speaking back and I didn't think that was good. Finn seems all right. I've let him rest where he is. But you need to feed now. You're not going to die on me, my sweet Theo. I can't allow it. Not after all the trouble I've gone through to stay with you."

The scent of blood reached through the heavy blanket of pain and Theo wrapped his lips instinctively around offered skin. He drank, moaning at the taste of Limpet's blood, so unlike any other, salt and iron but sweeter by far. Just a little...just a taste...

He pulled his lips back on an anguished thought, licking at the wounded wrist. "You cut yourself. For me."

"It's just a little slice. Hush. You needed some and you weren't trying to drink on your own, even though I offered my throat, you silly thing. I know it hurts and you want to sleep, but I didn't think you wanted to die."

Theo turned his head into Limpet's shoulder and the pain receded just enough to make him aware of how bad things were. He couldn't move his legs and was too weak to lift his head. Every beat of his struggling heart sent molten spears through his chest.

"You didn't stay. Where I told you."

"No, the proper thing to say to me is *Limpet, thank you for coming to rescue me. I'm so glad that you decided to follow me after all to make sure I didn't die.* Scolding the person who saves your life just seems rude, don't you think?"

"Hmm."

"That's all right. You can say thank you later. You probably should just rest instead of talking right now. Not that you talk very much even when you're well, which is a shame. You have such a wonderful, soft voice. Drives straight through me."

"Limpet?"

"Yes?"

"Thank you. Now, shh."

"All right. For you." Limpet kissed his forehead and clamped his mouth shut.

In the sudden silence, they both picked up the squealing of the nearby portal and the thump as it opened.

"I think they're coming out now," Limpet whispered.

"Tell them...run for it. Reinforcements will come. Soon."

"Even flat on your back, you want to protect everyone. That's what I love best about you. But you're going to have to let me protect you for a little while here."

True. Since he was fading out again. *Wait? Did Limpet say he loves me?*

* * * *

Diego had expected Finn's head to pop over the open portal at some point. That he didn't make an appearance, either to say cheerfully that everything was under control or to warn them, was chillingly disturbing. It was all Diego could do to stay at the bottom of the ladder while he guided everyone else up. Every fiber in his body wanted to swarm up the rungs and find Finn, but if he did that, he risked chaos and the possibility of more casualties.

He counted as he guided humans to the ladder, making certain no one was missing. The ghoul shifted partially to stand on two feet, weary and unsteady, clawed hands clutching the rungs in white-knuckled desperation as he climbed. The griffin made a clumsy leap for the top and had some difficulty with the narrow opening, clawing and maneuvering his wings in painful ways to squeeze through.

When Asif's turn came, he slung his stone passenger over his shoulder and climbed halfway up where he tried his best to maneuver the petrified werewolf through the portal to Gavin and Josh. The kids didn't quite have the best hold, though, and the poor werewolf slipped from their grasps where he knocked against the side of the portal and lost a finger.

Diego retrieved it as it fell, hoping that was the extent of the damage if there was any chance to restore him. Nusair went up next to last. He refused to relinquish the phoenix and slung her over his left shoulder while he carried Gamila, a full ten feet long if she was an inch, under his right arm. The laws of physics said he shouldn't be able to make the climb one-handed with that burden, but he managed, clearly straining but not once losing his grip on ladder or passengers.

Finally alone in the dark corridor, Diego swarmed up, an unreasoning fear of something sinister following him gripping his heart all the way up. He broke through into the relative brightness of the moonlit desert night, forcing himself to breathe calmly. They were out. Every single prisoner was out.

His cohorts hadn't sat idle while he directed the evacuation. Tarek and Ethan were speaking to someone who wasn't dressed in prison pajamas, someone whose bright hair cascaded to his waist.

"Limpet?"

The selkie gave a glad cry and rushed him, throwing himself into Diego's arms. "Diego! Oh, I'm so glad to see you safe. We heard about your arrest at the place where the Swiss stayed. Kurt was so angry and he wouldn't listen to Theo, not one bit of it. But I heard Theo leaving in the night and followed him since—"

"I know. Finn told me most of all that. Where is Finn?"

"Of course, pardon, pardon. Finn was shot—"

"What? Where is he?" Diego turned this way and that, his chest tightening painfully the longer he couldn't spot Finn.

"It's not bad. He's resting by the square building where they had to break the door and where Theo was shot, too, but his is much worse. Theo says there are more guards coming because they used the...radio, and Diego? What are we to do with all these people now?"

It was a valid question, but he couldn't think. He needed to see for himself that Finn would be all right. He needed to see how badly injured Theo was. He needed to—

A sudden rising wind cut off his skittering thoughts. The horror of facing a sandstorm in the open had him moving back toward Tarek to get everyone to shelter, but the rising storm was oddly localized.

Nusair had put both his burdens down on the sand and walked off a few yards. He stood with his palms spread down toward the sand, his head back, mouth open in an expression of pained ecstasy. The sandstorm whirled around his feet, obscuring the bottom half of his body. With a sudden crack, his collar snapped open and fell to the ground. The cuffs followed a moment after.

Dark purple light danced over his skin, throwing ominous shadows on his handsome face. More menacing still, he began to grow. His hair, free of his shirt, whipped about his head in his personal storm.

"Nusair?" Diego shook off Tarek's hand to step toward him.

The djinn's eyes opened, staring golden lamps without pupils or irises. He bared his teeth in a parody of his bright smile. "Did you think you could hold me, little sorcerer? Make a fool of me with promises of friendship while you schemed?"

"I never intended to trap you, Nusair. Where would you get that idea from?"

"You're going to open a door to your enchanted island where your allies live. I know all about that island, Sandoval. Nothing leaves that the sidhe don't allow to leave!"

"They don't keep anyone there who doesn't want to stay."

"No sorcerer will ensnare me ever again, do you hear me? Never again! I'm the storm in the desert! The roaring of the wind! I'll destroy this place and all of you with it, filthy humans and your dogs!"

There was that odd note of anguish in Nusair's voice again and Diego wondered if the return to his native sands after so much pain had unhinged him, knocked the wall of his native paranoia down on top of him. Instead of retreating, Diego stepped forward again, hands held out wide.

"Nusair, you're free. I'm not. I'm still trapped in the evil bindings they put on me. What can I do to trap you? To hold you? You're free, Nusair. Do you understand? The darkness, the pain, it's over. I never wanted to keep you. Go, if you need to."

The winds didn't stop, but the roar decreased a fraction. Nusair frowned down at him from twenty feet in the air. "Why wouldn't you want a djinn? You could have whatever you wish! Bring down the governments who stand against you! Be the benevolent ruler of all mankind!"

Been down that horrible road, thanks. "At what cost? There's always a cost. Regimes would fall and chaos would engulf a country. That country would pull its neighbors into the darkness. People would die. Economies crumble. What good is ruling anything if all it brings is ruin? Want to know what I'd like to rule?"

Nusair regarded him shrewdly. "What do you wish, little sorcerer?"

"No, no wishes. No traps. No games. Just the longing in my heart that I'm sharing with you. There's a desk back home, where I would like to write. And a small plot of garden that Nathair might let me have as my own. And a bed that I'd like to share with my husband. This is the extent of the domain I need. All my heart desires."

"But you...have power. Such incredible power for a human."

"Which I'll use as I need to. When people need me to help them heal a wound or, oh, let's say, escape a prison." His last step put him at the edge of the sandstorm. "I kept my promise, Nusair. I asked for none in return. No debt. No contract. Not even the burden of friendship, though I would've given that to you, too, out of gratitude for your help and, frankly, because I liked your company. Go, if you want to. Go heal. Maybe I'll see you again someday, but not if you kill me and slaughter everyone here."

Diego knew he would wonder for many years after what part of his speech made a difference. In the end, it didn't matter, because some part of it obviously resonated. Nusair abruptly slid to the left on his self-sustained wind and scooped up the phoenix and his basilisk. All three vanished behind the storm, sand whirling thirty feet in the air. It hovered over Diego, moving toward him, sand stinging his skin. Fear gripped him as it advanced, but he held his ground, imagining he could still see Nusair's golden eyes watching from inside the tornado. A strange trick of the wind seemed to carry an exasperated sigh to him. Then the whirling sandstorm backed off and raced away, out of sight across the dunes.

"Certifiable, I swear," Josh said from behind Diego.

"Yeah, but that was pretty freaking awesome, eh?" Ethan added in an awed whisper.

Still shaken by the odd turn of events, Diego pulled in a few deep breaths before he turned back to his strange troop of refugees. He still had to get them all safe. "Limpet, take these three, please"—he indicated the Canadian students—"and bring Theo and Finn over here. Tarek, I need the circle reformed, and please ask if anyone speaks the language the griffin and the ghoul are speaking to each other? I need to ask if these are their home sands and if they want to stay or come with us."

Vadim ended up speaking to the two remaining nonhuman prisoners, apparently in Dari. He determined that no, the griffin was a mountain dweller and absolutely did not want to stay in the desert, and that, yes, the ghoul lived in deserts but this one wasn't home. They were both willing to go to Tearmann Island for resettlement assistance.

While Tarek herded humans, Diego allowed himself a quick check on Finn and Theo. Finn stirred when Diego bent to kiss his feline head.

"Oh, love, go shave," he muttered irritably. "Beard is fine. Smooth is fine. But this scruffy, scratchy in between you humans insist on is dreadful."

"When we get home. Promise." Diego smoothed the black fur along Finn's neck. "I'm glad you're not badly hurt but I'm still taking you to Eithne as soon as we get back."

Finn mumbled something incoherent about a watermelon before his eyes drifted shut again. Their other casualty hadn't escaped with minor wounds, though. A bullet had pierced through his shoulder and another had left a long gash on his thigh, but neither one of these compared to the chest wound. A few questions to Limpet confirmed that there was no exit wound. The bullet had lodged inside, with the entrance wound above Theo's heart.

"Theo, *mijo*…" Diego knelt beside him, stroking the tangled hair back from his forehead. "I'm so sorry. Hold on. Please."

"*Jefe*, you're safe. Good," Theo whispered and even managed a hint of a smile. "Silver. No promises."

"Silver? The bullet?" Diego looked to Limpet, who nodded. "*Mierda*. Feed him if you can, please. We need to hurry."

Limpet was babbling something about already feeding him and Theo refusing more, but Diego couldn't stay to listen. With reinforcements coming, most likely already in the air, and Theo dying, they needed to get moving. He took his position again in the circle, Tarek and Ethan with a hand on each of his shoulders to keep his own free to build the door.

According to the dragons, doors between places were uniquely human, a magic no other being could duplicate without a human involved. Even then, most covens never achieved it and he was the only human in memory to construct them alone. Without the blasted collar…but they had no time. It had taken half an hour to remove Finn's collar. They had to leave now.

Diego concentrated on gathering as much of the magic trickle as he could. Exhausted and shivering with anxiety, even that was a chore. Doorways required being able to feel the places between, the spaces where matter was not, and with enough of a magic spark and knowledge of one's destination, reaching through those empty places to open the way.

Outside the lead-lined walls, he could feel his way through the spaces again. He knew where they had to go, the call of home stronger than any other location. Desperate, every fiber of his being aching with the strain, he reached for his magic, enough to build a lightning ball powerful enough to punch through. *Almost...almost...*

His grip on the forming magic slipped and he gritted his teeth to try again. On the second try, he nearly had something, but again, he couldn't hold it. Four and five times he failed and he stood there with sweat dripping from his chin, trying to calm himself. *I have to do this. I can't fail. Not at this.*

On his sixth attempt, legs trembling so badly that his teeth rattled, he threw every bit of energy into creating the lightning ball. A spark formed on his fingertips. It grew to several dancing together, his heart pounding with the effort. The whirling sparks formed a ball over his palm...and fizzled out.

Diego collapsed to his knees with a sob, his legs unable to hold him any longer. Overhead, the sound of distant helicopter blades drummed a war beat against the night.

* * * *

"Listen up, everyone!" Zack adjusted his helmet strap and shouldered his rifle. "I want fae warriors behind the armored humans when we go through! We may be walking straight into weapons fire, so no breaking formation until we have intel on enemy positions!"

"Zack!" Nate cried out from the coven circle, situated to the left of the garden fountain. "We've got a fix on Diego! He's suddenly broadcasting loud and clear!"

"Thank God," Zack muttered, then raised his voice again. "You guys ready?"

"Opening now, Sarge," Brandon yelled back. "We'll hold here as long as you need us to."

Zack gave him a thumbs up and turned to where the magical winds rose directly in front of him. The hair on the back of his neck stood on end as Minky sent her web of magic lightning out and slowly, a huge picture window opened in front of Zack, showing him a sky filled with brilliant stars.

With Balor at his side and armed men he trusted all around, Zack stepped from a beautiful sunny afternoon in the consulate's garden into the chill black of a desert night and a profound sense of wrongness. There was a glowering, blocky building bathed in spotlights that was obviously a prison. But there should have been guards and gunfire, or at least the threat of gunfire. Instead, a surreal scene greeted Zack, with a circle of tired, dusty pajama-clad people holding hands, a mangy griffin and a god-only-knew-what creature, and right in front of him, Diego, on his knees, clearly ready to pass out.

"Well...hey? You okay there?" Zack held his rifle at the ready in case the expected gunshots were about to start.

Diego blinked up at him, obviously having trouble focusing, then he leaned his head against Zack's thigh. "*Qué alivio*. About time you got here, Morrison."

"Had a little trouble with the GPS. Everyone here coming through?"

"Yes." Diego nodded against Zack's leg. "But you need to rush Theo through. Get him right to Eithne. Silver bullet. Might be in his heart."

"Got it. Where is he?" When Diego pointed to where a prone figure lay on the sand in Limpet's arms, Zack called two of his men from the back with a litter and told them to double-time it back through. "Who's your other casualty?"

"It's Finn. Shot creased his head, but I think it's not too serious."

"Marcus! Finn goes next!" Zack patted Diego's shoulder. "Princess Eithne's standing by in the garden. Thought there might be some wounded before the day was over."

"We have to move, Zack. Helicopter's on the way with reinforcements for the prison."

Zack cocked his head and picked up the *whup-whup-whup* of chopper blades. Three of them. "All right, people! Let's move out! Don't run. Walk with purpose and get yourselves through into the garden."

A handsome young man directly behind Diego turned to shout at the others in Arabic and the former prisoners began to walk toward the door, some hesitantly when they saw Balor, but they all moved. One guy toward the back did an odd thing, stopping to pick up a man-sized statue before he hurried toward the doorway.

"You're taking a statue?" Zack asked Diego softly.

"Yes. It's a person. Please find a safe place for it for now."

Diego still hadn't moved off his knees.

"You, too." Zack nudged him. "Time to go."

"I can't get up." Diego laughed helplessly. "All that and now I can't get up."

"Oh, now, that's an easy fix." Zack shouldered his rifle and lifted Diego in his arms. "Morrison Transport, at your service. You're gonna get some rest, then you'll have a lot of things to fill me in on. Looks to me like things got pretty weird."

"Just save our courageous Theo. We would've all been shot dead the minute we escaped if he hadn't been here." Diego was on the last bit of his strength, his head rolling on Zack's shoulder. "And thank you for saving us. Right on time as always."

The door closed behind them as Zack was the last to step back through, shutting out the roar of the helicopters as they crossed over the final dune. "Looks to me like you mostly saved yourself."

Chapter Fifteen

Ghoul
Classification: magically altered human
Appoquinimink social scale: 3
For ghouls, physiological changes take place much as they do for vampires – in a hibernative coma that slows metabolism to a point mimicking death. Because of this, ghouls were long labeled as 'undead,' a misconception exacerbated by their tendency to procure the carrion they require as food from graveyards.
The Compendium of the Magically Sensitive, 4th Edition, Dr. Nathan Cooper

The procession of feeders seemed endless, always another fae and another, but none of them Limpet. Theo drifted on Princess Eithne's soothing voice, telling him the bullet was out, that it had pierced the top of his heart. All his trouble breathing was because of the blood pooled in his chest. It seemed counterintuitive to drink more blood to take care of this problem, but she said since his body was good at healing itself, he needed to help it do so.

So he drank when she told him to and drifted off into his red-stained twilight in between, holding out some foolish hope that the next time he would catch Limpet's scent and taste his skin. Even his voice would have been some relief, something to clutch tight in the restless sea of pain.

Hours, days or years later—he had no way of knowing—he finally opened his eyes to blink stupidly at the walls of his own room in the fae caverns. He lay propped up on a mound of pillows in bed, his chest wrapped in bandages. Alone.

Stupid to become attached. Even stupider to have ridiculous fantasies that Limpet was sitting by his bedside all that time. He had heard the word *love* and misinterpreted it, willfully, wanting something he could never have. No matter how sensible he told himself to be, though, it still hurt in a terrible, hollow way that he hadn't felt since his mother had told him to get out of her house and never come back.

But the kid who'd cried and begged on his mother's doorstep was gone. He'd seen too much and done too much since then. Stoic, calm, nothing could shake him anymore. It might hurt, but it wouldn't rattle him. In a few days' time, he would be up and back on duty and the world would keep turning. Too bad his pack had been abandoned in the desert. He couldn't possibly care any less about the pack itself, but his stitching had been in there, the dragon scene. Irritating, to have all that work wasted, and he wasn't sure he had the heart to start over now. Limpet had loved that piece.

A drop of water ran down the side of his face to his ear, followed by another. *I can't cry over him. I can't. It's ridiculous and I'm going to shatter into tiny, jagged bits of darkness and the pieces will be too sharp for anyone to pick up to help put me together again. I didn't even like him. At first. Damn it.*

* * * *

Once the healers had seen to Finn and they were both clean again, Diego had tucked Finn in, curled up beside him and slept for over twenty-six hours. It hadn't been his intention. There was far too much to do. But Eithne reassured him that he had been dangerously exhausted and if he hadn't slept, she would have put him under herself.

Without an office of his own, he took the empty desk in the administrative office, happy to be around busy people. Carol told him that a small addition was being built on the back of the consulate, a special office just for him overlooking the garden. He tried to tell them it wasn't necessary. Everyone ignored him.

With painstaking care, he entered Tarek's handwritten information on each prisoner into the computer files — name, gender, age, family, occupation and education. Work had already begun to find placement for all the humans, with the Fae Collective scrambling hard behind the scenes to have families transplanted as well. Diego smiled as he finished typing Tarek's own file, his case already close to complete.

Placement: Sweden, Stockholm
Émigré employment: Resident, Karolinska University Hospital
Host family: Drs. Emma and Henrik Magnusson

"One of us could do all that for you, Mr. S., if you want," Dan said for the third time that morning, his forehead creased in concern, as if Diego might break something by doing clerical work.

"I'm almost finished, thank you. It's helped me get refocused."

Carol swooped in to set a fresh mug of coffee on his desk. "I can't even imagine what you and Finn went through. He tries to make jokes now, but it's been hard on you both." She put an arm around him for a quick hug. "Do you think he's having flashbacks to the time before?"

"I don't think so," Diego said carefully. "Nothing yet, at any rate. It was…different this time. I knew where he was. We could talk when we needed to. It was hard and there were bad moments, but the horrible despair from that first incarceration wasn't there."

He saved his work and shut down his computer. "I have to make some phone calls about our nonhumans this morning, but I need to see Theo first. Eithne said he woke up, really woke up, for a few minutes this morning."

"Go on. I think we can hold down the fort without you for a few minutes."

Diego laughed, since Carol meant it as a joke, but it wasn't a comfortable one for him. They'd managed just fine without him for over three years now. He took the coffee with him and made his way slowly down the stairs to the fae caverns. His legs still shook with the slightest exertion, nothing good food and sleep wouldn't cure.

"Theo?" He knocked softly on Theo's open door. "Are you awake?"

"*Sí, jefe, ven, ven. Cómo está?*"

"Recovering. How are you doing?"

Theo grunted as he tried to shift higher on his pillows. "Not bad for being shot through the heart."

"Very true." Diego turned his coffee mug in his hands, watching the little wavelets. "I'm so sorry, Theo. There should have been a better way to handle this mess. Better than nearly getting you killed."

"I had a job to do." Theo took a slow, shallow breath. "They wouldn't listen. So I had to go after you."

"I know. Limpet told me. Kevin's had a long talk with Kurt about that, believe me. And, please don't think I want to diminish what you did in any way. I'm so grateful that you came for us and that you were there when it counted."

Theo nodded, though something anxious lurked in his dark eyes. "Has Limpet...?"

Diego wasn't certain if those two hesitant words were meant to ask if Limpet had been there or if he had gone but the little crack in Theo's voice told him everything about how close they had become during their days in the desert.

"He was here, *mijo*. When you were still failing. When they weren't sure you would make it. He sat by you and held your hand. The healers wouldn't let him feed you since he'd already given you quite a bit before we got you through the doorway. But he was here."

"Oh." Theo turned his head away, obviously struggling as his chest hitched. Finally, he whispered, "Where is he now?"

Why hasn't anyone told you this already? Diego reached over and put his hand atop Theo's on the blanket. "His family was waiting. They were very upset that he was missing. I'm afraid they took him home."

"Family. His pod. That's good." Theo wasn't quite managing his usual stoic calm, his voice wavering.

"I know, as they say, where they live. I can always take you there to see him when you're better."

Theo wiped a hand over his face. "It's nice of you to say. But I don't think his family would want that."

The unspoken words *because his family took him away from me and doesn't want their nice boy in love with a vampire* lay heavy and cold between them. "I'm sorry, Theo. I'm so sorry. Maybe someday—"

"*Sí, jefe, tal vez.* I think I need to rest."

"Of course." Diego's heart ached at all the little fictions in those last few sentences, but he wasn't going to shame Theo and become a witness to his silent tears. "I'll be back later to see how you're doing."

He wished he could have talked to Cerith and Lyonsia before they left. Maybe he could have delayed their departure, reasoned with them about wresting Limpet away. But the pod had been gone by the time he woke and Eithne had implied there was subterfuge involved in Limpet's going with them.

When things calmed down and Finn was feeling better, they would go for a visit and have a serious talk with the overprotective selkie parents. Diego stopped on a thought on his way up the stairs. At least Theo was talking to him again.

* * * *

The waves of the home shore rolled toward him, speaking in voices both achingly familiar and suddenly alien.

I wanted so badly to come back here…

Limpet struggled to pin down the strange disconnection, as if everything were smaller somehow, duller, less tangible, but his mind couldn't wade through its storm of anger, hurt and worry. He was here, at home, where he had said he did not want to go. Theo was back through the doorway to the human world and Limpet didn't even know if his Nightwalker had survived.

"Don't you want to join us for a swim?"

His mother's voice jarred Limpet from his thoughts. He wanted to whirl around and scream at her, but he managed to sit still and quiet, jaw aching from how tightly he clamped his teeth.

"Limpet?" Now his father's voice joined hers, even worse. "Are you stone now, pup? Going to sit there for all eternity?"

He closed his eyes and thought of Theo, of his soft voice and how he always considered every word. Screaming and weeping would only make things worse. He needed Theo's strength right now, his calm in the face of every storm, large and small, even when his heart was breaking.

"Ma? Da? I need to talk to you," he forced out, still staring at the waves.

They settled on either side of him, his father with his broad-shouldered bulk and his mother with her beautiful sea foam hair.

Cerith ruffled his hair. "What is it, pup? Surely you're not still sulking about having to leave the island?"

Limpet pulled away, stood up and walked toward the ocean, letting the waves play across his feet. "That's the issue, Da. I'm not a pup anymore. What you did — drugging me so I wouldn't have a choice about leaving — that was a horrid thing to do."

"We're very sorry about that, sweetness," Lyonsia said, her voice full of hurt. "But do you have any notion how worried we were about you? Out there in the dangers of the human world all alone?"

"I wasn't alone. Theo was with me."

"Having a monster as your protector is no protection at all," Cerith growled. "You were lucky and came out of it whole, but you can't go around thinking with your small head, boy. One day that thing would have turned on you and killed you. We had to keep you safe."

Limpet pulled in a slow breath and faced them. His arms wrapped around his ribs were the only thing keeping him from shaking apart. "I'm sorry I left without telling you. That was wrong. I beg pardon for having worried you. But I'm grown now and need to explore on my own."

"You've never had the sense to keep you own head safe." Lyonsia nodded to his mangled ear. "We couldn't just leave you on your own."

"But if I had said I wanted to swim up the coast and find a mate? Start my own pod?"

"That's different."

"It is." Limpet nodded. "I agree. I would be with my own kind. You'd still be able to call to me whenever you wished. My poor muddled head would still have selkies to watch out for it. But I didn't. I went out to where things are happening, where people need help, and fell in love with a Nightwalker whose single-minded need to protect everyone nearly killed him."

"You don't love him," Cerith said on a snort. "Don't confuse lust heat with love. You can't love someone who only knows violence."

"Da, you never even spoke to him. You have no idea who he is, the terrible pain he carries with him without complaint, the selflessness, the sense of duty. You never saw how patient and kind he can be, the light in his eyes when he creates with his hands. I do love him." Limpet swallowed hard against the rock in his throat. He did love Theo and in that moment, he finally realized how deeply. "And I'm going back to him. You can slip something in my food again and carry me back here as many times as you like, but I'll turn right around when I wake and go back to him. Which will get ridiculous after a bit, since that's all we'll be doing is running back and forth to the *sidhe* lands."

He had run on a bit longer than he intended, but still his parents regarded him slack-jawed, as if he had sprouted extra fins.

"I love you both. I love all my family. But I can't stay here, not now when I don't even know if Theo survived. Come visit me at the consulate if you like, in the big, bad human world. I won't live in a net any longer and I have things to do. I'm going back to Theo."

Predictably, his mother started to cry and his father glowered, but he couldn't be intimidated any longer, or stopped short by manipulative guilt. He hugged them both and kissed their unhappy faces. Then he walked away over the grass-swept dunes without looking back.

* * * *

"We can reverse it, can't we?" Diego stared morosely at the stone werewolf under the wisteria arbor.

Lugh threw an arm over his shoulders and hugged him tight. "No."

"No? But if we—"

"Are you a necromancer now?" Lugh asked, raising one thick black brow at him.

"Of course not."

"That's what you propose, though. To raise the dead. Diego, there is no blood in the veins of this statue. No heart beats within. No mind cries out to us to be freed from its prison. The man is gone. There is only stone now."

"Damn it." Diego leaned into Lugh's offered strength. "I'd really hoped..." He turned to Asif, who stood nearby. "I'm sorry. I...asked you to carry out someone who had already died."

Asif shrugged, shoulders nearly as broad as Lugh's. "Not a big deal. Maybe he has family and shit."

"We'll try to find out. I'm sorry Mr. Werewolf Banker. I never even knew your name." *Nusair probably did, but I can't ask him and I'm still not certain he didn't engineer what happened to you.*

"You want him somewhere more private? I could move him."

Diego glanced up at Asif in surprise. He cleaned up well, no argument there. His gold-tipped black hair gleamed in the sun, pulled back in a neat queue since he could proudly display his tapered ears here. He had taken to wearing kilts as many of the *sidhe* did, so his black, giraffe-like tail could be free of the awkward confinement of pants.

"Thank you for offering. I'd appreciate that. Maybe in the pine grove at the back of the garden? If we can't find any next of kin, we could do a proper memorial back there, I'd think."

"Sounds like a plan." Asif hefted the statue easily and snorted at Diego. "Don't look at me like that. I feel kinda responsible for him." He lifted his chin toward the consulate. "Your pooka boy's looking for you. Of course you're together. Haven't seen this many gay fuckers in one place in my life."

"Most of the fae are bi, more accurately."

Asif actually smiled, the first one Diego had seen from him. It put a faint light of mischief in his violet eyes. "Best island ever," he muttered before he stalked off with the unfortunate werewolf over his shoulder.

Finn jogged up as Asif disappeared down a tree-lined path. "There you are."

"I am." Diego stood on tiptoe for a swift kiss. "Good to see you up. Did you eat?"

"Like a starved bear. But that's not what I came to tell you."

"I'm glad you did, anyway. Finn, if you hadn't—"

"Don't start that now, love." Finn stroked the side of his face. "You'll have us both in tears. What's done is done. Now then, Herself says the griffin is welcome to travel through *sidhe* lands to get back home to his mountains in the Otherworld. But she confirms what you suspected. The ghoul is not fae, and she forbids him entry."

"I was afraid of that. I haven't been able to find any government programs anywhere that offer support to ghouls. But I do have a call in—" Diego's phone buzzed against his thigh. He checked the number and glanced up at Finn. "I know you still hate him, but I have to take this call, *caro*. Agent Pulaski?"

Finn sniffed in mild offense but didn't stomp off. An improvement, at least.

"Yes, Mr. Sandoval, good to have you back. Checking into your placement issue. We may be able to offer territory in the Sonoran Desert, west of Phoenix, pending some licensing issues and his tolerance for the climate."

"It sounds ideal. Hot, dry, plenty of wildlife, right? Should be good hunting for him."

"Yes." Chill and dust-dry as always, it was hard to know what Gerry Pulaski was really thinking. "We'll send a Dari translator to collect him when everything's in place. But he needs to understand that the minute he strays into human lands, attacks some hapless tourist or decides to dig up a graveyard, all agreements are cancelled."

"Understood. We'll make sure he understands beforehand. Are there any other magically altered beings out that way?"

"That, Mr. Sandoval, is classified."

"Of course. Thanks, Gerry. The Fae Collective, as always, appreciates the support of the US Government."

"If you were anyone else, Sandoval, I'd accuse you of sarcasm. We'll be in touch."

Diego was still chuckling as he sat down with Finn under the arbor. Part of him still had difficulty with Gerry for what he had done some years ago. But he was one of those men who followed orders unflinchingly, whatever they might be. Always better to have that type of man on your side rather than opposing you.

"All settled, then?" Finn stretched his long legs out, lounging like a big cat on the garden bench.

"We're getting there. Some of the humans still need placement, but we'll find a place for everyone."

"Where will Asif go?"

Diego flopped down on the bench with his head in Finn's lap, content to have those long fingers stroke through his hair for a moment. "I'm not sure. Danu says he's welcome at the *sidhe* court, since he's half fae and not what she considers dangerous. But he didn't like the idea. Said it sounded too stuffy and full of politics."

"Interesting. Most humans wouldn't find half-naked, beautiful *sidhe* stuffy."

"For now, I think he's fine here. We'll see what he wants to do when he's had some time to adjust."

"But wasn't he a thief?"

"That's rather judgmental, coming from you."

"Your pardon." Finn lifted Diego's hand to kiss the fingers. "I'm sure he'll not cause a whit of trouble and all will be well."

"I hope so. You and I could use some boring, peaceful, non-traveling for a while."

"Is this what they call a staid-cation, then?"

Diego chuckled and nuzzled Finn's stomach. "Yes. Because we're not going anywhere."

* * * *

Pants. He'd managed the pants. Socks were optional, or they could be for once. Theo struggled to button the shirt, but his fingers were like inflated party balloons and he couldn't keep his arms up long enough to manage. He gave up and stomped into his boots without socks instead, but then realized lacing them up might not be possible.

"Where are you going? And why are you so angry at your boots?"

Theo's head jerked up. The figure in the doorway had to be a fever dream, except he never ran fevers anymore. No, the selkie was back, but it didn't matter. "Limpet."

"Hello." In a flurry of wild hair and near-nakedness, Limpet flopped down on the bed beside him. "I'm glad you're not dead. That was what I worried about on my way back. Though I suppose that was silly. It's not that you would die from me not being here and you're simply too strong for that. But I did worry and it's so good to see you awake. They too—"

"Limpet. Hush," Theo said softly. "I have to get to the security office and get back on duty."

"But you can barely sit up. They can't expect you to patrol yet, surely not. I could go ask them for you. I'm certain they'll say no…" Limpet trailed off suddenly, the hitch in his voice stabbing at Theo's still-healing heart. "You're not glad to see me."

"I'm glad you're safe. I have work to do."

Limpet grabbed his jaw and yanked his head around. "Theo Aguilar, I ran and swam like a sailfish in heat to get back to you, so worried about you I couldn't think of anything else. They tell me you asked for me, again and again. They tell me you… Well, no matter. And now you don't want me here? At least tell me why."

Dizzy from even that little bit of manhandling, Theo took a few slow breaths, which pulled Limpet's scent deep inside his lungs. *Damn it.* "It doesn't matter. What I want. Your family took you back. That's only right. You should be with family."

"I don't know whether to kiss you or to knock you flat," Limpet said in a too-even tone. "My family kidnapped me. I didn't go willingly, which I told them I would not tolerate. And I came back to you."

"You shouldn't have." Theo pulled away and went back to buttoning his shirt. *There. One button. Wrong buttonhole.* "You shouldn't have done that."

"Of course I should! Perhaps it's daft but I've fallen in love with you!"

Theo surged up, stumbled away, and fetched up hard against the wall. "You shouldn't! You can't!" Panting, he lowered his voice, "There's only darkness with me. No hope of children or a real life. Just endless rounds of blood feedings and darkness. I go where I'm told, when I'm told, because the structure helps contain what I am. And even that doesn't keep me from killing."

"That's why you push me away? Out of nine prison guards you helped take down, you killed one — because he would have killed Finn — and still you think yourself a monster?"

"Limpet, *épale*! Don't you see? I kill. That's what I do. It's what I am now. I can use it in ways that aren't as bad as others, but I can't be something else. It's all I have left. And I can't corrupt something as bright and beautiful and wonderful as you with all that filth." Theo choked on the last word, clutching at his heart, determined to stay upright despite the searing pain in his chest. If only Limpet had stayed away, he could have pretended the hole in his heart was healing. Having him here just ripped it wide open and staked it out in the sun.

Limpet rose from the bed slowly and approached him with cautious steps, as if he were a wild animal. "It's not all you are, my sweet Theo. You forget I've slept in your arms. Heard your pain. Seen what your hands can make. I've seen all you are and you can't pretend to be a vicious killer to hide from me. If this life hurts you, let's find another. But I'm here, Theo. To hold you up. To hold you close. To share as much of both the moon and the sun as you can manage."

A desperate moan echoed off the walls as Limpet's arms slid around him. *Oh, shit, that was me.* "Limpet…"

"Shh. Just tell me you love me."

Theo let his head fall onto Limpet's shoulder since he couldn't hold it up anymore. "But you're…but I'm…I do. I didn't want to. But I do. Love you."

"There. That wasn't so hard. I have you. Lean on me. Everything's going to be all right now."

It was a bit of an awkward shuffle back to the bed but Limpet got him there and drew his boots off gently before putting him back under the covers. "Now, no more of this *I have to get back on duty* nonsense. You can't even stand yet. Never fear. I brought you something that might help pass the time. Well, besides me, of course."

Limpet skipped out into the hallway and returned with something wrapped in plastic that he dumped on Theo's lap. He stared at the familiar packet, at the orange and yellow skeins of threads peeking through the stained film.

"You…how?"

"It was in my shirt. I had the odd feeling we wouldn't come back to the truck. So I tucked it in there for safekeeping. Carol had it for me in her desk."

"You clever little twerp." Theo brushed the back of his hand over his eyes. He really had to do something about them leaking so much. "I don't know what to say."

Limpet climbed onto the bed beside him, his grin absolutely blinding. "Oh, you're much better at not saying. I think we should have some not saying now."

Theo tipped his head up and met Limpet's kiss halfway, those soft lips a balm and benediction, washing away so much of the pain of the past five years. Thank God he was in love with someone who didn't know how to let go, and he said so.

"Ha." Limpet winked at him. "They didn't give me my name for fun, you know."

It wasn't that funny, but Theo laughed harder than he had in a long time, until his chest hurt and he couldn't breathe. But Limpet was there to hold him and he began to think about living in the light again.

Epilogue

Webs break. The tendrils float and brush hearts. Echoes of tendrils. Always.
From a bane sidhe lullaby, *Conversations with the Wild Fae* by D. Sandoval

Embassy parties were often deadly boring. Diego was actually enjoying this one. Looking ridiculously good in his charcoal gray suit, Finn held court in one corner of the ballroom, telling stories that might or might not have any basis in reality to a group of captivated diplomats and aides. Both men and women watched him with the same shining eyes and Diego knew better than to be the least bit jealous. He raised his glass to Finn from across the room and received a wink in return.

When he turned to set his empty glass on a passing server's tray, he spotted a flash of purple on the opposite side of the room. Danish embassy affairs did attract some interesting characters, but this particular shade of purple gave him pause. He approached the long way around the perimeter so he wouldn't appear to be marching across the floor to a confrontation. The man turned as he neared, his bright purple hair in a neat tail down his back, his black cutaway stunning on his tall, athletic frame. He nodded to Diego and smiled, his golden eyes catching the light in eerie reflection.

"Good evening, sir." Diego held his hand out and waited for the man to take it. "I'm Diego Sandoval, with the Fae Collective."

"A pleasure to meet you, sir. I'm called Nusair."

Diego managed a smile of his own. "It suits you. What brings you here tonight, if it's not rude to inquire?"

"It is." Nusair leaned in closer to murmur in Diego's ear, "I'm sleeping with the Swedish ambassador."

"Ah." Diego followed his gaze to a stunning woman in the middle of the dance floor who overtopped him by at least a foot. "I hope that works out well for both of you."

"I like the variety these international parties provide." Nusair snagged a canapé from a passing platter. "And what are you doing these days, sorcerer?"

"The Fae Collective has named me their liaison to the wild fae. The duties are rather varied but I suppose I'm the most qualified human alive right now."

"Sounds about right."

They stood side by side in a strange, companionable silence watching the ebb and flow of the partygoers until Nusair cleared his throat. "Diego, I'm a bit embarrassed over my behavior. The last time I saw you."

"We were all a little desperate and things were…unsettled."

"Hmm. I was in that place too long, I think. It wasn't good for me. Suddenly having the sand under my feet, getting that collar off, the power surge, made me a little crazy."

"I thought it might have," Diego said diplomatically. It was the perfect place for such things. "Thank you for not flattening me into a little sorcerer sand pancake."

"Heh. You're welcome."

"How's Gamila?"

"She's doing well. Back in my Otherworld palace."

"And the phoenix?"

Nusair took a sip of his champagne before answering, "Had to self-immolate before she could recover. She won't remember any of it for a number of years."

"Ah." It was impossible to tell from Nusair's airy tone whether that was good or bad, so Diego kept to non-comments and small talk about other guests for a few minutes.

"Amazing how much espionage goes on at these things." Nusair nodded to a couple against the wall. "He just slipped a thumb drive in her cleavage."

"Really? Incredible. I suppose if the Fae Collective ever wanted an espionage unit, I'd have to offer you the job first."

"My dear sir, that could only end in tears. Nobody trusts a djinn."

"You make certain of that. I suppose it keeps everyone at a distance."

"It does." Nusair gave him an appraising look. "You know, you're not so bad for a human."

"Thank you. I think."

"Ah, her nibs is signaling. She wants either to show me off or to leave the party early, which I'm looking forward to. She has the most amazing vibrating cock ring. If you weren't so disgustingly happily married, I'd invite you for a threesome."

"I'm flattered, but no thank you." Diego touched Nusair's arm as he turned to leave. "I'm glad you're all right and it was good to see you again."

"You, too." Nusair gave him a jaunty salute and swaggered off to his mistress of the evening.

It had been a strange encounter, certainly, but Diego felt the world steady beneath him. No one might trust a djinn, but for whatever strange reason, a djinn trusted him. He was where he needed to be, doing what he needed to do. Meddler, mediator, advocate—it was good to find his feet again.

* * * *

Theo crawled under the workbench after the rolling washer. He could just let it go and pull another from the 3/16 drawer in his washer caddy, but it would nag at him that one was missing.

"There you are. Bad thing."

"Theo?" Limpet called from the doorway. "Are you talking to small metal bits again?"

"Yes."

"That's all right then. So long as you don't have another lover under there."

Careful to avoid the common mistake of slamming the back of his head against the workbench as he got back up, Theo eased out from under and resumed his fussing with the battery pack. "I'm elbow deep in this, little bit. What is it?"

"I brought you lunch."

"What do you m—" Theo glanced over and froze. How his throat could go dry and his salivary glands could go crazy at the same time was a mystery, but they did. Limpet stood there in nothing but what he was born in, if one remembered that he was born with a seal pelt as well. He stood with his feet in the tail of his pelt, the fur pooling obscenely low around his waist, revealing his Adonis lines and the base of his hairless cock.

"Lunch," Limpet said with a sweet smile. "You haven't fed all week."

"You're trying to kill me."

"Not at all. I'm trying to keep you strong and healthy." Limpet shuffled closer, his voice low and husky. "It's better when you're strong and can pick me up. And toss me on the bed. And —"

"Quiet time. Definitely quiet time." Theo sank to his knees before his brain could explode and peeled the pelt down until Limpet's beautifully curved cock bounced free.

"No whispering?" Limpet asked, panting as Theo ran his tongue over the crown.

"No. But moaning is good," Theo murmured as he licked his way up and down the shaft, Limpet complying perfectly with a ball-tightening moan.

"Stay very still, love. So very still," Theo whispered against the silken skin of Limpet's cock.

His selkie lover twined his fingers in Theo's hair and hung on as Theo swallowed him down, sucking hard. Limpet let the pelt drop entirely, spreading his legs so Theo could reach between. He gasped as Theo pressed behind his balls, his head dropping forward and back in an extremity of ecstasy.

"I'll have to stop work if I feed," Theo growled.

"A two-hour nap," Limpet gasped out. "You need to rest."

Theo hummed as he took Limpet back into this mouth, tongue swirling over his skin. When he felt Limpet's balls tightening, he undid his jeans with his free hand and stroked himself hard, though he knew he wouldn't need much.

Fangs extending, teeth aching with need, Theo pulled back and found the large vein on the underside of Limpet's cock with his tongue. His hand around Limpet's base to keep him steady, he scraped the skin gently with his fangs and bit down. Above him, Limpet cried his name, coming all over Theo's neck and chest. The blood hit his tongue and he groaned at the sweet glory of it, like drinking bottled starlight, like tasting laughter. The sheer joy of it made him dizzy and had him coming within seconds, feeding and orgasm crashing together in exquisitely painful ways.

When he could think again, he licked the little wounds carefully and held on to Limpet as he sank to the floor. His selkie nuzzled at his throat, murmuring soft, soothing nothings, snuggling into his arms.

"You'll be sore for a few days."

"Worth every moment of it." Limpet kissed his jaw. "We'd best get you lying down before you fall."

Drunk and stumbling from the feeding, Theo half walked, half crawled to the cot in his workroom, and pulled Limpet down on top of him. Once down, the spinning stopped, but the happy lassitude remained and he found he was giggling as Limpet tried to get comfortable.

"Vampires don't giggle." He tried for a menacing tone and just started snickering again.

"As you say, love. So what are you making in here?"

"Besides some really good sounds?"

Limpet swatted him gently. "Yes, besides those. What machine thing are you making?"

"Ah. Jasper and Nate are getting married. Finally."

"Yes, I knew that. It's a wedding gift?"

"Sort of. Jasper wants an afternoon wedding outside. Family tradition. So. Outside. Daytime. Vampire. Not good."

"All true. Is it some sort of sunshade?"

"Better." Theo stopped to snicker again. He couldn't help it. "Sun's bad because a vamp's core temp goes up too much. Something about solar radiation. Anyway. Cooler body, no sunstroke."

"That sounds like a lovely idea for you as well, but I'm not following. I'm sorry."

"Don't be sorry, *corazón*. 'Cause it's genius. It's a body fridge."

"Like the one in the kitchen? That would look odd at a wedding, don't you think?"

Theo laughed helplessly at the thought of strapping a full-sized fridge to Jasper's back over his tux. Limpet had to shush him with kisses and petting before he could go on. "No…no. A tiny one. That could go under his shirt. Around his chest."

"Oh! That is a good idea. Does it work?"

"It will. It will. I'm getting there. Just have to work on the battery pack. Too bulky."

"Theo." Limpet gave him a soft kiss, angling up to look into his eyes. "I'm so very proud of you."

"For making a micro-fridge?"

"For trying to be happy. For not settling for the life you thought yourself doomed to."

"I couldn't settle anymore, you know," Theo said softly as he brushed the wild hair back from Limpet's eyes.

"Why was that?"

"Because it's not me now. It's us." Theo settled Limpet's head on his shoulder, his eyes closing in drowsy bliss. "Had to do better for an us."

There were a lot of maybes still out there. Maybe Limpet's family would never accept him. Maybe Theo's family would never agree to see him again. Maybe another crisis would see him back out with the security team again. All the maybes could wait. He wasn't a lone soldier in the dark any longer. *Us. It's a good word, the best word.*

He could have the sunlight, the starlight and Limpet all at once, and never have to choose again.

Want to see more from this author? Here's a taster for you to enjoy!

Wild Rose, Silent Snow
Angel Martinez

Excerpt

A hard gust threw dry leaves against the kitchen window, their pale, tattered lobes scratching questing fingers against the glass.

Rowan shivered at the unwelcome image. Bad enough a storm was moving in, but his brother had gone out into the wind to secure the back gate. *He's taking a godawful long time…*

The back door slammed open. Snowden stood there panting, as if he had raced for the house.

"Snow?" Rowan went to him, trying to peer around him into the dark. "What is it?"

He only glimpsed eddies of snowflakes whipping around the yard before Snowden set his shoulder to the door and shoved it shut. He shook his head, chest still heaving. "Don't."

"Don't what? Don't go out there?"

Snowden nodded as he slid the deadbolt home. "Tracks. Back gate."

He brought his brother a chair and made him sit so he could help him off with his snow-caked boots. "They were…someone's tracks?"

"No."

Trying to get information out of Snow was hard most times, but when he was upset, it bordered on impossible. Rowan understood his twin better than anyone else could, though, and he remained patient. "Animal tracks, then. Something big."

"Bear," Snowden muttered.

"You're sure it wasn't just a big dog?" Snow lifted dark eyes to glare at him. "Okay. Not a dog. But we haven't had bears around here in forever."

Snowden shrugged, a gesture that clearly meant, *Fine, don't believe me.*

"I'm not saying there wasn't one. Just surprised. Guess the weather's been bad west of here. Poor bear."

A snort indicated that Snowden's sympathies weren't with the bear.

"Must be hard, though." Rowan put the soaked boots on the mat by the door and hung Snowden's fleece-lined jacket on its hook. "Trying to find food to get through the winter…"

He trailed off, the statement a little too close to home. Snowden's calloused hand closed on his arm with a little shake.

"I know. We'll be fine. Of course we will." He shook off the momentary gloom. "We're safe in here while poor Mr. Bear's outside in the storm. And I made soup from the rest of the rabbit. We can have some tonight. Freeze the rest. We're good for a long while. There'll be a break in the weather soon and we'll get into town for supplies."

Neither one of them mentioned that one usually needed money for that sort of thing. At least if the shopper wanted to do more than just look. *We'll figure something out.*

In the summer, they had the honey to sell from their mother's apiary and the berries from the huge, tangled patches of blueberry and raspberry bushes on the island. They took seasonal jobs as river guides, too, as long as the weather held. The first winter hadn't been so bad, since a small life insurance policy had come through. But things always came up. Between repairs for the truck and the generator, an unexpected tax bill, and Rowan getting pneumonia, the money was long gone.

Their parents had put a sizeable chunk of money aside — investments, annuities, and so on — but several relatives had come forward to contest the will. Their inheritance languished in probate.

He ladled out the soup into his mother's blue stoneware bowls, trying not to think of how she had always laughed when he told her they matched her eyes. *God, I miss them both.*

They ate at the kitchen table in companionable silence. No matter what else they did during the day, they had always eaten dinner together, as a family. It was a tradition they sorely needed now, the comfort of each other's presence in the evenings.

"Bear, huh?" Rowan finally broke the silence. "Probably won't stay too long. Not much for a bear to eat here on the island in the winter."

"Honey," Snowden muttered darkly.

"Yeah, he probably smelled it. But he can't get through the enclosure to the hive boxes. He'll give up and go away. I mean, it's just a black bear."

Snowden shifted, staring at his soup.

"What? Oh, come on. It has to be a black bear. We don't have any other kind. Not like we live in Alaska with the Kodiaks."

He would just have to go out in the morning and look for himself. Not that he disbelieved Snowden. His brother wasn't in the habit of exaggerating. But if it was an unusually large black bear, or something bigger that had wandered down from Canada, he might have to call animal control.

That they might be trapped in the house, with him unable to hunt, was a sobering thought.

"Satellite's probably not going to pick up much."

"Nope."

"Wanna play some Fae Mongrels after dinner?"

Snowden's grin said *You bet your ass I do* loud and clear. As a rule, they didn't have extra money for games, and evenings passed with TV or reading. But Fae Mongrels had been a gift from a neighbor across the lake, in gratitude for help with her raccoon problem. They had tried to be noble and refuse, but the new game from Thaumaturgy Inc. had proved too much of a temptation.

The wind whined in the gutters as they settled on the sofa.

"You want to start new characters?"

With a little frown, Snowden shook his head.

"But I thought the wings were bugging you?" An RPG with real depth and variety, the game swiftly taught the unwary player that every advantage came with liabilities and every action had consequences. Building characters became half the fun, so the player could find out how a spiked tail might affect balance, or how wings might become disastrous during ground battles. *No two journeys the same* boasted the back of the box, and if that couldn't be literally true, there were enough variations built in to make it effectively true.

Snowden kept his wings on his mountain sprelf and Rowan stayed with his clawed, shapeshifting lycanoni.

The evening passed in near silence, the characters speaking for them onscreen as they battled a horde of ogre bats and reached a seedy border town.

Another angry gust rattled the windows and Rowan couldn't help thinking of the poor bear out in the storm.

* * * *

"Yep, boys, that's a bear." Mike tipped back his broad-brimmed hat.

The storm had let up in the small hours of the morning and a call to the nearby park station had brought two curious rangers out to have a look.

"Black bear?" Rowan asked, though from the size of the tracks all around the house, he was afraid he knew the answer.

"Nope. Too damn big." George scratched his white hair before replacing his hat. "Unless it's some new mutant kind of black bear. Gotta be something bigger. Probably a grizzly, though I've never seen one this far east."

"You won't have to...shoot it, will you?" Rowan swallowed down rising nausea. Killing to eat was one thing, killing a bear just struck him as horrible.

"Not usually necessary," Mike said as he reached for the radio mic in their Snow Cat. "Pretty good success rate with getting the bear tranked and relocated. With the black bears, we only do it if they start being a nuisance. Raiding garbage cans. Wandering the streets in town. But something this big... We'll keep an eye out for him."

George pointed to the tracks leading away from the house and out onto the frozen lake. "Anyway, your visitor didn't find anything interesting here. Looks like he left the island after the snow stopped."

Mike was speaking into the radio, "Heading back from the Hadley place now…"

George bent to take a last look at the tracks, shaking his head. "Just don't know what would possess a bear to come all that way…" He straightened, aiming a sharp glance at Rowan. "You boys all right out here?"

"We're fine." Rowan made sure to smile, though a war raged inside him between bristling at the implication of helplessness and craving that same implied help. "Just waiting out the winter."

A soft grunt was George's only commentary. Rangers came and went for the nearby state park, but George had been on the job since before Rowan and his brother had been born.

Mike turned back to their conversation. "You give us a yell if your visitor comes back. Just keep your distance and head inside if you see him."

"We will."

Snowden gave his brother a hard look.

"We will!" Rowan threw up his hands. "I'm not messing with a grizzly."

"Good call." George eased back into the driver's seat of the Snow Cat, then leaned out to tap Rowan on the arm. "You boys have some room in your freezer chest? Margie over-baked again this year when the grandkids came to visit and I'd like some room in our fridge for a good steak or something instead of the never-ending pies."

"We'll take some off your hands." *There. Gracious all around.* "What are friends for?"

Snowden gave him a too-serious nod. "Saving…George. From…pies."

And now Snow makes jokes. It's raining surprises. He knew there would be other groceries most likely sneaked in with those troublesome pies and he made a mental note to have Snowden write it down so they remembered to pay the Larsens back in the spring.

They took another tour of the windblown tracks around the house while the rangers made their slow way back across the frozen lake. The huge paw prints circled the apiary enclosure once, but there were no signs that the bear had tried to paw his way in. The shed, likewise, had a single circle of tracks. The house had three overlapping circles and a puzzling depression in the snow outside the living room window.

Rowan shivered. He had the oddest impression that the bear had sat there in the storm, watching them play.

PUBLISHING

About the Author

The unlikely black sheep of an ivory tower intellectual family, Angel Martinez has managed to make her way through life reasonably unscathed. Despite a wildly misspent youth, she snagged a degree in English Lit, married once and did it right the first time, (same husband for almost twenty-four years) gave birth to one amazing son, (now in college) and realized at some point that she could get paid for writing.

Published since 2006, Angel's cynical heart cloaks a desperate romantic. You'll find drama and humor given equal weight in her writing and don't expect sad endings. Life is sad enough.

She currently lives in Delaware in a drinking town with a college problem and writes Science Fiction and Fantasy centered around gay heroes.

Angel loves to hear from readers. You can find her contact information, website details and author profile page at https://www.pride-publishing.com